BLACKOUT

ANNUM GUARD 2

MEREDITH McCARDLE

SKYSCAPE

SKYSCAPE

Published by Skyscape, New York

www.apub.com

Amazon, the Amazon logo, and Skyscape are trademarks of Amazon.com, Inc., or its affiliates.

ISBN-13 (hardcover): 9781477827123
ISBN-10 (hardcover): 1477827129
ISBN-13 (paperback): 9781477827116
ISBN-10 (paperback): 1477827110

Cover art by Cliff Nielsen
Jacket design by Cyanotype Book Architects

Library of Congress Control Number: 2014912445

Printed in the United States of America

For my family. Thank you for always believing in me.

CHAPTER 1

I've watched my father break the law three times already this month, and let me tell you, it's nothing like in the movies. On the big screen, the bad guys always seem to meet with shady associates in the back rooms of crowded Chinese restaurants, glancing over their shoulders while being slipped a padded envelope under the table, but that's not how it works in real life. At least, that's not how my father does it.

Once there was a clap on the back at gate C14 at Logan Airport. That was in 1975. Another time there was a handshake in the Capitol Hill offices of a junior Illinois congressman. That was in 1902. And now there's the clinking of two beer mugs at McSorley's on Seventh Street in Manhattan. It's 1939.

I keep my head down as I check my gold watch before tucking it back in the pocket of my vest, along with the chain. It's just another part of the costume. I pick up one of my own mugs. There are only two drink choices at this bar—dark ale or light ale. I opted for dark, and they plunked down two mugs in front of me. I have no idea why they gave me two. I didn't even want one, but I had to get something. The glass is warm on my fingers, so I set it down, still untouched from a half hour ago, as I lean into the corner of the bar.

The bartender sets down his rag and nods at my mug. "What's the matter, buddy? Not to your likin'?" There's no friendly camaraderie in the way he says it, no "Hey, pal, why don't you try the light ale instead?" It's more of a threat hiding behind a simple question. I need to get out of here soon.

I start to shake my head but stop myself. The bobby pins keeping my hair tucked under my hat feel a little loose. The last thing I need is for my hair to tumble down past my shoulders. I'd certainly be the center of attention—my dad's attention included—and I'd have a lot of explaining to do. After all, it's going to be another thirty-one years before women are allowed in this bar.

"It's fine," I mumble in a heavy Romanian accent I throw in for the hell of it. "Not thirsty."

At a table a few feet away, my dad stands and extends his hand to the man with him. I'm not sure who this guy is, but based on precedent, I'm going to guess he's upper-level management at a company that manufactures war goods. Guns, tanks, bombs, airplanes. Turns out war is extremely profitable if you get the right person to sign on the right dotted line. Life lesson courtesy of my absentee father.

The man hands my dad a business card, and he tucks it inside his inner jacket pocket. Dammit. That's going to make things more complicated. My eyes snap back to my mug as my dad saunters past me, but I don't feel him give me a second glance. Just like in 1975 and 1902. I wonder if my dad would be ignoring me if he were still alive in the present, whether he'd be drawn to me in the past by some inexplicable parental force or something. I don't know. He died when I was a baby, and I never learned how normal parent-child relationships are supposed to work.

I give my dad a head start before I fish out a couple of coins and plunk them down on the wooden bar. The bartender jerks his head at me in a "Glad you're finally getting the hell out of here and freeing up some bar room on a Friday night" kind of way. I don't give him any sort of gesture in return.

I follow my dad out onto the street. I need to get that card before he projects back to the present. Well, his present. He left for this mission in 1991. I left decades later.

A woman walks past wearing a sweater that's probably two sizes too small and a tight pencil skirt that leaves very little to the imagination. *Please don't*, my mind begs, but sure enough my dad's head turns to follow the lines running up the back of the woman's stockings as she walks away.

You have a wife at home, I think. But at least it gives me an opportunity. I grab a rumpled copy of the *New York Times* off the top of a trash bin and hustle over to my dad. I unfurl the paper and pretend to stare at the headline:

GERMANY AND RUSSIA SIGN 10-YEAR NON-AGGRESSION PACT

And then I snort. Because that was a waste of paper.

I lift my head at the last moment to see my dad turning around, then focus my eyes back on the paper. My dad runs smack into me.

"Oh, sorry!" he says as I slip my hand into his jacket pocket and take out the card. His smile is warm and friendly. And entirely phony.

"My mistake," I say in a gruff voice. I've dropped the accent. I'm sure my dad would recognize it, and we are so not having the "Hey, are you from Romania? My wife's mother is Romanian" conversation. If there's one thing I've learned from these past months I've been tailing my dad, it's that he's the kind of guy who talks to everyone about everything. Lots of small-talk schmoozing, just like a politician.

I tuck my chin and keep walking, so he won't have the chance to recognize me from the bar, accent or not. I duck into the next street and toss the paper into another bin. Then I whip out the card.

HENRY GRAHAM

VICE PRESIDENT

IBERIA HOLDINGS

Iberia Holdings. This is a new one. Iberia. That has something to do with Spain. Crap, I hope that doesn't mean it's a foreign company. Those records are so much harder to trace. The Narc will not be pleased.

I repeat the man's name and title in my mind a few times, then peer around the corner. My dad is jogging down the stairs into the Eighth Street subway stop. He's on his way to Penn Station. I follow him down to the platform but leave about twenty feet between us. The train rumbles forward, and I watch my dad get on before I jump into the same car, different door.

During the ride, my dad grins and ogles at least three more women. He strikes up a conversation with a young blonde with a bad root job, and I hate this. I hate everything about this.

The subway pulls into Penn Station, and my dad takes the young woman's hand and kisses the top of it. Actually puts his lips on her skin, which makes my own crawl. I roll my shoulders back once, twice, like I can shrug off this feeling. But it lingers, wrapping around me like a scarf I can't take off. Or won't.

I hop off the car and spot my dad several paces ahead. The station is packed with evening commuters, which makes this a helluva lot easier. Then again, after I had to sneak a briefcase away from my dad in a not-crowded Logan Airport, photocopy the entire contents, then sneak it back without him noticing, anything looks like a piece of cake.

I pick up the pace and fall in line behind my dad as he makes his way toward the stairs. He's trying to get to Boston to project, which is exactly where I'll be heading myself soon. On a different train. There's a backup of commuters ahead, a throng of people pressed together, fighting one another through the turnstile. Perfect. I position myself to the right of my dad, then step toward the turnstile at the same moment he does. My dad elbows me out of the way to go first—*nice*—and I slip the card into his pocket before stepping away to let him through.

Done.

This mission is freaking done.

I turn and fight my way against the mob of people anxious to get home on a Friday night, then plop myself onto a bench. I have a ticket for a train that departs at 7:15, but I'm really in no hurry. I know what getting back to the present means. For a second, I let myself imagine I "accidentally" miss the train and spend a night in New York, but then the thought pops like an overinflated balloon when I realize the amount of paperwork that would create.

Plus, I want to see Abe. It makes me feel a bit codependent, but I crave Abe's company whenever I finish one of these missions. Like my brain can finally recognize how dysfunctional my old home life was, and now that I've had a taste of normalcy, of stability, it's become a part of me.

One train ride home and I'll have my fill. But first I'm starving. I'd kill for a soft pretzel. Something full of carbs, with no nutritional value. I'm not sure when pretzels were added to America's snack vocabulary, but a quick lap around the station tells me it wasn't 1939.

I sigh, buy myself a hot dog for ten cents, and park myself on a bench. And then I take a bite and remember why I don't eat hot dogs. They smell like sweat and taste only marginally better.

I chuck it in the nearest trash can and stand. I've given my dad plenty of lead time. He's probably on his train already.

It's well after eleven when my train pulls into South Station. I hail a cab. It looks like a prop from a movie. The car is long and shaped like a bubble, and painted this yellow-orange color with bright red fenders and a black-and-white checkerboard trim running the length of the doors. I ignore the driver's wrinkled nose when I toss myself into the backseat. *Look, dude, I just spent almost five hours on a train. I know I smell like cigarette smoke and other people's body odor. No need to remind me.* I'll never get used to how people in the past smoked everywhere they went and didn't let a silly thing like transportation or other people's health get in the way. Nope, the world was one giant ashtray.

"Thirty-four Beacon Street," I tell the driver before settling into the seat. The trip is short, and before I know it, I'm standing on the side of Annum Hall, staring at the door that leads into the gravity chamber, where I can project to the present without feeling like I'm getting stretched on the rack.

I unlock the door and step into the tiny broom closet. Then I tug on the chain hanging around my neck until a small, circular pendant pops out of the top of my shirt. An owl is etched on the front of it. I press the top button, and the pendant opens, revealing a watch face. This is my Annum watch, which is what allows me to travel through time. I press the button again, and the hands automatically fly around the dial. I'm going back to the present.

Peace out, 1939.

As soon as I shut the watch face, I'm yanked up like a reverse bungee jump. A few seconds later, I land on my feet inside the gravity chamber. It's hard to believe I used to find these jumps challenging. But I guess after you spend several days on the run, making dozens of unassisted jumps, your perspective changes.

I slip the watch over my head and take a breath. I can already hear the impatient *tap-tap-tap* of a pair of well-worn, sensible heels coming from the other side of the door. Time to get this over with.

I open the door with my left hand while holding out the watch with my right. Almost immediately, a tall woman in a pastel-green sweater set with frizzy brown hair pulled into a low ponytail takes the watch from me and places it into an open aluminum attaché with such care you'd think she was placing a premature baby into an incubator. Then she clicks the case shut and locks it. An electronic *beep* echoes in the hallway, and the woman withdraws from the attaché a security token bearing a set of numbers (which just changed and will continue to change every thirty seconds), then tucks the token into her pocket. The only way you can open the case is by entering her own personal password and the combination from the security token, which she never lets out of her sight. She holds up a tablet, and I dutifully place my hand on top, although I have to refrain from rolling my eyes.

"Obermann, Amanda. Code name: Iris. Annum Guard employee number 0022," an electronic voice states.

Yeah, security's changed just a bit around here lately.

I withdraw my hand. "Am I done?"

She narrows her eyes at me. "You know you're not," she says with all the patience of a post-office employee. "The memo I sent around on Monday has already gone into effect. I expect you—all of you—to begin your reports immediately upon your return."

I don't point out that it's nearly midnight on Wednesday. I left for this mission at one p.m. on Monday. I don't tell her that I'm so freaking tired, any report I'd try to write now would be a jumbled mess. I don't say anything. Instead I nod once and wait for her to spin on those beige heels and march back up to her office. The Annum Guard leader's office. What used to be Alpha's office but is now *hers*.

Jane Bonner. She's our interim leader, plunked here by the secretary of defense until the investigation into the Eagle Industries mess is completed. Forget making sure that every *i* is dotted and every *t* is crossed; Bonner expects—no, demands—that every *i* is dotted with a perfect circle, and you'd better whip out a ruler to make sure those crosses are exactly perpendicular.

I wait a minute to make sure she's gone and there's no chance of running into her. My eyes are drawn to the chipped paint above the gravity room door—to where the "Enhancement, Not Alteration" plaque used to hang. Our old motto. That plaque got ripped off the wall a few months ago, after everyone finally admitted there's no difference between enhancing the past with a small tweak and materially altering it with something huge.

Enough stalling. I trudge up the stairs into the grand foyer. The chandelier is still there, but the marble table with the flowers is gone, replaced with two back-to-back desks, each with a computer. A rotating team of initials sat there every day for months. FBI, CIA, NSA. Everyone wanted a crack at us. They haven't removed the desks, so I wonder if they're coming back.

I'm tempted to flip the bird toward Bonner's office, but I know that she's probably watching me on camera right now, so instead I keep all my fingers where they should be and head up the stairs to my room on the third floor. She can't stop me from taking a shower before she forces me to start this damned report.

There's a yellow Post-it stuck to my door.

Come find me when you get in.

It's not signed, but I'd recognize Abe's handwriting anywhere. I glance two doors down, to my boyfriend's room. I want to go now, but I just need to get out of these clothes and scrub my father's corruption from my skin with a loofah. *Five minutes, Abe.*

I pull my keys out of my pocket and open the door. A figure leaps off my bed, and I jump back into the hallway, crouching down and readying myself for a fight. Then I see who it is. Yellow.

"Whoa there, Bruce Lee, simmer down with the judo moves," Yellow says.

I take a breath and relax my shoulders. "I don't think Bruce Lee did judo."

Yellow cocks her head. "You know what? I don't think so either. Darn it. Witty line *fail.*"

"What are you doing in my room, Yellow?" I shut the door behind me and plunk my keys on the dresser.

"Waiting for you."

"The door was locked."

"And I am totally insulted that you think I'm not capable of picking a simple lock. How did it go?"

I fling my hat across the room, where it lands on a pile of dirty clothes in my closet, then I free my hair from the last few bobby pins holding it in place. A wavy mess of dark-brown hair tumbles around my shoulders. "I got the information I was looking for, if that's what you're asking."

Yellow pauses before plopping herself back down on my bed. "It wasn't."

I sigh and take off my vest before tossing it sideways into my closet. It lands on top of the hat. Now all I'm wearing is a men's white dress shirt and itchy brown trousers. "I swear to you, that woman keeps sending me on missions my dad was involved with on purpose. It's like she has a personal vendetta against me. She enjoys turning that screw as tightly as she can."

"She's heinous," Yellow agrees.

I laugh bitterly. "Yeah? She seems to love *you.*" I pull a pair of comfy sweatpants and a tank top out of my dresser, then toss them on the bed, next to Yellow.

Yellow grins and brushes a lock of pale-blonde hair from her shoulder. "What can I say? Everyone loves me."

I kick off my shoes and pull off my socks and leave them at the foot of the bed. I have to get out of these clothes.

My mom blessed me with strong bone structure, and I got broad shoulders and narrow hips from my dad. The flat chest is all me. Put all these features together, and it's easy for me to pass as male with the proper accessories. And while my old Peel professor, Samuels, assured me this was a definite plus for my future CIA career plans, it never really sat right with me. I crane my head toward my shower.

I unbutton the top of my shirt to let my neck breathe. "Look, I don't mean to be rude—"

"Like that's ever stopped you before."

"But I'm flipping exhausted, and I smell like a train depot from an era before antiperspirant became common hygienic prac- tice, *and* the Narc is making me draft my report *tonight.*"

Yellow scrunches her nose. "Tonight?" She glances at the clock. "Doesn't she realize it's after midnight?"

"Of course she does," I say, starting toward the bathroom. "But apparently that memo she sent around about starting imme- diately wasn't a joke. I'm taking a quick shower. I assume what- ever you wanted to talk about can wait until the morning?"

There's a knock on the door.

Abe.

The door opens, and Indigo walks in and shuts the door behind him. He stops in front of me. Like Yellow, he's ridiculously good-looking. Her hair is blonder, but they both have the same piercing blue eyes. The first time I saw Indigo, I was instantly attracted to him. It's one of those things you can't control—like when you're walking down the street and you pass a guy who looks like he could walk a runway. Your heart rate speeds up, your face flushes, your hands get clammy. It's a natural human reaction.

But then I actually got to know Indigo, and it didn't take me long to figure out that we're only friends. He's more like a brother to me, actually. And he's way too wholesome—too *aw, shucks*—to handle me.

"You kind of smell," Indigo says.

"Then get out of here so I can take a shower." I glance over my shoulder at Yellow. "And take your sister with you."

"Ouch," Yellow says.

I grab the towel from the bar and whip it over my shoulder. "You know I like you both, but—"

"I just got in," Indigo interrupts. He looks at Yellow, who's looking back at him with wide, eager eyes. I get the distinct impression I'm missing something here.

I look from Yellow to Indigo. "What? Hot date with one of the FBI analysts?"

Indigo shakes his head and drops his voice to a whisper. "I had dinner with my godfather."

Yellow claps like someone just told her she won a lifetime supply of cotton balls. And, trust me, that girl goes through *a lot* of cotton balls. She spends most Saturday nights flipping through trashy celeb magazines with a jam-packed makeup bag in her lap, copying red-carpet looks, then scrubbing her face and starting again. She's been hounding me to let her make me up as "vintage Elizabeth Taylor," but I've declined. Repeatedly.

I sigh. "Look, unless your godfather is someone seriously important—" Indigo's face lights up with a mischievous smile. "Your godfather *is* someone seriously important, isn't he? Why am I not surprised?"

"He and my dad go way back," Indigo says.

"*Who* and your dad go way back?"

"Ted Ireland. Regional FBI field director for the Boston office. Super-high clearance. I asked him about my dad."

My chest feels light, and I forget how exhausted I am, how much I have to do, how desperately I want to shower. I drop down onto my bed beside Yellow.

"Start talking," I say.

It's been four months since Alpha, Annum Guard's former leader, was killed. Shot in front of me by my old headmaster—Vaughn—at the Peel Academy because I discovered that Alpha was selling Annum Guard missions on the side and that his biggest client was Vaughn and a company called Eagle Industries. Four months since Zeta—Yellow and Indigo's father—was removed from his position as temporary leader of Annum Guard and replaced with Jane Bonner. And two months since anyone has heard from Zeta. The official word is that he went to a breakfast meeting with a friend in government contracting—and then just vanished.

I decide I don't want to wait for Indigo to start talking. Let's cut to the chase. "Does the Narc know?"

"Are you kidding me?" Indigo says. "Of course she doesn't know. I told her I was going for an evening jog and that I'd be gone a few hours. She knows I used to run cross-country. I promised I'd be a good boy and not make any detours. She didn't seem suspicious."

"How far did you go?" Yellow asks.

"Newton Centre," Indigo says. Yellow opens her mouth to protest, but Indigo adds, "I cabbed it home. I had the driver drop me off on Arlington Street. I jogged the last few blocks to work up another sweat. Stop giving me that look."

"You shouldn't be running all the way to *Newton* with your bad knee."

"Dude, calm down. You're not my mom."

I hold up both hands, one pointed at each sibling. "You guys, stop. What did your godfather say? What's his name again?"

Indigo crosses his arms over his chest. "Ted. The investigation is pretty classified—more than even his clearance will allow. But he pulled a few strings at Quantico, and he found something." He reaches into the zippered side pocket of his running shorts and pulls out a phone with a familiar cover—an ivory background with a handlebar-mustached penguin in the middle, wearing a top hat and monocle.

"Your phone?" Yellow asks in a clipped tone. "He found your phone?"

"Will you both have a little patience?" Indigo types in his code, and the phone unlocks. "They found something in Dad's study. The FBI did. It was in a sealed envelope set perfectly in the center of his desk. They think it's some kind of message or warning. Here, I took a picture of it." His finger swipes across the screen as he scrolls, then he holds up the phone so Yellow and I can see.

And then I stop breathing.

It's a picture of a plain white piece of paper with two even creases, from where it was folded. The only thing on the page is a small handwritten symbol:

I see it right away. *XP.*

The code name Alpha whispered to me before he died. The code name of the person behind Eagle Industries. The code name I've been ordered by everyone—Bonner, the defense department, even the vice president—never to mention because it's "sensitive information." And I haven't. Among the rest of my team, XP is still my own little secret.

"What the heck is that?" Yellow asks.

My mind is racing. Is Zeta dead? Did XP have him killed, just like Alpha? No. I refuse to accept that. But still, my hands are shaking.

"Ted didn't say," Indigo answers.

Yellow raises an eyebrow. "Didn't say or *wouldn't* say?"

"I got the impression that it was *wouldn't*, although he tried to pass it off like he didn't know."

"What does it mean?" Worry creeps across Yellow's face.

It means Zeta is in some serious trouble.

"I don't know," Indigo says.

I do.

Indigo looks at me. "Iris, what do you think?"

"I don't know either," I lie, and I feel like such a bad friend. Maybe I should tell them what I know. But then again, leaking sensitive information is a federal crime, and our government doesn't look too kindly on that. If I were to be prosecuted and convicted, there would be no slap on the wrist. No, it would be years in a supermax prison for me.

I decide to change the focus. "Did you ask Ted about Bonner?"

"I did. He knows nothing about Bonner. Literally nothing. He's asked all of his contacts at Quantico *and* Langley, and no one's heard her name before. It's like she just appeared out of nowhere."

"That's weird," Yellow says. "Who gets a high-profile appointment from the defense secretary out of nowhere?"

"That's more than weird," I say. "That's suspicious."

None of us say anything for a few moments. We're all trying to come up with some reason why our new leader doesn't have any sort of paper trail, and I'm trying to get rid of that sinking feeling in my stomach that I'm the worst friend in the world. But then there's another knock, and the door opens a second later. I jump off the bed as Abe looks from me to Yellow to Indigo, then pulls the Post-it from my door.

"Sorry," I say. "I just got in, and I'm so gross. I was going to take a quick shower, then come find you, but Yellow found me first, then Indigo, then—"

"McLean called while you were out," Abe interrupts. "I fielded the call for you."

And just like that, all the air is sucked from the room.

Yellow stands up. "Yeah, okay, we'll just let you guys talk. We can finish this conversation tomorrow."

Indigo nods. "See you, New Blue." Yellow squeezes my shoulder as she leaves, and Indigo shuts the door behind him.

I look into Abe's eyes. I know he hates being called New Blue. Officially, he's just Blue, but the rest of the Guard has taken to calling him New Blue since he replaced Tyler Fertig. Tyler never wanted to be a part of the Guard—not after he watched the physical effects of time travel slowly kill his mother—but Alpha forced him. After Alpha's corruption began to unravel, Tyler lost it. He shot Yellow, then tried to shoot himself. He'd probably be dead if I hadn't deflected the shot at the last second.

I don't know if it's the association with Tyler or the "New" part of the nickname that bugs Abe, but right now, it's like he didn't even hear Indigo say it. His eyes are focused only on me, and they're filled with sympathy.

"Did they say why?" I ask, even though I know the answer.

"They wouldn't tell me, but . . ."

"They're kicking her out." I flop backward onto my bed and shut my eyes. It's the same damned show I've been watching for years. Mom starts treatment. She swears it will be different this time, that *this* time she'll stick with it. All is well for a few weeks. Then Mom decides her art is suffering, goes off her meds, and slips back into our regularly scheduled bipolar programming. I've been tuning in for over ten years.

"They didn't say that." Abe sits down next to me.

"Oh, come on, what else is it?" I snap. Immediately I add, "I'm sorry. I'm tired." And incredibly overwhelmed. My dad. My mom. XP. Zeta. Bonner. "Thank you for taking the call. You didn't have to do that. You don't have to do any of this."

Abe reaches out and touches my knee. It's such a simple gesture. Fingertips against cotton, nothing more. But it fills me, grounds me. Reminds me I do have some stability in my life, even if it doesn't come from family.

I look up at him. His eyes are the color of roasted chestnuts, the kind you can buy from street vendors in the fall. And they're looking at me with the same warmth and comfort. But there's something else hiding behind them. A hesitation. An uncertainty.

"Just say it," I whisper.

There's more hesitation. "It's just . . ." Abe's fingers find mine, and he interlaces and squeezes. "I really hate seeing you this way. Over and over again. All the pain, all the sadness. It kills me to watch."

I squeeze his hand back. I know there's more he wants to say. Abe's a problem solver. I know he wants to fix this, fix my mom. We've talked about it before, when we were both at Peel. Late nights in my dorm common room, afternoon study breaks in the library, Saturday morning jogs across campus. I can't tell you how many times I've said to Abe that enough is enough, that if she pulls her crap again, I'm done.

But I'm never really done. She's my *mom*. And Abe's never called me out for my repeated empty threats.

Until now.

"Maybe it's time," he whispers. "You're almost eighteen. And really, you've been on your own for three years. Your mom's had more second chances than—who am I thinking of? That actress with all the DUIs and arrests? The one who got kicked off the plane after getting all pilled up and making a bomb joke?"

"I don't know." I untangle my fingers from Abe's. "I just . . . I *can't*, Abe. Trust me, I want to. More than anything in the world, I wish I could walk away, but . . ." My voice trails off as memories of Mom flood my mind. The trip into Boston to see Cirque du Soleil when I was ten, the Sunday morning yoga classes we took together in the park some summers, the paintings that fill our Vermont home. My crappy seven-year-old paintings, mixed with her MFA-trained paintings, hanging on every wall of our house.

It would be a different story if every memory I had was negative, if all my mind could dwell on was the drinking and the mania, or the cruelty that could come from a low. But that's not how it is. And I can't help but feel like my mom is a victim in all of this, too. She knows about Annum Guard. We had a long talk about it the first night she was in Boston. But she has no idea about the corruption. In her mind, her husband died a hero. And I'm not going to shatter that illusion for her. Not now. Probably not ever.

There's another knock at the door. Three short, hard raps. Anger erupts in my chest because I know who it is this time. She's always there. Always interrupting. Always pulling me back, pulling me away.

"What?" I growl as I jump up and swing open the door.

As expected, it's the Narc. She's still wearing the same matchy-matchy sweater set she had on earlier, not a hint of tiredness on her face. Instead, she's wearing a smug smile. "All done with the report?"

"Working on it," I say.

"You understand the new policy, do you not? That all mission reports are to be completed—"

"Immediately. While the mission is still fresh in the Guardian's mind. Yeah, I got it."

"Do you have any questions about what the word 'immediately' means?"

"Nope."

"I trust you should need only, what? Two hours to complete it?" She glances at the clock on my bedside table. "I'm going to retire for the night, but I'll look for the time stamp on your report to be no later than three a.m. Is that clear?"

I swallow the bile rising in my throat. "Crystal."

"Excellent," Bonner says before turning her attention to Abe. "Blue? Are you lost?"

"About to retire for the night myself, ma'am. I just wanted to make sure that Iris returned from her mission safely." I'm realizing my boyfriend is kind of like the male version of Yellow. Everyone inherently likes him, and he's so much better than I am at masking his disdain for certain people.

"How touching," Bonner says. "Well, good night."

Abe and I hear her stupid, boxy heels stomping down the staircase to the second floor.

Who is she?

"Remind me again why I thought staying in Annum Guard was a good idea?" I say.

Abe jumps up and kisses me on the forehead. "Because you want to bring integrity back to the Obermann name and get to the bottom of this conspiracy." I close my eyes and lean into his chest. He's right. "And because you are a good person, a strong woman, and you're always going to rise above whatever challenge life throws at you."

"I must have been really good in a past life to deserve you in this one."

Abe squeezes my shoulders, then scoots around me and into the hallway. "Hang on, I almost forgot." He reaches into his back pocket and slides out a protein bar. The kind of thing that tastes like a chemically enhanced piece of tree bark with a vague hint of peanut butter. Abe buys them in bulk with his parents' Costco card, and even though I usually rag on him for eating these, I swear I'm about to tackle him to the ground if he doesn't hand this one over. He smiles and tosses it to me, and I rip open the wrapper.

Abe reaches out and wipes a crumb from my lips. "Bang out your report and get some sleep." All talk of my mom is gone. Not forgotten, but I know Abe won't bring it up again.

It's what I need.

"Love you, Abey Baby."

"Love you always, Mandy Girl." He turns back to me. "Oh, but maybe take a shower, too. You smell like the urinal trough at Fenway."

And then he shuts the door before I can chuck the rest of the bar at him.

CHAPTER 2

My alarm wails at six and I want to cry. I open one eye, only to find it burning in pain. The other follows suit. Yep. This day is going to blow.

I push myself to a seated position and drop my head to my chest. I'm dizzy. Not nearly enough sleep. I open and close my mouth a few times, then stick out my tongue and make a clucking sound. Dehydrated, too. It takes every ounce of strength I have—physical and mental—not to lie back down. But the Narc is serious about her 6:30 a.m. daily debriefings, and I still haven't taken a damned shower yet.

I let the hot water rain down over me, but it doesn't wash away the fact that I've had only two and a half hours of sleep. There isn't enough time to find my blow-dryer, much less use it, so I pull my hair into a messy bun at the base of my neck and throw on a pair of gray pants, a baby-blue button-down, and black flats.

That's another recent change around here. Alpha didn't really care how anyone dressed unless we had a specific mission scheduled. Then the Narc came in and immediately set up a boring, corporate dress code. She actually used the word "slacks," and that's when we knew we were screwed. There's no wiggle room with people who use terms like slacks.

I run into Yellow on the stairs. She's dressed in a tight, black pencil skirt, which she's paired with a cream cardigan, lace tights, and black kitten heels. Her hair is perfectly flat-ironed, not a strand out of place.

"Are you freaking kidding me?" I ask her.

"What?" she says.

I give her a grunt in return and follow her down to the briefing room in the basement. There's a lectern at the front of the room and two rows of two tables facing it. Facing her.

At least there's a nice breakfast spread out this morning. A few days ago, it was lemon Danishes and French vanilla coffee. Gag. I grab half of an everything bagel, fill a Styrofoam cup with strong black coffee, and slip into the empty seat at Abe's table.

His hair is still wet, and he smells like my Abe—like the same "adventure-scented" bodywash he's used since freshman year. I stifle a laugh as I remember the number of times Abe walked into Peel's dining hall for breakfast, hands on his hips like a superhero, and proclaimed himself "Ready for adventure!" Somehow, it only got funnier every time he did it.

I smile and let my leg brush against his, then I look down at his hands, at the small metal box he's tinkering with. That's Abe. Always tinkering with something. When he was about six, his parents left him with a babysitter, only to come home to find their

DVD player in about three hundred pieces on the living room floor. He hasn't stopped dismantling and re-mantling things ever since. (And I'm pretty sure that babysitter was fired.)

"I'd ask how you slept, but you look like the *Night of the Living Dead*," he says, greeting me with a familiar half-grin.

Ugh. Abe and his old roommate, Paul, were obsessed with that stupid zombie movie. I can't tell you how many of our Saturdays went something like, "Hey, want to watch *Night of the—*" "No." And then I'd have to listen to Abe and Paul launch into an argument about how that movie started the entire zombie genre and how George Romero is a genius and blah blah blah. There was no reason to point out that the movie really isn't as scary as they thought.

I nod at the box he's holding. "What's that?"

Abe looks down for a second. "It's a feed-through scrambler. I need to tweak the oscillator a little more. The signal isn't quite right."

"I don't understand a word you just said."

He smiles. "I realized I don't have a good scrambler in my toolbox, and you never know when you're going to need to jam a signal."

Ah, right. Abe's toolbox. More like junk drawer full of contraptions—anything from small robotic vehicles to cameras hidden in pushpins. Abe really is just a younger version of Ariel, his grandfather and the man who invented the Annum watches.

I open my mouth to respond, but close it as the door shuts behind us. Abe drops the scrambler into his lap, out of view, as Bonner walks past us to the front of the room. Bonner hands a stack of stapled papers to the front row. Violet and Green each take a packet and hand them back to me. It's my report, the one I wrote last night. Wait, I mean this morning. I stare at the 2:58 a.m. time stamp, then scan the top page and notice there's a typo in the first damn paragraph. A bad one. Inwardly I groan as I toss Abe a report and pass the stack to Orange behind me.

As I do, I catch sight of Red. He's slouched in a chair at the back of the room with his eyes toward the floor, and I feel for him. That should be Red up there, giving the briefing. Red's at least ten years older than I am. He was being groomed to take over Annum Guard as its leader, but now he's been shoved into the position of underling to a mystery woman.

Red's had only one job lately, and that's to keep Bonner informed about our agency. When she first arrived, Red had to give a daylong briefing on how time travel fundamentally works. I rolled my eyes when I got the memo slipped under my door, mandating my presence, because I thought I knew how it all works— a Guardian travels back in time, tweaks the past, and then when she returns, the entire world has shifted up into a parallel present and has no idea about history before the tweak. Only we know.

I also knew that we travel by wormholes and that the opening is large in the present and gets smaller and smaller the further back you go. That means when you project back, more time passes in the present than it does in the past. If you go back twenty-five years, you lose two hours in the present for every one you spend in the past. A hundred years back, you lose eight hours. Two hundred, you lose about four and half *days* per hour.

But turns out there were also a lot of things I didn't know about time travel. I knew about dual projection—when one Guardian forces another to travel with him to a destination, no matter what date the other's watch is set to—but I didn't know you could only dual project into the past, and not use it to return to the present day. It's because we all travel inside our own wormholes when we dual project. It doesn't matter how far back you go, or when. You only have catching up to do when you try to return to the present, so you can't dual project to the present because each Guardian has her own catch-up time to complete.

And you can't trick the wormholes. Red looked right at Yellow and me when he said this. You can make a number of jumps, throwing yourself back and forth in time—like Yellow and I did when we were running from Alpha—but you can't undo all of that like it's a spiderweb you can bat away with a broom. It's more like a series of tunnels—hard, steel tunnels. That's part of the reason Alpha wasn't able to send a Guardian back to the moment I first ran away, to stop me from going in the first place. I was already inside my wormhole, tunneling my way through time. The only way to catch me was in the past—on *my* timeline. At the end of the tunnel.

The wormholes keep us safe while we're flying through time, but they're also a prison. There's no cheating the system.

Bonner clears her throat, and I swivel around in my chair. She tilts her head back with this stupid, smug grin on her face, like she's a monarch about to address her subjects. She casts her eyes down and starts reading my report aloud, word for word. I hate when people do that. Everyone in this room can *read*. Stop wasting our time.

"'I arrived at McSorley's at approximately four thirty p.m.'"— Bonner frowns and looks at me—"I thought I'd made my position clear on approximate times. Iris, exact times please from this point forward." She locks her gaze with mine, as if we're in some kind of staring contest. One I know I'm supposed to lose. It takes every last bit of effort I have to swallow my pride, but I do. I nod. Bonner gives a thin-lipped smile and looks down. "'I located the subject shitting at a table near the bar'"—I hold my breath as Bonner's head whips up and she stares at me again— "I trust that's supposed to read 'sitting at a table'?"

"Clearly," I mumble.

"No, clearly you need to exercise more care when drafting official documents."

Abe squeezes my leg. It's a gentle squeeze, one of reassurance and solidarity. But it doesn't make me feel any better. I zone out as Bonner talks about my dad entering the bar and starting his shady dealings. Living it once was bad enough. Reliving it is just unnecessary. I've been struggling for months with the knowledge that my dad was in on Alpha's scheme.

I let my thoughts wander to my mom. Maybe this time I can get her to change her mind and stick with a treatment plan. She owes this to me. She promised this to me. I reach under my sleeve and tug at my charm bracelet until it slides down onto my wrist. I finger the one charm on the bracelet my mom gave me—the bird that's supposed to signify a fresh start for us. I refuse to let that be garbage. My mom will do this.

I think of the Christmas when I was twelve. My mom wasn't very religious. Her mother raised her Romanian Orthodox, but it was a pretty half-assed religious education. By the time I came around, we mostly celebrated the Holy Church of Santa Claus at Christmas and the Gospel According to Chocolate Eggs at Easter, and that was it. But the year I was twelve, my mom decided we had to go to church on Christmas. We got all dressed up and walked to the community church down the road. I still remember like it was yesterday how they dimmed the lights and handed out candles. The sound of "Silent Night" being sung by a hundred different voices. The feeling of safety as my mom took my hand in hers, a tear rolling down her cheek as she sang.

And then I remember the Christmas when I was thirteen. My mom didn't even get out of bed. There were no presents under our tree, which had turned brown and shed its needles because I didn't know you had to water it. I knocked on the bedroom door around six that night to tell her I'd heated up a can of soup and to ask if there was anything she needed, and she told me to bring her a razor blade. I pretended not to hear.

Abe nudges me under the table, and I look up. Bonner is staring at me with raised eyebrows, the universal sign that she's just asked me a follow-up question about something in my report.

"I'm sorry, could you repeat that?" I ask.

She pauses a few deliberate seconds. "What else have you been able to ascertain about Iberia Holdings?"

Oh really? That's my job now? Because last week I got reprimanded for trying to look into corporate tax records on my own instead of letting the FBI analysts do their job. Good to know there's consistency. But also good that I spent about five minutes doing a quick Internet search at two in the morning.

"Iberia appears to still be in existence. It's an American company, first registered in Delaware in 1935. It's filed the required corporate accounting forms with that state every year since. Current registered agent is a woman named Claire Schuller, who also serves as the registered agent for an LLP called Rodkin &

Associates, which is a law firm in Waltham, Massachusetts, founded only about ten years ago. I'll make sure our analysts have all of this information so they can check into any other potential links between Iberia and Rodkin, and learn as much as they can about Schuller."

(Spoiler alert: None of this is going to have anything to do with Eagle Industries, the company connected to XP. Nothing Bonner has us doing is remotely related to Eagle Industries.)

I smile weakly at Bonner, and in return I get a glare. "Yes, that's what our analysts should be doing at a minimum. You stick with the field work, and I'll handle the intelligence portion of your job."

Abe's hands ball into fists on the table, and his nostrils flare. So this time it's my turn to reach under the table and give his leg a reassuring squeeze. Something to let him know that I'm not letting Bonner get under my skin, even though that's a lie. She's slimed her way through my pores, through my veins, into my bloodstream.

Bonner asks, "Does anyone have additional questions for Iris?" The room stays silent, but the tension hangs there like a dense morning fog. "Very well, then. You are dismissed. Iris, a word?"

She's got to be kidding. What does she want to do, berate me some more in private after doing it in front of all of my peers? *I will not let her get to me, I will not let her get to me.* I make that my mantra as I walk to the front of the room, where she's waiting behind the lectern like a professor.

"Yes?" I ask.

"Schedule change for the day," Bonner tells me. "I had you sitting in with the analysts this morning, but your presence has been requested elsewhere."

That's a relief. Just as I start to wonder who could possibly have requested my presence, a smile creeps across Bonner's icy pink lips, and I know. Whatever this is, it's not going to be a relief. Best-case scenario, an annoyance. Worst-case, physically painful.

"Who am I meeting with?"

"Whom."

"Excuse me?"

"The correct question is 'With *whom* am I meeting?'"

Oh my god.

I don't take the bait. I just keep looking at her, knowing eventually she's going to have to tell me.

Bonner's eyebrows crease ever so slightly. "The vice president is in town on behalf of Congressman Durrin's reelection campaign."

I clench my fists. *Oh no.* This is worse than worst-case.

"The vice president has requested a meeting"—*No no no no no*—"for this morning. Nine o'clock." *Why, dear god, why?* "Secret Service will meet you in the lobby of the Taj and escort you to the vice president's suite. Do you have any questions?"

I have plenty. I've told the vice president and the investigation committee everything I know about Peel, about former headmaster Vaughn (who's currently living in a federal detention facility in Maryland and refusing to talk), about Alpha, about my dad, about Eagle Industries. Everything. But they won't stop. When is enough going to be enough?

"Nope, I'm all set." I smile and turn before she has a chance to chide me for saying "nope" instead of "no, ma'am."

This is going to be a long day. I grab my coffee and untouched bagel, and I don't try to cushion the speed of the door slamming on my way out. I gasp as I go flying into Orange. The coffee sloshes in the cup, and I'm seriously glad I opted for a lid today.

"Hey," he says, jerking his head back to get the tips of his hair out of his pale-blue eyes. His hair is longer than normal. Usually, he has it buzzed pretty close to his scalp, but today there's no mistaking its bright orange color. I've always thought that Orange got the short end of the code-name stick.

"Um . . . hi." This is odd. I literally can count on one hand the number of conversations I've had with Orange since I've been in Annum Guard. Actually, make that one finger. And even then it was an awkward moment when we both found ourselves on the stairs and neither of us felt like playing that weird game where one person pretends to slow her pace while the other acts like he's in a rush because we don't feel like chatting. I think the difference with Orange is that he's older. He was the first new recruit after Red, and he was here for years and years before the rest of us were added. I'm not sure how old Orange is, but maybe late twenties? He's friends with Red, not so much with the rest of us. I don't even see Orange that often anymore, not since he moved out.

That's another thing I learned recently. I always thought it was a little odd that everyone *lived* here—like, don't we need some work-life separation?—but then Yellow told me that was an Alpha mandate that had been in place for less than a year. It makes sense. Alpha got a little crazy and paranoid toward the end.

After Alpha died, Orange and Green had moved out by the weekend. Red stayed as a show of solidarity toward the organization. Zeta left for home, but made Yellow and Indigo stay for "safety reasons" that didn't make any sense then but do now. Violet and I both stayed because we're in the same boat—nowhere else to go. Abe has plenty of options, but he laughed at me when I suggested he move home.

"You're my home," he'd said, nestling closer to me on my bed.

"That was total garbage what happened in there," Orange tells me, snapping me back to the present. His jaw tenses. "I know Alpha had his flaws"—*you think?*—"but there's no way he would have let that happen to you. To any of us. Make sure you stand up to her. Don't get pushed around."

I'm not sure what to say. I feel like I'm getting a pep talk from my big brother after a playground bully told me I couldn't go down the slide.

"You're strong, Iris. You've certainly proven that. You don't have to take this." He pauses, looks at the door to the briefing room, then adds in a much louder voice, "None of us do."

And then the door next to the briefing room opens, and Red pokes his head out of Situation Room One. He scowls. "Orange. Discretion." He jerks his head back into the room.

Without another word to me, Orange follows Red into the Sit Room.

"Thanks?" I say as the door closes. I'm not sure if he hears me. I stare at the closed door for several seconds.

What just happened here?

But then I brush it off and head for the stairwell. Abe is waiting for me at the top of the stairs.

"Vice president wants to meet with me," I say.

"Again?"

I shrug and take a bite of the bagel.

"I set up a meeting with Dr. Netsky at ten thirty. Will you be able to make that?"

I stop and swallow the bagel. It's way too big of a bite to manage in one gulp, and it scrapes the inside of my esophagus as it goes down. "Dr. Netsky? Really? How did you manage that?"

Dr. Netsky is the chief psychiatrist at McLean Hospital, where my mom has been living for the past couple of months. I've been trying for weeks to get him to meet with me, ever since my mom started pulling all her old tricks and telling everyone who would listen that she doesn't really need the treatment she desperately needs. The man is impossible to get on the phone, much less in a face-to-face. Suddenly, this day is looking up.

Abe flashes me a coy smile but doesn't say anything.

I look at the clock hanging in the hall. "Seriously, it's seven a.m. How did you do this in six hours?"

Abe shrugs. "Hacked into McLean's server and found the personal contact info for all staff. I called Netsky at four in the morning and pretended to be from the Vermont Department of Children and Families. It's amazing how fast someone will respond if you call them in the middle of the night about the welfare of a minor."

"I'm legally emancipated," I point out.

"I didn't see a need to include that little detail."

I shake my head. I can't believe this. "That was ingenious."

"Well, Ingenuity is my middle name."

"And all this time, I thought your middle name was David." I link my arm through Abe's and lean my head on his shoulder. "Thank you."

"You can do ten thirty?"

"I'll be there at ten thirty even if I have to break several international laws in the process."

"Let's not go crazy. It would be hard explaining to people that my girlfriend is a UN-sanctioned criminal." He kisses me on the cheek, then walks toward the library.

Before the door closes, he winks at me, the same cocky wink he flashes any time he wants me to smile. Because Abe is so not cocky. He tries it on for size every once in a while, but it never fits. His strut is more like a limp, and his pout looks like he's having an allergic reaction to a bee sting.

I laugh as Abe shuts the door. Then the smile disappears as I think about what awaits me.

Okay, it probably won't take longer than half an hour to get to McLean. As long as Abe and I leave Annum Hall by ten, we'll be fine. The Taj is a five-minute walk from here. I can't imagine what the vice president has to talk about that would take more than an hour. There can't be any questions left that haven't already been asked. And if push comes to shove, I'm not above being a teensy bit rude and excusing myself.

You have to come first sometimes, Amanda. That's one of the things Dr. Becker, a family therapist at McLean, keeps telling me. Over and over, week after week in the sessions I've been attending with Mom.

I'm important, I tell myself. *I'm allowed to come first.*

I just hope the vice president agrees.

CHAPTER 3

I arrive at the Taj hotel a few minutes before nine, and there are already two Secret Service agents waiting for me. You can spot these guys from a mile away. The movies get them exactly right. Short hair, dark suit, sunglasses, big old earpiece, standing around and staring in the most conspicuous way possible. Unlike the CIA, the Secret Service doesn't want to blend into the background. They want you to know they're there, and they want you to know you'd be an idiot to mess with them.

It smells like floral air freshener in here. I'm getting a headache. I walk up to the two guys standing by the curved staircase that leads to the ballrooms.

"Iris," I announce myself.

The bigger of the two nods. "Miss. We'll escort you upstairs." The three of us pile into the elevator, and we make our way to the presidential suite. I think I'd be insulted if I was the vice president and hotels kept putting me in the presidential suite. It's like a constant reminder that you are not, in fact, the president.

There's another agent stationed outside the double doors. He's enormous—his biceps are so big, I don't think he can touch his shoulders—and his neck is the same width as his jaw. He looks down at me and nods. "Miss." That's another thing that drives me crazy about most government agents. The "miss" thing. I'm not eight years old, and this isn't the nineteenth century. Just call me by my code name. "You're expected."

"Well, I would hope so," I say with a smile as the agent opens the doors for me.

The suite is huge. Easily bigger than my whole house back in Vermont, which immediately makes me feel out of place. I walk into a light-blue, carpeted living room–dining room combo with massive, gold-curtained windows. A man stands with his back to me, gazing out over Arlington Street and the Public Garden below. He's wearing a navy suit, has salt-and-pepper hair, and could really benefit from logging a couple of hours in the hotel gym downstairs. Also, he is very clearly not the vice president. He turns to greet me.

"Amanda!"

"It's Iris."

"Oh right, right, of course," he says as he extends his hand and grabs mine in a weak handshake. "It's been, what, a month since I last saw you?"

"I'm sorry, I thought I was meeting with the vice president."

The man smiles. "And indeed you are. My wife is running a bit behind schedule, but she should be along here any minute now. Until then, you've got me for company. How's that sound?"

About as good as a bullet in my brain. I sigh. I've learned in the past few months that "running a bit behind schedule" to a politician means "running about six hours late" to the rest of the free world. The first time I met the vice president one-on-one, I was so nervous I didn't care that she kept me waiting for hours on an empty stomach. But now the allure has completely worn off. I think I'd rather opt for dental surgery than meet with another politician.

"I'm sorry, Mr. Caldwell, but if the vice president is going to be really delayed, I think I'll have to reschedule. I have a meeting at ten thirty I have to get ready for." I start for the door. The VP's husband holds up his hand to stop me.

"Nonsense. Caroline is only a few minutes away. She had a breakfast speaking engagement this morning downstairs in the Adam Room."

"So she's in the building?"

"In the building," he repeats.

I inhale through my nose. The breath is long and exaggerated and meant to let this man know I'm annoyed. This certainly is not the first time I've met Joe Caldwell, husband to the most powerful woman in the country. He's a Texas transplant, born into a New England family that had money to invest in a small oil company that hit the jackpot back in the eighties, when everyone was obsessed with drilling, shoulder pads, and TV shows that featured both. I don't think he's had a real job since. According to his official White House bio, he's spent the last twenty-plus years working as a "consultant," whatever the hell that means.

I think what's really throwing me is that I can't figure Joe Caldwell out. I don't know if he's consciously being a douche bag or if he's just one of those people who means well but completely lacks any sort of self-awareness. The more time I spend around him, the more I think it's the latter.

The doors open and I exhale a sigh of relief. Maybe I won't have such a time crunch after all. I turn, but it's not the vice president. It's a guy maybe a few years older than I am. He looks like a trim mini version of Joe. With the same fake smile tinged with an air of superiority.

"Colton!" Joe greets him with a clap on the back. "I'd like for you to meet Amanda."

"Iris," I growl, and now I'm back on the douche bag side of the fence. I doubt Joe would be playing so fast and loose with sensitive information if I was a forty-year-old CIA operative. But no. I'm just a seventeen-year-old girl. He clearly doesn't get that I can think of at least seven different ways to kill him with my bare hands. I glance at the doors again.

"Iris," Joe says, "this is my eldest boy. Colton is going to be a sophomore at Harvard." His tone is more than proud father. It's obvious I'm meant to be impressed.

I look at Colton, and he's still smiling that canned smile at me, and I wonder what the hell I'm doing here.

"Did you hear me? I said Colton is a sophomore at Harvard."

"Oh, well . . . good for him. I really think I need to reschedule if Vice President Caldwell isn't available."

"Nonsense!" Joe turns to Colton. "Why don't you run down to the Starbucks and get Iris one of those pumpkin coffee things all the girls are crazy about?"

I hold up my hand. "No, that's—"

"Iris, you're probably thinkin' to yourself, 'But, Joe, it's the middle of summer. They don't have those pumpkin coffees until the fall!' And you'd be right, except that there are a few perks to being the vice president that aren't available to the general public." He winks at me.

Except that you aren't the vice president, you total, total tool.

"I don't need any coffee," I say. I look at the clock. It's 9:15. Not yet time to start panicking about missing the McLean appointment, but every minute definitely counts.

Then the door opens a third time, and the vice president sweeps into the room. She unloads an armful of papers onto the edge of the dining table and turns to us. Caroline Caldwell is a very petite woman. I probably have six inches on her. She has on a pale-pink skirt suit with three-quarter length sleeves. Her ash-blonde hair is coiffed in a neat bob with blunt bangs, and her makeup is flawless. Not too much but certainly enough to mask a few of her fifty-some years.

"Iris!" she greets me. At least she got that right. "I'm so sorry to have kept you waiting. So many photo ops with Congressman Durrin's constituents. I was not expecting the turnout we had."

The vice president kisses her husband on the cheek. "And I see you met our son Colton. He goes to Harvard, you know."

"Yes, as do a lot of people." Damn, that came off a little ruder than it sounded in my head. I clear my throat to try to cover it. "What can I do for you, Madam Vice President?"

She motions to the dining room table before turning to her husband. "Joe, darling, the daffodils in the Public Garden are truly breathtaking. And the *Globe* is downstairs in the lobby. I'm sure their photographer would love to get a picture of you strolling through the scenery."

Yeah, I'm pretty sure a professional photojournalist is not actually clambering to get a picture of a grown man out *strolling* through the daffodils, but I'm grateful Joe is being dismissed. He smiles and bids me a "good day," and then clasps Colton's shoulder.

"Nice to meet you," Colton says in a soft Texas drawl, and I don't buy his polite niceties for one second.

"Yeah, you, too," I say, even though I'm not sure if I actually *met* Colton. This morning is very weird. And it's ticking away. After they leave, I put my hand on the back of a silk chair, the only cue I can think of to show the vice president that I want to sit and start this meeting already.

She obliges me and lowers herself into the opposite chair. "So, Iris, you're probably wondering why you're here today."

"Yes." I drop down into the chair. "I assure you, Madam Vice President—"

"Call me Caroline, please."

Well, that's a bit awkward. And also not going to happen. I clear my throat again. "I assure you . . . ma'am . . . that I don't have any more information than I had a few weeks ago. If I did, you certainly would be among the first to know."

Caroline smiles. It's warm, but it's a politician's smile. All pizzazz and no meaning. "Oh, I know. Trust me, I'm kept very up to date on the inner workings of your agency." She's still smiling. *What is this?*

"O-kay." I drag the word out.

And then Caroline laughs this throaty laugh, and I squirm. "Iris, I know this investigation hasn't been easy on you." Understatement of the millennium. "I know you've learned a lot about your . . . er . . . family dynamic that I'm sure you were unaware of previously."

Like that my father is a corrupt murderer who I don't think ever told the truth one day in his life?

The VP drums her fingers along the chair's arm. "I'm sure you're aware that I didn't exactly have the most . . . er . . . normal of upbringings." I guess this is true. She comes from a very old political family. Her grandfather was a senator. Her father was secretary of state. "When you're raised in the political climate I was raised in, you learn to play by different rules."

An electronic version of a classical song I've heard before (but couldn't name if my life depended on it) fills the air. The vice president lunges for her phone and her eyes go wide when she sees the screen. "Sorry," she mumbles as she leaps out of the chair and heads toward the bedroom. "Have to take this." The door slams shut, and I hear a terse "Hello?" from the other side.

I sigh and stand up. The VP has dropped her voice so low that all I can hear is a whisper. I have no idea who she's talking to or how long this call will take. I glance at the clock. Still plenty of time, but ugh.

I pace back and forth a bit, but it's clear this call isn't going to be a short one. One more glance at the clock. 9:30.

9:40.

9:45.

9:50.

Dammit.

You have to come first sometimes.

Screw it, I'm leaving. I'll jot a quick note to Vice President Caldwell, and she'll have to understand. On the desk by the window, I find a cheap hotel pen but no pad of paper. I open the top drawer of the desk. There's a hotel information binder but no paper. Great.

Then I look over at the table, where the VP dropped that stack of papers. Maybe there's a notebook or memo pad. The top stack of documents has a cover sheet from the Office of Management of Budget. It's a Statement of Administration—something about coal miners. Looks important, and I probably shouldn't tear off the front page to scribble, *Call me!*

I don't mean to snoop, I really don't, and I could just tell the Secret Service guy waiting outside the door that I have to leave, but instead I flip to the next stack of documents. And then my gut does a somersault. This one also has a cover sheet.

IN RE: MATTER OF JULIAN ELLIS

Julian Ellis. A name I didn't know until four months ago, but one I've heard way too many times since then. Alpha's real name. There's a subheading under that.

Testimony of Noah Masters

Masters. Also a name I've gotten to know very well these past few months. Elizabeth Masters. *Yellow.* Nick Masters. *Indigo.* Noah must be their father. This is Zeta's testimony before the closed-door Senate committee analyzing every little thing that Annum Guard has ever done. I glance at the date. He gave this testimony only two days before he disappeared.

"CONFIDENTIAL" must be stamped across the cover page at least a dozen times.

This is playing with fire. And I'm pretty sure it's also illegal. But damn me if I don't flip open to the first page. It looks like hearing testimony, where a senator asks questions and a court reporter copies down Zeta's answers word for word. I know this because I had to read through the transcript of my own testimony and sign off that I actually said what the reporter wrote down.

I take a deep breath. I really should close this, tell the Secret Service I have another appointment, and bolt. But instead I pause and strain to listen. Vice President Caldwell's hushed voice is still audible from the bedroom. And so I whip out my phone, open the camera, and snap a picture of the first page. Then I flip to the second and snap again. And again and again and as many times as I can until the vice president's voice becomes louder. The call is ending.

I flip the testimony shut, toss the coal-mining report on top, then straighten the pile into a neat stack.

Is that too neat?

But I don't have time to fix it as the door opens and the vice president walks into the living room, holding her phone to her chest with a pained expression. She sees me standing by the table.

"I'm sorry," I say before she can dwell too much on what I'm doing over here. "I have a very important personal appointment that I'm going to be late for unless I leave right now."

Caroline looks from the table to me, then shakes her head and drops her phone onto the chair where she'd been sitting before. "Of course," she says, sounding frazzled. "I'm very sorry to have kept you waiting." And then she comes over to me. "What I'm going to say won't take but a minute."

I hesitate. Somehow I doubt that. I glance behind the vice president at the stack of papers. They're definitely too neat.

"Like I was saying before we were interrupted, there are certain . . . er . . . unpleasantries that come with living a life in the public eye. Times have changed, and in this era of global media, it becomes harder and harder to exercise . . . discretion."

What is she talking about? "Okay?"

"I know that you're deep into the investigation of Eagle Industries and other personal ventures that the former leadership of Annum Guard might have dabbled in."

She pauses, like she wants me to confirm this. So I do. "Yes?"

"Just as I am deep into the investigation from the other side."

Another pause. *Jesus, woman, just spit it out.* But then I glance at those too-neat papers again and decide riling her up isn't in my best interest at the moment. "Right."

"You're a very young woman with your entire life ahead of you, Iris, and I want to make sure that the past dealings of your father don't irreparably tarnish your reputation."

Yeah, me, too.

"In the same vein, should you uncover any information that you deem"—pause—"sensitive"—another pause—"I ask that you exercise discretion in who you share that information with and why. Am I making sense?"

Of course she is. I raise an eyebrow. "You scratch my back, I'll scratch yours."

The vice president's face softens into a smile. "If that's how you want to put it. I'm sorry I kept you so long. Please, I hope I haven't made you too late to your appointment."

I nod and turn to go. But the vice president reaches out and grabs my arm.

"Oh, and there's one more thing."

I look at her hand on my arm, then back at her. "Okay?"

"Colton and a couple of his friends from school are starting at Annum Guard on Monday."

I blink. "Colton . . . your son?"

"Yes. Just for the summer. It's never too early to start building your résumé. I wanted to place him in a more high-profile agency in the capital, but Colton protested that he didn't want to leave his friends for the whole summer, and then Joe told me I was being too hard on him and to let him stay in Boston, and so Annum Guard was the compromise."

Is she for real? The *compromise*? Her pampered little son is being *forced* to work at one of the world's most secret agencies?

"Okay," I say again.

"They're just going to be reviewing the documents you've uncovered so far, nothing too important, and of course they have no idea about the investigation. They assume they're reviewing paperwork from previous missions and doing so under the strictest of confidentialities. But I'd really like it if you kept a close eye on Colton."

"No problem," I say with what I hope comes off as a sincere tone.

"I'm trusting you on this."

She lets go of my arm, and goose bumps dot my skin because that's a really strange choice of words. *Trusting* me. With what? Her son? Or her secrets?

With one final nod of my head, I'm out the door.

Secret Service escorts me to the lobby, and once I'm on the street, running back to Annum Hall, my mind replays everything that just happened. But I can't for the life of me figure out what the vice president wants me to do. Or why.

CHAPTER 4

"Discretion?" Abe says as the government-issued Chevy he's driving zips across Route 60. "You're sure that's the word she used?"

"Yep." I stare at the clock on the dash. 10:25. No way we're making it on time. I've spent the whole car ride telling Abe about my meeting. But I haven't told him about finding Zeta's testimony because . . . I'm not sure why. Maybe because of the XP thing I've been ordered to keep quiet. Or maybe because the pictures currently sitting in my phone are burning a hole in my pocket, and that's enough for now.

"Well, that's weird," Abe says.

"You think?" I close my eyes for a moment and replay the scene for the twentieth time. Then I open my eyes and turn to my boyfriend. "You don't think the vice president is behind Eagle Industries, do you?"

"Uh-uh. No way. Not a chance."

"So you want to take a second to think about it, then?"

Abe cracks the smallest smile as he turns onto Olmsted Drive, which leads us to the hospital. "If the vice president had anything to do with Eagle, she'd be doing everything in her power to bury the investigation, not spearheading the whole thing."

"True," I admit, checking the speedometer. He's going ten over the speed limit, but it still feels like we're crawling. "So what's she hiding?"

Abe shrugs. "That's a really good question. And stop looking at the dash."

It's 10:30 exactly when we pull into McLean's parking lot. I sprint full steam to the front door, terrified we'll be too late and Dr. Netsky will move on to his next appointment.

"Hey," Abe pants as he catches up to me. "Slow down. He's not going anywhere."

I shake my head. I just want to be there. *Now.* And you never know how long security is going to take.

The clock outside Dr. Netsky's office door reads 10:42 as I rap my knuckles against it. I hold my breath, praying there's an answer on the other side.

"Come in," a pleasant voice says.

I open the door and stop in my tracks. Dr. Netsky isn't what I was expecting. I pictured someone grandfatherly, but the man before me is a lot younger than that, with hair that's only starting to gray. He's sitting behind a mahogany desk, gazing at me with a polite smile on his thin face. But that's not what stops me. It's the fact that I'm staring at the back of my mom's head. In hindsight, I should have been prepared to meet her here today. After all, she's the patient. She has the right to be informed about her medical care.

My mother turns, and she has none of Dr. Netsky's pleasant warmth. This is not the mom I like to remember, but this is a mom I know all too well.

I look like her. A lot like her. We both have the same dark brown hair, the same olive skin, the same small nose, the same high cheekbones. But our eyes are different. Mine are a deep brown, like my dad's, but my mom's are the vivid green of polished peridot, her birthstone. When my mom is well, her eyes—her entire presence—is striking. But today her eyes are dull, angry.

She's lost weight. Too much weight. Skin stretches over her clavicle, and I can count the ribs peeking out above the deep V-neck of her shirt. She has on her skinny jeans—the ones she can fit into only during the periods of mania when she doesn't eat. They're loose around her waist.

She looks past me to Abe. "He can't come in."

I open my mouth to protest, but Abe interrupts. "It's fine. I'll just wait outside." He squeezes my hand before he slips away. My hand dangles by my side, empty and cold. I feel like it's been amputated.

"Amanda." Dr. Netsky motions to the chair next to my mom. "Please sit. Your mother and I were just going over her medical file for her stay with us."

"Uh-huh," I say as I lower myself into the chair. There's a canvas resting against the side of my mom's chair, but it's turned around, so all I can see is the back of the frame. I don't take my eyes off my mom. She's staring straight ahead at the wall behind Dr. Netsky. She's mad about being here. I bet you anything she thinks I went behind her back to set up this meeting. Which, you know, I did.

"Joy has been living in our Appleton extended-care facility for"—he flips back a page—"over three months now."

My mother stays silent, so I say, "Correct."

The doctor flips forward a page. "And in that time, we've tried"—he blinks—"a very wide variety of pharmaceutical combinations to help treat your mother's illness. We had initial success with lithium, but after a few weeks, Joy refused any further treatment." Like always.

The doctor scans the rest of the page. "After a number of unsuccessful combinations, we settled on carbamazepine and sertraline."

"Oh," I say. Because I know where this is headed. I know exactly what happened.

"Joy showed great improvement during the first two months on carbamazepine and sertraline, combined with intensive psychotherapy, but soon thereafter, she . . ." Dr. Netsky looks up at my mom, as if he just remembered she's here. "I mean, you, Joy, decided to stop the medication and refrain from trying any further combinations."

My mom doesn't say anything. She doesn't move, doesn't even blink.

I reach over and touch her arm and try not to be hurt by how she tenses. "Mom?"

My mom yanks her arm away. She leans over, grabs the canvas, and shoves it into my hands. "Look at that," she practically spits.

I'm scared to. But I do. It's a painting of a white sailboat gliding across a glistening aquamarine sea. I lean in closer. She's used about a dozen different shades of blue for the waves. It's a level of depth and detail I haven't seen from her work in a while.

"What do you see?" she snarls.

I look at Dr. Netsky, who has his eyebrows raised, then back to my mom. "Um . . . a boat?"

And then she rips the canvas from my hands and cracks it over her knee. I jump in my seat. "It's a *boat*. The most literal, piss-poor, goddamned boat you've ever seen. The kind of stuff that talentless hacks paint, then mass produce so *doctors* can hang it in their offices." She throws Dr. Netsky a look filled with venom more poisonous than a black widow's, then she whips her head back to me. "Do you think I'm a hack, Amanda?"

"Of course I don't." My voice is barely a whisper. "Mom, that painting is really good."

"Oh, what do you know? You don't know anything. I don't paint *boats*."

And this is sort of true. My mom's known for being an abstract painter. She'll throw down a dab of yellow, a swirl of blue, and she'll blend it all together until you can't help but stare at it. She'll tell you it's a boat, and you'll think she's crazy, but then you'll squint—and you'll see it. Some semblance of a boat peeking out from beneath the globs of paint.

"It's like five years ago. *Exactly* like five years ago!"

And there it is. What I knew was coming. This conversation is over. My mom has checked out.

Dr. Netsky looks from me to my mom, then down to his chart. Out of the corner of my eye, I see him flip back a page, then one more, trying to match the dates. "I'm not seeing anything in the notes that details any incident from five years ago." He looks up at my mom. "Can you enlighten me?"

My mom leans forward in her chair.

"Carbamazepine and sertraline. Let's just call them by their real names. Tegretol and Zoloft. The medication that nearly killed us."

I slowly shake my head. "Mom," I say in the softest voice I can. "You know that's not true. The art world is cyclical. Even Adam said that."

"Cyclical," my mom sneers, pushing herself back in her chair. "Right."

Dr. Netsky is staring at me. I swallow the lump in my throat. "We've tried carbamazepine and sertraline in the past. And you're right. It's a great combination for my mom." I pause. I don't want to say anymore.

"But?" the doctor prods. "Five years ago?"

I glance over at my mom. She's not looking at me. "Five years ago was when we first started the combination. Five years ago was also when . . . we kind of had a rough patch."

"I didn't sell a goddamned single painting for an entire year," my mom says through gritted teeth.

"It wasn't because of the meds, Mom. I heard what Adam said. He said it was some of your best work yet and that the lack of sales was just due to a dip in the market. We were in a recession! Adam said you were going to sell soon and even bigger than before. He practically promised us!"

"Who's Adam?" the doctor interrupts.

"Her publisher. Kind of like a manager."

"Former publisher," Mom adds.

Dr. Netsky flips through the file. "I don't see any of this noted in your file, Joy. Did you tell Intake about your history with this drug combo?"

Mom doesn't answer, and I wish I'd gone with her that day, now more than ever. But I didn't. I was stuck in 1917.

Of course she didn't tell them—being honest wouldn't let her play the victim card she loves to throw out. Five years ago, when I was twelve, was the best year of my life. Mom met with her medication manager every month, like she was supposed to. She was happy. She was healthy. She slept. She ate. She kept a normal schedule—not painting for twenty hours in a row, only stopping when she passed out from exhaustion on the living room floor.

That was the year I had a mother.

I want it back.

"You're just scared, Mom," I whisper. "I am, too. But you promised this to me. Remember how you *felt* that year."

"Destitute? Like I didn't know where the next rent payment would come from?"

"No, Mom. Healthy. Stable. *Happy*." My breath catches as I remember the late night talks we had that year. How my mom made me swear I'd remind her to take her meds every single day. And then I remember how no amount of begging is ever going to get her to refill the prescription now. "You promised me you'd try again."

"Well, I take it back." My mom drops the broken canvas to the floor. "You remember what happened when I stopped taking those drugs, right? I sold a painting the next month. And it took me only two weeks to paint, not two months." She kicks the broken canvas across the room and looks to the doctor, nodding her head forcefully, like she's waiting for him to acknowledge that she made the right decision.

"Yeah, to pervy old Mr. Jotkins, who only bought it because you practically gave it away and because he liked to stare at your boobs!"

She narrows her eyes and looks away.

"Mom, if it's money you're worried about, I'm making a salary now, too. I mean, it's not a *ton* of money, but I can cover rent and utilities." I have been, the whole time she's been here at McLean. Sending money each month to a neighbor to hold onto for my mom. But telling her that would only make things worse.

"I don't want my *daughter* to take care of me. I can handle myself. I just need things to be like they used to be."

I take a breath to compose myself. "Mom, things can't be like they used to be. Deep down, you know they can't. Maybe we should just listen to Dr. Netsky. Maybe he has some suggestions for us?" I give him my best pleading stare.

He clears his throat. "Yes. Our options." Another throat clear. "Joy, I really think we shouldn't be so quick to give up on medication that's proven successful in the past. However, I've asked a colleague to be available to join us, if you should wish to speak with her about a more permanent type of option." Dr. Netsky hesitates and looks at my mom. I hold my breath. "Dr. Singh is the director of our electroconvulsive therapy service—"

Dr. Netsky is still talking, but you can't hear a word he says because my mom has jumped up so fast her chair bangs to the floor.

"No!" she yells. "Absolutely not!"

I'm frozen in my seat.

"You want me to do *shock therapy?*" Abe doesn't have to be in the room to hear this. I'm sure they can hear her down in patient check-in.

Dr. Netsky is on his feet, holding out a hand to my mother. She doesn't take it. "Joy, we don't call it shock therapy. What you're thinking of is a fiction of movies and television shows. The service we provide is a safe and effective procedure—"

"Safe and effective, my ass!" My mom grabs my arm, and I gasp. "Is this what you want, Amanda? You want them to strap me to a board and run an electrical current straight into my brain?"

I don't answer her because . . . Yes? No? I have no idea.

"You would be anesthetized," Dr. Netsky points out.

My mom flings my arm to the side and shakes her head with such force I'm scared she'll give herself a concussion. "I'm not doing it." She turns to me and wags a finger in my face. "I'm not doing it!"

Cautiously, I say, "Mom, it might not hurt to meet with this doctor. Dr. Singh, was it?" I look to Dr. Netsky, and he nods in confirmation. "We don't have to make any sort of decision right now, but maybe we should hear from her whether she thinks it's a good option."

"It's not." My mom's voice has gotten small. She's gone inside herself. I've seen this before. So many times I can't count. My mom is gone.

I touch her shoulder. "I want you to be well."

She recoils from my touch. "Fuck you." And then she throws open the door and leaves, slamming it behind her.

I look at the chair lying on the floor, at Dr. Netsky's diplomas, which are now hanging crooked, at the broken canvas she kicked across the room. I quickly right the chair and mumble an apology.

"It's quite all right," the doctor says calmly. "I've seen worse, I assure you."

That doesn't assure me of anything. I look the doctor in the eye. "So where do we go from here?"

Dr. Netsky purses his lips. "We can't force treatment on your mother."

"I know that."

"And we can agree that psychological care is not enough to combat your mother's illness, correct?"

"Yes," I say, though I hesitate. Not because it isn't the truth—it is; shrinks alone do nothing for my mom—but because every statement I agree with seems to be putting another nail in the coffin of my mom's McLean stay. And there aren't any other options on the table after this.

"We'll gladly keep your mother at Appleton for another week or so, to continue with the psychotherapy and to give her a chance to reconsider her options, but after that, she's best suited elsewhere."

The final nail bangs down with a thud. This conversation is over. My mom's time here is over. The relationship I'm trying to rebuild with her is over. Over over over.

"I understand," I say as politely as I can. "Thank you for taking the time to meet with me today." My voice is cracking. I bite my bottom lip—hard. The pain centers me. "I know you're a very busy man."

Dr. Netsky takes my outstretched hand and shakes it. "I'm truly sorry, Amanda. I've seen your exact situation time and again. But you're young and optimistic, and if there's anyone who can convince your mother, it's you."

And now we've gotten to the bullshit portion of the meeting. Optimistic? Me? Yeah, no. But there's no point in arguing.

"I'll do my best. Thank you."

Dr. Netsky lets go of my hand, and I can't get to the door fast enough. Abe is waiting right there, but I don't stop. I walk toward the elevator, and I punch the button so hard that pain spirals down my finger. "Dammit!" I shout as the doors open.

Abe slips in behind me and quietly presses the button for the first floor. The doors slide shut.

"Dammit!" I turn and punch the air, stopping just short of the back wall. Then I open my hands and press them against the wall.

"Hey," Abe whispers. His fingers graze my shoulders. Lightness courses through my body, making me feel warm—and guilty. As if I shouldn't be allowed to feel anything but pain, anger, and sadness right now. I step away.

The elevator stops and the doors open, and I whirl around to get out. But then I pause. Because we're only on the second floor. And because I'm staring at Tyler Fertig.

Old Blue. I haven't seen him since he tried to kill himself four months ago back at Peel, right after he shot Yellow.

"Tyler!" I gasp.

He looks lost. He has on a long-sleeved thermal and baggy jeans that hang low on his waist. His sandy hair is thin and unwashed and desperately in need of a cut. He stares right through me.

And then I notice the plastic bracelet dangling so far down his wrist that it's about to slip off. It's the same bracelet my mom had on. Tyler's an inpatient here.

The doors start to slide shut, and I'm not sure whether to put my hand out to stop them.

"I can wait," Tyler says.

And then I'm staring at silver metal. The elevator lurches, and after a few short seconds, the doors open into the lobby. I look back at Abe. He doesn't need to say anything.

I'm sick of this. All of this. Tyler is just the icing on the cake. Annum Guard did this to him. Alpha did this to him. And we're not even trying to make sure it never happens again. I push through the doors into the parking lot, and I'm running to the car and I want to punch things.

Abe's footsteps are right behind mine. I don't fight him off when he grabs onto my arm and spins me around into him.

"Can just one thing go right in my life? Just one!" My hands are shaking. I really, really want to punch things. I ball my hands into fists.

"Hey," he whispers, and this time I lean into him, let myself feel. His arms wrap around my shoulders and I don't know how much time passes, how long I spend with my cheek pressed into his chest, inhaling the lingering scent of bodywash. But before I know it, I'm full, complete. Everything I never felt growing up and everything I ever hoped for.

"Do you want to stop at Mystic Valley on the way home?"

I keep my head tucked into his chest. My face is flush with anger, and my thoughts are a swirling mess, but an unexpected laugh escapes my lips. I can't help myself. Mystic Valley is a shooting range just outside of Boston. Trust Abe to know the one thing that would make me feel better.

"You are the best thing that's ever happened to me," I tell him as I gently pull away, ignoring how sappy I sound. "But I really think we should just head back. I'm tired."

Guilt bubbles in my chest because this is a lie. I'm not tired. Not anymore, not since I found Zeta's testimony. The only reason I want to get back is so I can go through these pictures on my phone, then delete all trace of them. I'm keeping secrets from Abe, from my friends. I know I can trust them, but I still don't say anything. And I'm not a hundred percent sure why.

Abe unlocks the car. "Well, if not Mystic Valley, you know what would make you feel better? Tonight Coolidge Corner Theatre is doing a special midnight showing of *Night of the*—"

"Not a chance." I slide in and buckle my seat belt.

Abe clutches his heart as if he's been shot. "I'll remember that." He slips the keys into the ignition, and the engine roars to life. He throws it into reverse. "Yep, I will definitely remember that."

We ride most of the way home in silence. We don't mention my mom; we don't mention Tyler. It's like we're both going to forget any of that ever happened, which is exactly what I need right now. Selective memory loss.

Abe pulls to the front of Annum Hall, and I hop out.

"I'll park and meet you inside?"

I shake my head, then gesture across the street to the Common. "I'm going to take a quick walk. Clear my head a little."

Abe nods. He understands.

"Love you," I whisper before I close the car door. I watch him turn onto Joy Street, then into one of the four parking spaces behind the Hall. Once the Narc realizes Abe is back, she's going to ask where I am, so I need to get moving.

I tap my foot as I wait for the light to change. It's the middle of the day, so traffic isn't as bad as during rush hour, but there's a steady stream of cars, trucks, and Duck Tour boats barreling down Beacon Street. Finally, the walk sign lights up, and I jog into the Common. I head to the Greek Pavilion, looking over my shoulder several times to make sure I'm not being followed. I seem to be okay, so I trudge up the steps, plop myself next to a pillar, and whip out my phone.

Deep breath.

The first few pages of testimony are all background, stuff I could have guessed. Zeta's father—Yellow and Indigo's grandfather—was one of the founding members of Annum Guard—first generation. He was code-named Five. Zeta didn't join the Guard until after he had obtained an undergrad degree from Harvard with a concentration in physics. He then joined the Guard and started working on a PhD at MIT in theoretical nuclear and particle physics—which makes my head hurt just thinking about it—but had to abandon it due to time constraints. It was during the MIT years that he devised the idea for the gravity chamber to lessen the physical trauma of projection, and the government funded a research and development team at MIT to design a prototype for the chamber. Zeta remained a part of the team.

I skim through these pages. Interesting, but not what I need.

There's a little bit more on a failed marriage that produced two children, which I already know, and then around page thirty, it starts to get really interesting. I slow down and take my time, relishing every word of the transcript.

Sen. Wharton: Are you aware of any covert operations that took place during your tenure at Annum Guard?

Masters: Well, that's a pretty broad question, Senator, considering our entire agency is covert.

Sen. Wharton: Allow me to rephrase. Are you aware of any operations outside the scope of Annum Guard's stated purpose?

I flip to the next image.

Masters: Are you asking me again whether I was aware that Julian Ellis was selling every mission he could on the side to the highest bidder? Because the answer is no. Just as it has been the last hundred times you've asked me this question over the past two months.

Sen. Wharton: Let's put this matter concerning Mr. Ellis to the side for a moment—

Masters: Put it to the side? The one thing you brought me here to talk about? Again?

Sen. Wharton: Mr. Masters, I would like to know whether you are aware of the existence of any covert operation teams within the confines of Annum Guard.

Masters: Covert op teams *within* Annum Guard? I don't know what you're talking about.

My hands tremble as I flip to the next image.

Sen. Wharton: Really now? So if I said the words "Operation Blackout" to you, that wouldn't ring a bell?

Masters: Nope. Like I said, I have no idea what you're talking about.

Sen. Wharton: Please let the record reflect that Mr. Masters took approximately thirty seconds to answer the question and then did so with a clipped tone.

Masters: No, let the record reflect that this line of questioning has nothing to do with the pretext under which you brought me here today.

Whoa. Next image.

Sen. Wharton: With all due respect, sir, I am the one asking the questions, and I will lead the questioning in the direction I feel it needs to go. Are we understood?

Masters: (silence)

Sen. Wharton: Are we understood?

Masters: I understand what you're saying, yes.

Sen. Wharton: Good. So now be truthful with me, Mr. Masters. You have heard the term Operation Blackout before, correct?

Masters: (silence)

Sen. Wharton: Don't feel like answering? Fine. You do have two children who are still members of Annum Guard, do you not?

Masters: Are you threatening me, you son of a—

I flip to the next image, but there isn't one. No! No no no!

I sit back and take a breath, then look up to see a young couple with linked arms laughing as they walk toward the small concession in the park. I read through those last pages again. Operation Blackout. My brain is zooming straight to one idea, and I don't want it to be right.

Blackout. Like black ops. Elite special forces. Unknown, unseen, unrecognized.

And in many cases, an assassination squad.

CHAPTER 5

My brain wages a million intense debates with my heart over whether to tell Yellow and Indigo what I know. My heart says they have a right to know—and maybe they even have some information—but my brain always clobbers my heart with a quick right hook. I have no business even knowing Zeta's testimony exists. I have *negative* business telling anyone about it. That could earn me a one-way ticket out of Annum Guard and into a federal detention facility.

And so I try to stay focused on doing my job—on reading thousands of boring documents that I only marginally understand. And on waiting for Colton.

On Monday morning, there's a knock on Annum Hall's front door. Abe and I are in the library going through a box marked "SPECTRA CAPITAL TAX RECEIPTS," which is about as interesting as it sounds. We both look at the door, then back at each other.

"Was that . . . the *front* door?" Abe asks. "Shouldn't they be going through the security entrance downstairs?"

"Probably." I look toward Bonner's door. It's shut, so I grunt and stand. "I'll pay you to do this."

Abe shakes his head. "Oh, hell no." And then he smiles. "Just imagine what the vice president would say if she found out you were trying to pawn your babysitting job off on me."

"Babysitting job. That's the most accurate description ever for this."

I swing open the door. Colton is standing there, his hair flopping in front of his aviator sunglasses. He's wearing a concert T-shirt, khaki shorts, and flip-flops, and he has one shoulder shrugged up high, like he's posing for a catalog.

There are two people behind him. A guy with olive skin like mine, dark hair, and dark eyes, and a girl with wildly curly red hair. They're both dressed like they're showing up for Day One of an important government internship. Corporate casual. That's the term Bonner used when she described what she expects us to wear when we're off the clock. The guy has on navy pants and a dress shirt with rolled-up sleeves, and the girl, like me, has on black pants and a blouse.

"Hey there," Colton says. "We're here."

"I see that. We were expecting you down through the security entrance." For a moment, I debate being a stickler for the rules and telling them to go through the alleyway to the back door, but I decide against it. No need to start off on the wrong foot, and, besides, rules have never really been my thing. I stand back and let the three of them pass.

Colton walks into the foyer and pops his sunglasses up on top of his head. His mouth chomps open and closed like he's— hang on, he *is* chewing gum.

"Nice place you got here," he says in a condescending voice. Like he's telling us that his house is better than this. More square footage, higher ceilings, more expensive furnishings.

The redhead shoves her hand out. "Thank you for the opportunity. Really and truly. I'm looking forward to working with you. I'm so sorry about the door thing. I didn't know. Colton handled the arrangements."

She's staring at me with these intense green eyes that are laser focused on mine. Then they flick down to her outstretched hand, which she moves just a few inches toward me. I take the hint and shake her hand.

"Paige Wharton," she says, grasping my hand so firmly I feel a bone pop.

I twist my hand free. "You can call me Iris."

The other guy steps forward and extends his hand. "Mike Baxter." I shake it, even though this is totally weird. I mean, all of them are in college. They're at least two years older than me, and yet they're looking to me like I'm their leader.

I'm so not their leader.

I clear my throat and walk toward the library as Yellow bounces down the stairs. "Hey, Iris."

Colton's gaze lingers on her as she walks toward the back door, then down toward the situation rooms.

"Who's that?" he asks.

I continue on as if I didn't hear. "Let me get you guys all set up. You'll probably just be in here going through boxes of financial documents. I can promise it's going to be really boring."

Paige pushes past Mike to get shoulder-to-shoulder with me. "I'm sure it will be fascinating. And I aced both macro- and microeconomics, so I hope my skills will be useful to you."

Is this chick for real? She could benefit from a Xanax.

And now I'm thinking of my mom. McLean called yesterday. They're pressed for space, so she only has until Friday to vacate her room.

In the library, Colton immediately plops down into one of the desk chairs.

"Oh, hey, are these chairs Herman Miller? They look like the one my parents bought me for my desk in our summer house when I was, like, eight." He rises and pushes his palms on the chair's arms a few times before wandering toward the bookshelves.

"I don't know, Colton." My eyes travel to Abe sitting on the floor, then I roll them so hard they practically disappear into my skull. Abe smiles and hops up. "This is Blue." It sounds weird as I say it. I know I'm not supposed to call him by his real name, but . . . he's my Abe.

Paige nearly leaps over a box as she shoves her hand forward. "Paige Wharton!"

"Um, hi," Abe says.

I tip my head to the side. "Mike Baxter and . . . Colton Caldwell." Colton has his hands on his hips, loudly smacking his gum as he looks at the books.

"Nice to meet you," Abe says. "I'm sorry I can't stay"—a flash of panic hits me—"but I have a briefing."

I look at him and my mouth drops open. Because he most certainly does *not* have a briefing.

Liar! I mouth.

Payback, he mouths as he gives me a wink and jostles his shoulder into mine on the way out. I stare at the door after he's gone. Damn you, *Night of the Living Dead*. I sigh and turn around.

I look down at the list Bonner gave me. Set up e-mail, show where documents are, teach cataloging system. "Okay, over here." I show them the two computers on the far wall.

I flick the mouse around to light the screen, then go to the page where I can add a new user. I type in Colton's first name. "Colton, come pick a password. This'll be your log-in to get on our system."

"Ooh, access to national secrets," he says as he flops into the chair.

"Not even close. Pick something with letters and numbers. The system requires it."

Just as I suspect, Colton doesn't bother to hide what he's typing. I watch him pick a password. And then I just can't help myself.

"Callaway007. Are you freaking kidding me?"

"Hey! You're not supposed to watch me type that!"

"Of course I am," I say. "You're not supposed to be dumb enough to let me see it." I didn't mean to say that. It just slipped out. But then Mike chuckles, Paige cracks a smile, and Colton relaxes and laughs, too, so all seems well.

"Pick another password, double-oh-seven. Callaway, aren't those golf clubs or something? Who are you, the secret agent of the clubhouse?"

"It's my middle name," he says as he hunches over to shield the keyboard, which is a nice try, but I'm better than that. He types in HC1013LX3V and hits "Enter." Interesting.

"Hang on. Your parents named you Colton Callaway Caldwell? Do they hate you?"

"Callaway is a family name. After my dad's mom." His voice is suddenly stiff, which makes me feel the teensiest bit of regret. Maybe I took it a little too far. Then I look at his flip-flops and what appear to be pedicured toes and forget it.

Mike slides into the seat next. "Hey, man, I feel you. I got stuck with Teremun, which is a family name, too. No one can spell it or pronounce it." And then he types in 2TREXARMS, which takes me a second to get, but then I do. I choke back a laugh that I try to cover up as a cough.

"My middle name is Alexis," Paige says as she sits. "My parents just liked it." She hunches so far over the keyboard that I don't even know how *she* sees the keys, then she stands and pushes the chair in. "I made sure to pick a combination with a mix of upper- and lowercase letters, numbers, *and* special characters."

I resist the urge to sigh. I knew plenty of girls like Paige at Peel. Bright-eyed and way too eager for their own good. "Come on, I'll show you the documents."

Paige whips something out of her purse and has it in my hands before I even finish the sentence. "Wait, here's the confidentiality agreement we were asked to sign."

I look down at it. "Um, okay." Bonner didn't mention confidentiality agreements, but that makes sense. I look back up. Mike fishes one out of his pants pocket and unfolds it.

I take the paper. "Colton, do you—"

"Nope." He tosses his head back to get the hair out of his eyes. *Shocking.*

"I'll print you another one. In the meantime"—I point to the mound of boxes taking over the library floor—"have at it."

At the end of the day, Bonner calls me into her office. Red is slouched in one of the chairs; Bonner sits behind the desk with her arms folded. Red kicks the chair next to him over in my direction.

"So," he says as I lower myself, "how are our interns?"

I look at Bonner, who has her lips pressed together in a line and one eyebrow raised, then over at Red, who has one elbow casually resting on the arm of his chair, his thumb and forefinger cradling his face.

"Do you want total honesty?" I ask, still looking at Red.

"Why would we want you to lie?" Bonner clucks her tongue. "Accurate reporting is part of your job."

I don't even look back in her direction. "Paige is intense, but I haven't quite figured out if that's a good or a bad thing. She got through the most documents today by far and tabbed and highlighted everything she thought was important, but we'll need the analysts to check that she's on the right track and not just highlighting nonsense."

Bonner clucks her tongue again. "Well, obviously."

I grip the arms of my chair. "Mike seems to be a good fit, I guess? He's personable and easy to work with, and he's also really bright." I think of his password, and it makes me smile. Then I think of the third intern and clear my throat. "Colton is useless. He's barely literate. He asked me where the bathroom is twice.

Who has to ask where a bathroom is *twice*? You did drug test him, right?"

Red smiles, but Bonner makes a loud harrumph that causes both of us to look at her.

"Do not antagonize Colton Caldwell. You know who his mother is."

"I'm not antagonizing him," I say, even though I don't think that's the truth. "And besides, you asked for total honesty."

Bonner presses her lips together.

"What I don't understand is why we even have interns in the first place. I mean, I get that the vice president wants me to babysit Colton for the summer, but bringing along his two friends? To an agency that's supposed to be a complete secret? Confidentiality agreement and background checks aside, is this really something we should be doing? What about XP? Are we just forgetting about him?"

Bonner's chair scrapes back on the wood floor as she stands. Then there's a finger in my face, and I flinch.

"That is classified information and you are not to mention it. *Ever.*" Her eyes flick to the chair next to me. "Red, you can leave us."

I watch Red's reaction. He was being groomed to take over Annum Guard back when Alpha was still around. He spent three years training for it, from what everyone else has told me. And then at the last minute, the DoD swept in and replaced him with an outsider. Red's nothing more than Bonner's puppet these days, here to take orders and follow them, no questions asked. That can't be an easy switch. There's a moment when it seems he wants to protest—probably to point out that he should be the leader of Annum Guard right now because that's what he was hired to do—but then his face relaxes into a look of resignation. He stands without saying a word, and the door closes behind him.

Bonner lowers her finger. She rests both hands on the desk and leans forward.

"I must say, I'm disappointed. You didn't figure out who the other two are?"

"I . . ."

"Michael Baxter, son of renowned venture capitalist Layla Baxter, and, more importantly, grandson of Francis Howe."

My mouth drops open. "The defense secretary?"

"And Paige Wharton. As in daughter of Senator William Wharton out of Philadelphia, ranking member of the Committee of Homeland Security and Government Affairs, the committee which, I don't need to remind you, is presently investigating this agency's indiscretions."

Senator Wharton was the one who questioned Zeta. He *knows* about Operation Blackout.

"I assure you, I did not say yes to babysitting a bunch of college kids this summer. I hired three promising young people whose performance this summer could *save* Annum Guard. Do you know how close you are to being shut down for good?"

I blink. Once. Twice. Because I caught that—how close *you* are—not *we*. And everything about Bonner's body language is telling me she's anxious. She's fiddling with a ring on her right hand, and she won't make eye contact for more than a second. She's pale, and her breathing is heavier than usual. *Good.* The upper hand is mine.

"Why didn't you tell me this before? Don't you think that's kind of important information for me to have?"

Bonner drops back into her seat. "No, I just presumed you would act like the professional you allegedly are. You need to make sure our guests are well taken care of, do you understand?"

I stare at her until she looks away. It takes only a few seconds. Is she setting us up? Is the vice president?

"You're dismissed," Bonner says without meeting my gaze. I wait a few more seconds to make her squirm, then I turn and put my hand on the doorknob. "But, Iris . . ." I glance back. Fear has taken the place of anxiety. I've never seen her look like this before.

"Don't let me down," she says. "You can't afford it."

CHAPTER 6

"So when do we get to, you know, do stuff?"

I stop and set my pen on top of the notes I'm taking concerning a mission in 1945 when my dad took a bribe from the president of an energy company. I look at Colton. "What?"

"You know." Colton waves to the back staircase, leading down to the gravity chamber and situation rooms. "Stuff. Like what the dude with the orange hair and the guy with the crooked nose are doing."

I'm sitting on the library's burgundy Persian rug with about a hundred documents spread around me and a yellow legal pad on my lap. It's Wednesday. Only two days left until my mom has to be out of McLean. I'm trying not to think about that because I don't have a solution. Hell, my mom hasn't even returned my call from last weekend.

But then again, that's not unusual. When she's manic, she has way too much going on to think about making a phone call, and when she's on a low, she can't bring herself to press the numbers.

Paige is sitting next to me. She bites her bottom lip and reaches into the box for another stack of documents. Mike is spread out on the couch and doesn't bother to look up either.

Yellow and Green were both summoned to meet with federal investigators downtown this morning, and the only other Annum Guard member around is Indigo. He's sitting at one of the two computers in the corner. He looks at me for a half second, his eyebrows shoot up in disbelief, then he turns back around.

"First of all," I say, "the guy with the orange hair and the guy with the crooked nose have names. They're Orange and Blue." *As I'm sure you know.* As I say their names, a feeling of jealousy pricks my skin, because both Orange and Abe were sent on reconnaissance missions this morning by Bonner. Orange's has something to do with Eta—Violet's mom—rigging a gubernatorial election, while Abe is at a riot in Providence in the 1800s. It seems like my teammates are going on missions left and right, and I haven't been on one since I stalked my dad in 1939.

I shake my head—like that will get rid of this feeling. "And second of all . . ." I think about how to word this. *Be nice to Colton. Be nice to Colton.* I swallow my pride. "Second of all, only very select people can project, if that's what you're talking about. And I hate to break it to you, but you're not one of them." And then I laugh this phony, contrived laugh that no one joins.

"Well then, when do we get to sit in on briefings and stuff?" Colton asks.

Never, jackass. NEVER.

"That's not up to me."

"No offense, but this is boring." Colton waves his hand at the piles of paper stacked all over the library.

"Dude," Mike says, finally looking up. "Chill."

"Shut up, Baxter." Then Colton looks at me. "I mean, don't take this the wrong way or anything"—I brace myself—"but we're all kind of VIPs, you know?" He waves his hand around the room again. "So I thought we'd get to do more interesting stuff. I'm sure the White House wouldn't have us reading about"—he looks at a paper and squints—"alternative minimum tax."

At least three different responses flash through my head, but they all involve four-letter words or an insult to Colton's manhood, so I think a little harder. I draw a complete blank.

"Hey, Iris, I have a question for you." Mike scoots down off the couch and hands over a sheet of paper. "This here." I look down. It's a balance sheet from the 1970s.

Colton scowls and whips back around in his chair.

I squint at the paper. I don't understand half of it. Three quarters of it. "Er, I'm not sure what this is. Which box did it come from?"

"Oh, don't worry about it." Mike leans in closer to me. The stubble from a day-old shave brushes my shoulder. "I don't really have a question." He shoots a half-glance at Colton, then drops his voice to a whisper. "I know he can be difficult. It's part of the culture he grew up in."

"Mm-hmm," is all I say. Because that's such a BS excuse. Mike and Paige grew up in the same culture, and somehow both of them are perfectly capable of acting like normal people.

"I think we're going out to grab a bite to eat later tonight," Mike whispers. "You should come." But before I can answer, he slips back onto the couch.

I reach down and grab a stack of papers. It's a stack that Paige worked on. I can tell immediately because it's highlighted and tabbed with about eight different colors—as if a gay pride flag mated with a bag of Skittles, and their baby threw up all over the pages.

Paige looks over and sees me holding her papers. "Do you need the key I made again?" She grabs a three-by-five index card and thrusts it into my face. "Pink highlighter means an economic issue. Yellow highlighter is political. Blue tabs are companies to investigate, while green is—"

I hold up a hand to stop her. "I've got it," I lie. I don't look very hard at Paige's work. I learned early on that she's the kind of person who highlights 90 percent of the page, which completely defeats the purpose. But seeing as how none of these documents have anything to do with Eagle, I haven't called her out for it.

"It's fine, Paige. Really." I set down the stack and pick up another. Colton's initials are in the top-right corner, but other than that, the first page is untouched. I flip to the next, then to the next, then to the rest until I've hit the end. No highlights, no tabs, no notes, nothing.

Colton is now sitting with his back against one arm of the couch. One leg is tucked underneath him, while the other is splayed straight out. He has on headphones—the big, bulky kind that don't actually make the music sound any better but are meant to advertise that you dropped a grand on them—and is moving his head back and forth with his eyes closed.

"Colton!"

I don't get a response.

"Colton!"

I ball up a piece of paper and send it flying. It bounces off his forehead, and his eyes spring open.

"What the hell?" He pulls his headphones down so that they rest on his neck and glares at me.

I hold up his papers. "You didn't mark anything on these."

He shrugs. "I didn't think there was anything worth marking." He slips the headphones back onto his ears and looks down. It takes him only a second or two to get the sway back.

I clench my hands together. Not because I don't agree with him—there's basically *nothing* worth marking in any of these documents—but because I don't think there's been a second in Colton's presence that I haven't wanted to punch him. I stare at him for so long that he has to feel my gaze. He has to know how annoyed I am. And yet he doesn't look up.

I reach for the next stack. Mike's initials are on the top. I scan the first page. It's one of Orange's missions. He tracked my dad's 1968 meeting with some guy named Xavier Portis who worked for RA Enterprises. Yeah, whatever. I drop the stack onto the floor, then stop.

Wait.

I grab it and check the name again. Xavier Portis.

XP.

"Hey, Mike, come here a second," I say without looking up. Out of the corner of my eye, I see him get up and sit down next to me. I hand the page over and let him scan it.

"Oh yeah, the RA thing. I remember this."

"When did you look at this?"

He shrugs. "Two days ago, maybe?" And then his face lights up. "Is it important?"

It's the best lead we've had in four months. But I can't tell him that. I can't tell anyone that. Bonner and Red are the only people in the Guard who know about XP.

So I give him a shrug of my own. "Where are the boxes of documents on this?"

Mike leans in closer to the page, and his shoulder brushes against mine. He smells good. Like expensive cologne and peppermint. His fingers find the middle of the page. "Boxes 347 and 348. I'll see if they're still in the library."

But before he can even move, an alarm blares.

This isn't the security alarm, which is loud and chirpy. This is two low, slow blasts, like a siren.

"What is that?" Indigo asks, jumping up from behind the computer.

Both of us scramble to the door as two more blasts sound through Annum Hall. Violet rushes down the stairs and jumps into the foyer.

"What's going on?" she asks. "I've never heard that before."

I look back into the library. Paige is sitting on the floor, with her mouth open, and Mike hasn't moved an inch, but Colton is up and heading for me.

I hold out my arm. "You stay there! All of you, stay there!"

Then Bonner's door bangs open. She looks at us for a split second, and her face says it all. Something is very wrong. She rushes past us to the back stairwell. Her heels *stomp-stomp* down the concrete staircase.

"Stay there!" I yell again into the library, then I glance from Indigo to Violet. The three of us react at the same time. I nudge Indigo out of the way as I race to the back door, while Violet straight-up bodychecks me, flinging me into a table. I steady myself and follow her down the stairs, Indigo right behind me.

It's not hard to figure out where Bonner is. The door to Situation Room One is wide open, and the three of us barrel inside. Red is standing at the front of the room, staring at a computer projection screen that's totally black except for the words "ERROR: SUBJECT NOT FOUND." His shoulders are tensed, like he's forgetting to breathe.

"What do you mean it just deactivated?" Bonner yells over the blare of the alarm. "It can't just deactivate! And shut the damned alarm off!"

"I'm telling you, it did!" Red shouts back. "And I'm working on it!" He bends over a laptop and punches the keys.

"Do you have anything?" Bonner asks. "Vitals? A location?"

"Nothing! I have nothing. All I have is—" Then Red's head snaps up and his eyes narrow at the sight of me, Indigo, and Violet. "What the hell are you all doing here?"

Bonner turns around, too. But surprisingly, she doesn't look mad at the intrusion.

Violet takes a step back. "We just wanted—"

"What's going on?" I demand as the alarm blares again.

"Red, turn that blasted thing off!" Bonner says. "You three, come inside and shut the door."

Red grunts in frustration, taps a few more keys, and the alarm shuts off, midblast.

"Sit," Bonner says, her eyes still on us. Indigo and Violet drop into chairs. I take a little more time. The three of us stare at her and wait.

Bonner takes a slow breath. "Orange's tracker deactivated about two minutes ago."

I gasp, and I hear Indigo and Violet do the same. That's another new thing around here. After Yellow and I proved just how easy it was to get rid of the old trackers, one of Bonner's first orders of business was to insist on new ones. Better ones. Trackers that required a surgical procedure and general anesthesia to implant computer chips at the bases of our necks. There's no cutting these things out without risking death. And there's no deactivating them either. This can mean only one thing.

"Orange is dead?" Violet whispers.

"No!" Red says. "We don't know that. We don't know anything at this point."

"We need to send a team in immediately to assess the situation," Bonner says. "The three of you won't have much time to prepare."

"We don't need time," Indigo says. "What was Orange's exact mission?"

"Simple reconnaissance," Red answers, but his eyes shift to the left, which makes me sit up straighter. He's not telling the whole truth. "Observing a previous mission in which Eta tampered with the 1904 Massachusetts governor election."

"No problem," Indigo says, jumping to his feet. "I'm very familiar with that time period. I've gone on a ton of early twentieth-century missions. Plus, Yellow never shuts up about it." This is the truth. We all have time periods we specialize in. Yellow's is the late nineteenth and early twentieth centuries. That girl will talk your ear off about corsets and courtesy.

Red nods. "Change and hurry back. I'll tell you where you need to go."

"No, *I* will tell you where you need to go," Bonner says, like she's reminding us she's still in the room.

Indigo and Violet exchange a glance and start for the door. "Wait!" I say, turning to Red. I ignore Bonner's scowl. "Abe—I mean Blue. Is his tracker still on?"

Red nods. "For now."

That's not the reassurance I need. "Should we send someone back to get him?" I hear the anxiety in my voice.

"No," Bonner says.

"I agree," Red says. "We don't know what we're dealing with. For all we know, we could be sending you into an ambush." The way he says that word—*ambush*—makes me pause.

I follow my teammates out the door. Indigo and Violet go up the main staircase, but I stop in the library.

"What's going on?" Paige asks with a worried look on her face.

"Alarm malfunction. It's nothing," I say. "Why don't you guys call it a day, go home, and we'll see you back in the morning?"

Mike raises an eyebrow, clearly not buying the explanation, which . . . *duh*. No one would buy that explanation. "Are you sure we can't help?" he asks.

"Positive. An IT contractor is on his way over. We'll see you tomorrow."

Colton slings his bag over his shoulder. "Whatever. Anyone want to go to a bar? I've got my fake ID on me."

"No, Colton," Paige says as she slides the handles of a brown purse onto her arm.

Mike doesn't say anything else. He just . . . stares at me. I can't quite read the look, but I don't have time to decipher it.

"The dinner offer still stands," he finally says to me.

"Thanks, but I really think I should stay here until IT shows up. Maybe next time?"

He gives me a smile that's equally warm and wary, then shuffles behind his friends. Paige nods a good-bye. Colton is already halfway down the block.

I shut the door after them and lock it.

My mind flies to Abe as my feet pound up the steps. *He has to be okay, he just has to.* But then I stop myself. Worrying about Abe isn't going to do any good. It's just going to distract me from finding Orange, which is what we have to do.

Orange can't be dead. There's like a zero percent chance of violence on these stupid recon missions. Okay, maybe not zero, but less than one. We get in, we watch from a distance, we get out. And if we're compromised, we abandon immediately. Them's the rules. No, there has to be another explanation.

I think of the weird vibe I got from Red. Maybe this *wasn't* just a simple recon mission. Red and Orange are pretty tight. What if they were up to something?

The sinking feeling in my stomach lingers as I step into a swath of purple fabric that Yellow refers to as my "afternoon dress," and I slip on a pair of low boots with pointed toes and buttons on the side. What if Orange *is* dead? What if we go back and find his body? I don't think I can bear it. I mean, I don't know Orange very well, but I certainly don't want to find him dead.

Violet's shutting her door as I open mine. Her dress is very similar to mine except that it's salmon pink. The color really works with her light-brown skin. She has her short hair pulled back into a tight bun and looks like she's about to puke. She's never been the best in high-stress situations.

Indigo's waiting for us by the stairs, in gray, high-waisted pants with a vest and jacket. He drops a top hat onto his head.

"Any problems letting me lead this one?" he asks. Violet and I both shake our heads. Now is not the time for a who's-better-than-whom pissing match. Indigo knows the historical period the best. We'll defer to him.

Bonner and Red are standing in the hallway outside the gravity chamber. Red clasps Indigo on the shoulder. I guess it's obvious he's leading this one.

"It's been eleven minutes already, so we need to hurry," Red says. "Orange was last tracked inside the State House, standing on the west side of the rotunda. By all accounts, the rotunda should be full of people, so someone has to have seen something. I would imagine you're walking into chaos and confusion. Can you do this?"

Beside me, Indigo swallows what I can only assume is a gigantic lump in his throat and nods. "We have to do this."

Bonner holds open the chamber door for us but doesn't make eye contact. I don't know if she's worried or angry or what. Red tells us the date and time to set our watches, and then he wishes us good luck.

I take a step closer to Red and whisper, "Are you sure there's nothing else I need to know?"

Red looks into my eyes, and I see hesitation and understanding. But all he says is, "Watch yourself."

I don't know if he's talking about the mission or my question.

I step into the gravity chamber, slam my watch face shut, and I'm tumbling down to 1904.

CHAPTER 7

As soon as we land in the past, we're on our feet and running. The gold dome of the State House hovers over us. A crowd is milling around the entrance on Beacon Street, and I shove a man out of my way as I race up the steps toward the door.

"We get in and we spread out," Indigo orders as his feet pound up the steps. "Iris, you head left; Violet, you head right; and I'll go straight. Keep an eye on each other's coordinates at all times. Got it?"

"Got it," I say. Behind me, Violet grunts in approval. *Left*, I tell myself. *That's west. The spot Orange was last seen in.* We approach the door and slow to a walk. Sprinting in like crazed monkeys would draw a bit too much attention. Time to dial it back.

Security at the State House is nonexistent in 1904. In present times, there are guards and metal detectors, but here we just walk on in and no one gives us a second glance. It's so weird the way people in the past just assumed they were safe.

We rush through Doric Hall, up the few steps into Nurses Hall, then weave our way through the crowd of people milling about the entrance to Memorial Hall. We enter a large rotunda, and I brace myself for chaos and confusion, just like Red said. But there is none. There are people running about, busy on this election day, but there's no mass hysteria. Certainly no police and onlookers crowded around a body. I look at Indigo, and he jerks his head left before heading through the arches toward the Hall of Flags.

I push my way through a group of men talking about whether a candidate named Douglas has the Socialist votes. Memorial Hall is a massive round room with arches held up by marble Ionic columns. There's a balcony level that circles the entire room. And Orange is nowhere to be seen.

I look over at Violet on the other side of the rotunda. She's weaving in and out of the arches, scanning every inch of the room. I do the same, going in the other direction.

Men wearing tall hats, men wearing funny suits, men shouting about this or that political issue on the ballot. But no Orange.

"Pardon me, sir." I tap a rather large man on the shoulder. He's talking to a short, thin man who looks like his polar opposite. They're standing almost exactly where Orange supposedly disappeared. "I'm trying to locate my brother. He said he would meet me in this spot twenty minutes ago, but I haven't seen him. Have you been standing here awhile?"

The large man reaches into his pocket and pulls out a gold watch hanging from a chain. "Dear me, is that the time?" He squints. "I suppose I have been here for a while. Half an hour at least." He looks at his companion and chuckles. "You're far too engaging, Norris."

I don't have time for this. "My brother. He's about this tall." I hold up my hand about six inches above my head. "Light-blue eyes, hair as orange as a carrot, face dotted with freckles."

I catch Norris staring at my dark-brown hair and olive complexion. He raises an eyebrow. "Your brother?"

I clear my throat. "Have you seen him?"

"I haven't seen anyone matching that description, miss. I'm sorry."

"Very well. Thank you for your time."

I ask a few more people, except this time I change "brother" to "cousin." But it's the same answer every time. No one has seen Orange. It's like he wasn't here at all, which makes no sense. He was tracked here. This floor, this spot. Right freaking *here*.

I look over to find Violet staring at me from across the rotunda. She shrugs. I can't see where Indigo disappeared to, so I look back at Violet and point at the balcony. She nods and takes off toward the stairs.

But then I stop. There's something on one of the pillars, right by where Orange was last tracked. It's small and rectangular and looks like a sticker, but I'm pretty sure they didn't have stickers in 1904.

No, this one was placed here by a modern traveler. The hair on my arms stands on end. I walk closer to the sticker, but I already know what's on it. I just *know*.

My gaze flies to the balcony. Violet's stepping off the last stair now. I look back and claw at the sticker. It peels off in one go, and I push up my sleeve, slap it onto my forearm, then pull my sleeve back into place. I race for the stairs.

The balcony is crowded, but not as crowded as the ground floor. I pretend to look over the edge, but I know I'm not going to find Orange.

"Did you see anything?" Violet hisses to me.

"Where is Orange?" I ask. I don't answer her question, but she doesn't seem to notice.

"Do you think someone took him?"

Operation Blackout. It's the only thought running through my head. They took Orange. They took Zeta. But *who?* And *why?*

"Why would anyone take him?" I say. "And that wouldn't explain why his tracker went off. You and I both know there's only one way those things deactivate now. So assuming people took him, they'd have had to kill him there, right there"—I lean over the edge of the balcony and point to the western arches—"and then smuggle his body out of this crowded building."

"That seems . . . highly unlikely." Violet chews her bottom lip.

"You think?"

"So then what happened to him?"

I remember the brief conversation I had with Orange just a week ago. How unhappy he was with all of the changes that have been made.

Blackout. Orange was blacked out because he was too vocal. Did Bonner have something to do with this?

"I don't know," I say.

I spot Indigo. He's back in the rotunda. He glances around, and I let out a sharp whistle. He sees us in the balcony and holds up both hands, palms up. He hasn't found anything either.

The sticker on my arm is making my skin tingle.

Violet and Indigo insist on spending the next forty minutes combing this place, which is just a waste of time. Every hour we spend here means that more than ten hours pass in the present. But I can't very well say no, so I join in the fruitless search. Indigo even manages to sneak himself inside the governor's office for a minute.

I should tell them we're not going to find Orange. But I don't. Not yet.

"Now what?" Violet asks as the three of us head down the stairs. Boston Common spreads out before us, and I notice the chill in the air. I wasn't thinking when I left. I dressed for the summer, not late fall.

"It doesn't make any sense," Indigo says. "There's not a trace of Orange anywhere in that building." Then he turns to me. "You've been very quiet."

I rub my arm. I can't tell them I found the sticker—can't tell them about XP—but I can say *something*.

"I'm just wondering whether Bonner had anything to do with his disappearance." I feel their eyes boring into me.

"That's quite an accusation." Indigo pauses. "Not that I don't think that woman is heinous, but where is this coming from?"

I tell them about my weird conversation with Orange. How he practically shouted to Bonner that he didn't have to take her crap rules anymore.

"But the door was closed?" Violet says.

"When he said it? Yeah. But he said it really loudly. There's no way she didn't hear him."

"So what's your theory? Bonner sent one of us back to kill Orange out of spite?" Indigo shakes his head. "Because apart from the three of us, the only people who can project are Yellow, Green, and New Blue. You think one of them killed Orange?"

And then I remember distant, drugged eyes staring out at me from an elevator lobby.

"Tyler can still project, too." My voice is a whisper.

"Old Blue?" Indigo says. "You think Old Blue did this?"

"I'm just kind of thinking out loud."

"I can guarantee you that Old Blue is never coming anywhere near the Guard again. Last I heard, he's an inpatient at a mental hospital."

I flinch. He is. And so is my mom, and dammit, I haven't thought of her and that ticking clock for at least an hour. I mean ten hours. I've lost so much time being here.

"I just think it's a little suspicious, that's all. Especially since there would've been an easy way to figure out what happened to Orange."

Indigo stares at me.

I sigh. "Send us back to *before* his tracker deactivated, right? Then we could see with our own eyes what happened."

"You know we can't actually do that. It's one of our key rules. No do-overs. You know that, Iris. Sending us back to before Orange disappeared would have tipped him off that something was wrong—he's too well trained not to notice us—and considering we don't know what the hell happened, that would have been a very, very dangerous situation. For all of us."

"Look, I just—"

"We need to get back," Violet cuts me off. "Standing around here sharing crazed theories isn't going to help us find Orange. He's obviously not here. So we need to follow protocol: go back and report everything we found."

She's right, of course. It doesn't help Orange at all, but we need to leave.

Bonner and Red are waiting outside the gravity chamber when we arrive.

"Anything?" Red practically barks at us.

Indigo shakes his head. "Not a trace. Nothing. Everyone at the State House was going about their business like nothing was wrong."

Red's brow furrows, while Bonner stays still as a calm sea. She's giving nothing away.

Red gestures down the hallway. "Back into Sit Room One. All of you. I need to know everything that happened from the moment you arrived in 1904 until now."

I touch his arm. "Blue?"

"Traveling back now. He's probably five minutes behind you guys."

Then there's a *ziiiiiiip* sound and a *whoosh*, and Abe steps out of the gravity chamber. I forget the rules, forget decorum, forget everything. I leap forward and fling my arms around his neck. I breathe him in, resisting the urge to kiss his jawline, my favorite part of him.

"Thank God you made it back!" I squeeze him closer to me.

"What are you talking about?"

Bonner clears her throat, and I drop my arms from Abe. "Blue, did you see anything unusual during your mission?" Bonner asks.

Abe's nose crinkles like it always does when he's confused. "Um . . . no? Unusual how?"

"Orange is gone," I say. "His tracker deactivated on a mission."

Abe blinks. "He's dead?"

"That is what we're trying to ascertain," Bonner says. "Blue, go upstairs and start on your report. Make sure you include a detailed summary of every person you encountered and pay close attention to any events that seemed out of the ordinary, no matter how small. A casual glance, a misplaced object. Anything."

I give Abe's hand another squeeze as Bonner ducks into the Sit Room with Red right behind her.

"Love you," I mouth, and he does the same.

As I enter the room, Indigo, Violet, and I exchange one quick glance that lets me know they're not going to reveal *everything* that happened. Our little conversation at the end will stay private. But I still can't shake the feeling that something is very off here. And that one or more of the people in this room might know what really happened.

Indigo and Violet take a seat, but I rip the sticker from under my sleeve and thrust it into Red's hands. He looks down at it, then up at Bonner, and shoves it into his pocket.

And that tells me everything I need to know. Red's been trained to hide his real thoughts. But I've seen them sneak out before, when I confronted him with Alpha's deception back at Peel. And I just saw a flash of them now.

He knows way more than he's letting on.

And now my mind is made up. I'm not keeping XP a secret any longer.

CHAPTER 8

I take a deep breath and look at my teammates. All of my teammates. Well, the ones who can project anyway. We're the only ones who have the genetic ability.

I look from Yellow to Violet to Indigo to Green and finally to Abe. We're all gathered in my bedroom. I've barely slept since we got back from 1904 last night. My last nerve is fried, and it's only six in the morning. Green's been complaining nonstop about being here early. I'm not sure why. I'd love any excuse to leave if I lived in that crappy basement studio in Allston that's all his government salary will allow.

"You're being weird," Yellow says. "Just so you know. I feel it's my duty as your friend to tell you that."

I ignore her. "Guys, we need to talk."

"About Orange?" Indigo says. "I agree. I don't understand how he could just disappear, no trace of him. Like, I don't get the physics of it. Unless he's dead, he'd show up on the tracking system, right?" He looks over at Abe. It didn't take long for everyone to view him as the authority on these things. Abe always assumed he'd be drafted to join the science and technology wing of the CIA. But he chose to be here with me.

"That's how I understand it," Abe says.

And now we're all business.

"You're sure he wasn't anywhere in the State House?" Yellow looks directly at her brother. "Like, one hundred percent confidence?"

Indigo narrows his eyes. "Thanks for second-guessing my ability to do my job. Yes, Yell, I'm one hundred percent confident he wasn't anywhere in the State House."

"I don't think we can ever be one hundred percent confident on anything."

I touch Indigo's arm because I think he's about to chuck something at his sister, but he waves me off and shoots Yellow a dirty look. "We checked every spot in the State House that we could find. Obviously, given the time constraints, we didn't have a chance to check blueprints ahead of time to make sure there weren't any secret rooms, but Violet did that when we got back."

Violet nods. "Nothing. We searched the entire place."

"And there's no way someone could have killed him and smuggled him out," Indigo continues. "It was an election day. The place was packed."

"Look." Violet motions to Yellow, Green, and Abe. "I know you guys weren't there, but you have to take our word that Orange just disappeared. There's no explanation for it."

"Of course there's an explanation."

All of our heads turn to Green, who's leaning with his back against my door, arms crossed. His shaggy brown hair has flopped in front of his eyes, but he doesn't make a move to brush it away.

"He's dead," Green says matter-of-factly.

No one else says anything.

Blackout. Blackout. Blackout.

I have to tell them.

Green uncrosses his arms. "Oh, come on, I know you're all thinking it. If what we've been told about the new trackers is correct, the only way Orange's could have deactivated is if his brain stopped functioning, and if his brain stopped functioning, he's dead. You all know it's true."

"Of course we know it's true," Yellow says. "But that doesn't explain how someone could have killed him or why there was no trace of Orange anywhere." She matches Green's sullen expression.

"Guys," I whisper. "There might be another explanation. I know some stuff you don't. Stuff that relates to Zeta, too."

Five heads turn to look at me, and I avoid making eye contact with anyone. Especially Yellow and Indigo. I drop my voice low so that anyone who might be lurking outside can't hear me. "If I was to say the word blackout, what would that make you think of?"

"Power outage," Indigo says. Yellow and Violet both nod in agreement.

"Okay, and what if I were to say the word blackout in a military setting. Same answer?"

"Of course not," Green says. "You'd think of special forces, obviously. What is this about?"

"Let's just say that I stumbled across some information that leads me to believe a blackout has something to do with the disappearances of Zeta and Orange."

"Stumbled across this where?" Green asks.

"That doesn't matter, but . . ." I look from Yellow to Indigo. "Your dad may have known about something called Operation Blackout."

Indigo's eyes go wide, while Yellow purses her lips.

"Wait, you think some kind of Annum Guard special ops team *took out* Orange?" Indigo says angrily.

I nod. "And I think your dad, too."

"You're saying you think my dad is dead?" Yellow asks in a small voice. Indigo takes her hand. "I mean, the idea was always in the back of my head, but I never wanted to . . ."

"I don't know," I say gently. "I'm really not sure what to believe. I hope no one is dead."

Yellow doesn't look at me. She stares at my bed.

Green pushes off the wall, and I brace myself. Green has never given me that warm, fuzzy feeling, and now that I know his father murdered mine—shot him shortly after they both orchestrated the assassination of President Kennedy on the order of Eagle Industries—getting to know Green really is the least of my concerns. Besides, he has that way of speaking where he tries to make himself sound like my superior, not my teammate.

But then he surprises me. He nods. "In the same vein, does anyone else think it's highly suspicious that we suddenly have *interns* connected to three very, very important people?"

Abe juts his chin in the air. "What are you saying?"

"Interesting timing, that's all," Green says. "A few days after the daughter of a senate committee member, the son of the vice president, and the grandson of the secretary of defense start combing through our secrets, Orange goes missing. I've thought it was suspicious since the first second they appeared. And now there's this? Operation Blackout? It's related."

"Where's your proof?" I ask, even though the same thoughts are running though my head.

Green turns to me. "I obviously don't have any, Iris." The way he says my name—sarcasm mixed with a hint of derision—this is the Green I know.

Yellow shoots her hand into the air, like we're in a classroom. "Hang on," she says. "Operation Blackout. I'm not sure why, but it's kind of ringing a bell."

"*Think*, Yellow," I say.

"I'm trying." She closes her eyes. "I can picture myself in my dad's office at home. I'm like twelve or thirteen. I'm looking for paper for the printer. I think we're probably out of it, but I'm opening all the drawers anyway, drawers I'm not supposed to open. I'm jumpy because my dad will kill me if he finds me going through them."

Indigo lets out a nervous laugh. "That's an understatement."

"I see . . . something. A file? A stray paper? Something. It has the word "Blackout" written on it. I remember that word made me curious because blackout was the name of that game we used to play at camp late at night, the one with the flashlights"—she looks at her brother, who nods—"but that's all I remember. I didn't read whatever it was."

I groan. "Come on. You didn't read it?"

"Um, hello, you know my dad. Would you go snooping through his personal things?" Her expression changes, like she just realized what she said. She shrinks back. "I mean, *knew* my dad? Maybe?"

"*Know* your dad. Let's think positively. We don't know what happened to him. Or to Orange. What are the chances that memo is still in your house?"

"Zero," Yellow says. "No, less than zero. Dad had—*has* a paper shredder in his office and he's not afraid to use it."

"Well, we need to get that memo somehow," I say as Green rolls his eyes at me, "and that's because there's something else I haven't told you. Something I bet is related to this whole mess." I pause. "Something about Eagle Industries."

I can feel the tension in the small bedroom grow.

"You found out something more about Eagle?" Indigo asks.

I nod. "Alpha told me."

"Alpha!" Violet exclaims, then winces. She drops her voice. "When?"

"Right before Vaughn killed him. He told me about someone else who's involved." I pause. "Someone code-named XP."

"XP," Yellow repeats softly. "Like the letter left behind on my dad's desk?"

I nod. "And there was a sticker in the spot where Orange disappeared. The same symbol."

And then there's a lot of talking at once. Indigo asks why I didn't say something when I found the sticker. Green demands to know what the hell is going on. Yellow barks at her brother to show everyone the picture on his phone.

Yellow turns to me. Her shoulders are hunched, like she's rearing for a fight, but her eyes show only hurt. "Why didn't you tell us this before?"

"Because I was ordered not to. *Ordered.* I'm, like, 90 percent sure I could be arrested if anyone finds out about this conversation."

"Does Bonner know?" Indigo asks as he passes his phone to Violet.

I stiffen. "Of course she does, but she's not authorizing any XP missions. It's like she's trying to keep the whole thing hush-hush."

Yellow blows out a short, loud breath. "So XP blacked out my dad, whatever that means, and now he's done it to Orange?"

"Or *she*," I correct her. "We don't really know, do we? But it looks like you're on the right track."

"But why?" Indigo demands.

"Maybe they knew too much? Or maybe we're getting too close to the truth?" I sigh with frustration. "I really don't know, you guys."

"Was there anything about XP in Alpha's notebook?" Yellow asks. "I can't remember."

"Me either," I admit. And I hate that I don't know. But I hadn't known about XP when I found the notebook. Now I wish I'd had the chance to go through the notebook and specifically ferret out XP entries while I still had it in my possession.

Abe stares at me. "Have you tried Samuels's method?" He's referring to our Practical Studies professor at Peel. "Opening your mind and letting the answer come to you?"

"I've tried, Abe. Really, I've tried *so hard*. I can't tell you how many nights I've lain awake, wishing hoping praying I could remember if XP was even mentioned. But I can't. It's not like I memorized the whole stupid thing."

"Okay," he says, and his tone takes me aback. There's more than a hint of annoyance in it. And he's not making eye contact with me.

"Did you try an online search for XP?" Green asks. He sounds like a kindergarten teacher asking a kid if he washed his hands after using the bathroom.

"Where?" I say. "The computers downstairs, which are probably alerting the Narc to every keystroke? I think she'd know in a heartbeat if I started Googling 'XP' for the hell of it. Besides, did you guys not hear the 'ordered to stay quiet' part?"

Abe springs up. "Seriously? Okay, now you're just being dumb." He's out the door in a flash. I'm sure he didn't mean it like that, but my boyfriend just called me dumb. I don't have time to dwell because then Abe's back and tossing a phone on the bed between Yellow and me. We both look down at it.

"Disposable smartphone," Abe says, stating the obvious.

"You have a disposable smartphone?" I ask.

"No, I have seven of them. I keep them charged and hidden in the back of my closet in case I need to use it and ditch it. The real question is, why don't you?"

Before I can respond—or beat myself up for missing such an *obvious* solution—Yellow grabs the phone, powers it on, and opens the browser.

"I have a small lead," I tell everyone while Yellow types. "Mike found a record in one of the boxes of a mission involving someone named Xavier Portis."

"Please," Green sneers. "Nothing in those boxes has anything to do with anything."

He's right—my gut tells me Xavier Portis is a dead end—but his statement annoys me all the same.

"XP," Yellow whispers, tapping the screen with her perfectly manicured fingernail as the search results load. "Here!" She holds the phone closer and frowns, then scrolls down. "Okay, most of this has to do with an old version of Windows." Then she stops and gasps. "Bill Gates! Maybe he's XP!"

I blink in disbelief while Violet laughs. But Yellow's not joking.

"Bill Gates?" I say. "Really? One of the world's biggest philanthropists is running a murderous, time-travel corruption scheme?"

"Maybe that's how he made all of his money?" Yellow's voice is weaker, like she knows just how stupid her suggestion is.

I sigh. "Even if you were right, don't you think 'XP' would be a bit of an obvious code name? The first hit on an Internet search?"

"Okay, fine," she says.

"What else is there?" Abe asks.

Yellow looks back at the phone. "Extreme programming? It's a kind of software development." She looks up at us, and we all look at Abe.

Abe shrugs. "Maybe? I don't see how it's relevant, but we can't count out anything at this point."

Yellow looks down and scrolls some more. "Um . . . we have a power supplier . . . probably not . . . a kind of digital camera . . . power saws . . . There's xeroderma pigmentosum. That's a kind of rare skin condition, apparently."

"None of this seems likely," I say.

"I know." Yellow goes back to scrolling. She's silent for a moment, then her face lights up. "Ooh, here's something. XP. The Greek letters chi and rho, often used by early Christians to mean Christ."

"So . . . Jesus is behind Eagle Industries?" I ask.

"Or maybe the pope? I don't know."

I cock my head. "So we have Bill Gates and the pope as our top two suspects? Yes, I'd say we're definitely on the right track."

Yellow looks back at the phone.

Green stares right at Abe. "Have we all forgotten that we still have access to the man who *invented* time travel? Anyone thought of asking him for his input on any of this? Orange? Blackout? XP?"

Abe tenses next to me. His grandfather is a sore subject these days. To say that Ariel wasn't happy when Abe decided to join the Guard would be an understatement. They're barely on speaking terms.

But still. If there's anyone who might have a clue what happened to Orange, it's Ariel.

"That might not be such a bad idea," I say slowly, looking over at Abe to gauge his reaction before I decide how much enthusiasm to throw behind this plan. His lips press into a thin line. Okay, so, annoyed but not angry. I can push this further. "We haven't been over there in a while. Maybe I could call Mona and set up a dinner—"

Too far. Abe's brow furrows, his eyes narrow, and little flames of red appear under them. Classic Abe. I've seen this face before—it's the face he gets when he's angry but knows he shouldn't vocalize it. The worst was back at Peel after Abe took second place in the sophomore-class combat challenge, even though the winner totally stepped out of bounds, according to Abe. But Abe didn't want to protest for fear of looking like a sore loser, so instead he sat and stewed. Which is way worse for your mental well-being, in my book, but that's Abe.

And then Yellow gasps again. Loudly. Her hands tremble as she holds the phone.

"You guys. It *is* Chi Rho. Jesus Christ. Whatever." She holds up the phone so we can see the screen. "This is its symbol."

I turn to Abe. "Do it. Set up a dinner, make a call, do whatever you need to do."

Abe huffs. "Fine."

There's a knock on my door. We all freeze. I whip the phone out of Yellow's hands and chuck it into my closet, where it lands behind the laundry hamper. Yellow gets up off the bed and opens the door.

"Hi!" she greets Bonner, who has her hands on her hips and a scowl on her face. Her eyes widen in surprise, like she doesn't understand why Yellow just answered my door. "We were just talking about you!"

I cringe but then force myself to relax as Bonner peers past Yellow into my room. After all, if there's anything I've learned since I became Annum Guard, it's that Yellow is the best freaking liar on the face of the earth.

Bonner takes her hands from her hips and crosses them over her chest. "I heard voices. What's going on here?"

Yellow smiles sweetly. "I'm sure you can understand that we're all worried about Orange"—Bonner opens her mouth to respond, but Yellow holds up a hand and flashes a grin—"and I know you totally are, too. I'm sure you've been working nonstop since last night to try to figure out what happened. You're probably concerned about all of our safety."

"Of course I'm concerned about your safety," Bonner says. But nothing about her tone or her body language agrees with her words.

"It's just . . ." Yellow pauses deliberately. "We're a team, you know? We want Orange to be okay."

"As do I." Bonner's voice is flat, the voice of someone who's reading economic reports on C-SPAN at four in the morning.

"Oh, I'm sure you do! But we all just want you to know that we're not afraid to go back to doing missions. We want the truth as much as you do, both about what happened to Orange and who's really behind Eagle."

And then I see it. A little flick at the corner of Bonner's mouth. I know what that means. She's worried. I look over at Abe as inconspicuously as I can, and he raises his eyebrows at me. He noticed it, too.

"We'll see," is all Bonner says before she changes the subject. "It's nearly time for our morning briefing. Are you all planning on attending?"

Indigo nods his head and stands. "Yes, ma'am." His eyes meet mine for one quick second as he walks past. Maybe he caught Bonner's look, too. Green, Violet, and Yellow follow him.

"I'll be down in just a minute," I tell Bonner, my hand on the doorknob.

She looks past me to Abe.

"Don't worry, I'll bring him with me," I say. I check the clock. "It's only six twenty-three. I promise we'll be there on time."

"Very well," Bonner says.

I wait for her to head down the stairs before I shut the door. "She suspects us, doesn't she?"

"Of course she suspects us," Abe says.

I lower myself onto the bed and touch Abe's leg. He doesn't bat my hand away, but he stares down at it like it's an intruder.

"Is it too early to call? They're both early birds, right? Do you want me to do it in case Ariel answers?"

"Really?" he says, still not looking at me. "That's what you want to talk about right now?"

I suck in my breath. "As opposed to?"

And then he looks up, right into my eyes. "Oh, I don't know. Any other secrets you're keeping from me?"

"That is not fair." I punctuate every word. "I was under orders not to disclose that information."

"You seem to have no problems breaking rules when it suits you, which, you know, is all the time. But the second you want to keep secrets, you hide behind the protection of the *rules*. You can't deny it."

I can't. I've always disregarded rules that didn't suit me in the moment. And I have no real answer for why I didn't tell anyone about XP sooner—why I didn't share it with Abe.

"Hand me the phone. My grandfather isn't going to answer. He's going to see the number on caller ID and make Gran answer."

I hesitate. Is he dropping this fight, right when it's starting? Part of me wants to press him, to hash everything out and get it over with. But instead I lean back and grab my cell off the nightstand. It's dead. Oops. So I grab the black handset—the kind of phone you'd find in an office conference room—wind the cord around the edge of the nightstand, and set it on the bed between us. I dial the number, then hand the receiver to Abe. His fist tightens around it for a second before he holds it up to his ear.

"Hey, Gran, it's Abraham," he says. "I'm good. How are you and Grandpa? . . . I know, it's been a while . . . She's good too . . . I . . ." I see Abe struggle with what to say next. He knows any call made from an Annum Guard phone is being recorded at the very least, if not monitored as we speak. "I was hoping we could have dinner and try to bury the hatchet . . . No, I know you don't have a problem with . . . Well, I wouldn't call it being ridiculous . . . Okay . . . I know . . . Okay . . . Okay . . . Sounds good. See you then."

Abe thrusts the receiver forward, and I take it and set it back in the cradle.

"Tomorrow night," he grunts. "Six p.m. It's done."

I know Abe's mad, so I definitely don't mention how ridiculous he sounds, saying "it's done" like he just ordered the assassination of a target who's only a questionable threat to national security.

"Gran's making brisket," he adds.

I almost smile. I haven't known Mona for very long. I accidentally saved her from an early death caused by lung cancer by snatching a cigarette out of her hands when she was nineteen, back when Alpha had me trying to convince Ariel to change the design of the Annum watches so that he would be able to travel through time himself, because Alpha didn't have the genetic makeup. The only people who can project are those people directly related to the first generation of Guardians.

I haven't told anyone about how I saved Mona. Another of my secrets. It's been hard, trying to play catch up. Trying to fake like I know all these things about Mona when really I've only known her for a few months. Everyone else has a complete memory of her in this new reality. But one thing I learned early on is that she's an amazing cook, and her brisket is the best of the best. I never had home-cooked meals growing up. At least, not after my grandmother died, taking with her memories of lamb soup at Easter and *gogosi* doughnuts at Christmas. Even when my mom was lucid, cooking was the lowest of her priorities.

Damn. My mom.

I shake my head. Later. I'll deal with that later.

Even though she's being discharged *tomorrow.*

I lean back so I'm lying on the bed and place the phone on the nightstand. We still have two minutes until the briefing, and it takes like thirty seconds to get downstairs. I roll over and put my hand on Abe's stomach as I nuzzle myself into the warm crook of his neck. *We're okay,* I tell myself. *We're going to be okay.*

Except that Abe's not having it. "We're going to be late," he says as he rolls off the bed.

I let him go, but when he's at the door, I tell him, "I love you. I'm sorry."

Abe turns around. "You hurt me. You hurt me today. You've hurt me before." He holds up a hand so I can't interrupt. "Yeah, I get it, you didn't have such a great childhood, but you've got to let me in. If we're going to have any sort of future together, you can't keep secrets from me."

It's like someone has shot me in the chest. I push off the bed. "*If* we're going to have any sort of future together? As in, there's a question about that?"

"I love you. But you are so incredibly frustrating, and you don't seem to realize it." He lets out a long sigh. "I think maybe joining Annum Guard was a mistake."

"What, you want to go back to the original plan and have us both join the CIA? Do you think they'd still recruit us?" I'm not committing to anything, or even thinking about committing to anything, but I want to know.

"I'm starting to think that if we want to have a future together, we shouldn't work together *and* live together *and* spend almost every waking second of our lives together."

I blink. "Are you breaking up with me?"

"No. Of course I'm not. I just . . . Maybe we need some space."

My heart sinks.

"Abe," I whisper. He's looking at me, and I *see* him. See the Abe I know and love. He's there, hiding behind a wall of pain. A wall that I've built myself, brick after brick. Abe has been nothing but supportive from the first day I met him. He provides me with the only stability I have in my life, and I haven't been very fair to him. I've taken and taken, and I can't think of a single thing I've given. Not since Annum Guard.

"Do you want me to stay here tomorrow night?" I ask.

"No." There's no hesitation. "I want you there. I need you there."

Need. The word is so short, so simple, but it gives me hope.

His hand is on the door.

"I love you, Abe. I know I haven't been very fair to you, but I really do love you."

He looks back at me and frowns. "Yeah, I know. We're going to be late for the briefing."

He doesn't wait for me.

CHAPTER 9

It's still light out when Abe parks the Chevy on the street, be-tween Ariel's rusted old Toyota and the next-door neighbor's 5 Series. Well, tries to park the Chevy. He grumbles and pulls forward so that he's next to the Toyota again.

"Are you sure you don't want me to do it?" I ask. I lean my head back against the seat. This is ridiculous. Abe can parallel park a car in his sleep. This is nothing more than a delay tactic.

He hits the curb and slaps the top of the steering wheel. "I do not need my girlfriend to park a car for me, thank you very much."

I shut my mouth. At least he called me his girlfriend. That's the most I've gotten all day. I'm starting to get angry, too. Yes, I haven't been entirely fair to Abe or treated our relationship with all of the respect it needs. But hello, relationships are a two-way street, and it's really unfair of Abe to wait until he's at the point of no return to say something to me. But I'm not in the mood for another fight right now. I need to keep my head clear.

"Just park the car, Abe," I say in my softest voice.

He relaxes next to me. A breath escapes his lips. He looks at me, and I see the guy I fell in love with three years ago. The guy who promised he'd keep me anchored to reality when the storm that is my mom started surging. He's still looking at me, not the road, when he zips into the spot.

I open the door. We're a perfect six inches from the curb.

"I don't want to do this."

I'm silent as I get out, mostly because I don't know if Abe is talking about dinner tonight, fighting with me, or our relationship in general. And I don't know if I want the answer. Instead I reach down and interlace my fingers with Abe's, like nothing's wrong. His fingers tense, but only for a moment. Then he squeezes mine. Even though we're in a rough patch, it makes me know we'll be okay. We have to be.

"We're in this together," I remind him. I'm not just talking about dinner.

Abe nods, and together we climb the three steps to the front stoop. Abe raises his hand to knock, but at the last second he turns to me.

"You sure you don't want to call your mom? Leave her a voice mail?"

My mom was discharged this morning. I haven't called her yet. I *should*, but I don't think she wants to hear from me. And I don't really want to talk to her right now either. The more I think about her, the madder I get. Because she *can* make herself well. She has done it. She's just too scared to try again, and screw that.

"Positive." I nudge past him and rap my knuckles against the door. "Stop stalling."

There's a shuffling inside and the sound of a chain being slid from a lock.

And then Mona is staring at us. I'm not sure when her last chemo treatment was, but she looks worse than the last time I saw her. A sweater hangs from her bony shoulders, and she has a blue-and-yellow silk scarf tied around her head, hiding the fact that she has no hair. I'm hit with a pang of guilt because this is my fault. I saved Mona from an early death caused by lung cancer, but then I plunked her down into a present where she has stage IV lymphoma.

"Hi, Gran," Abe says gently.

Mona smiles. "Abraham." She throws her arms around him, then opens her arms to pull me into the hug. "Amanda. I'm so glad you both came."

"Is Grandpa?" Abe asks.

"He will be," Mona says as she ushers us inside the living room and shuts the door.

The dining room-slash-kitchen is right off the living room, so I can see that there are only four places set. Part of me was hoping Abe's parents would be here, too. Ariel was dead set against Abe joining the Guard, but Abe's dad was for it. It would have been nice to have another buffer here.

Abe isn't saying anything. I see him trying to be inconspicuous as he peers into the kitchen to check if Ariel is there. This has to be killing him. It's his family. I like to think that *I'm* his family, too. And we're all in various states of turmoil.

No, I tell myself. *Not now*. I remember Orange and what we're here for. It's time to stop the pouting already. Both of us.

"What can I do to help?" I ask Mona as I sweep into the kitchen, knowing full well that she's going to tell me to sit down and relax. It didn't take me long to realize she's the type of person who won't let you lift a finger to help.

"Sit down and relax," Mona says, and I smile. Then Ariel wanders in from the hallway that leads to his office.

"Are we eating?" he asks brusquely. "Let's eat. I'm hungry."

Mona nods, and formalities are skipped as we all sit down at the table. Ariel takes the head seat, and Abe and I sit next to him across from each other. Mona sets a brisket on a chipped serving platter in the center of the table, and hands a bowl of vegetables to me and a bowl of roasted potatoes to Abe. Then she sits in the last empty chair.

Abe smacks a spoonful of potatoes onto his plate, and two of them roll from his plate onto the floor. Ariel's shoulders tense.

I gingerly set some carrots onto my plate. They smell like they've been cooked in the brisket juices, and my stomach growls. "How's work going, Ariel?" I ask as I hand him the veggies. I figure that's an easy, neutral question.

"Same as always." Ariel sets the bowl down by Abe without looking at him. I wait, but it becomes obvious that's the only answer I'm getting.

I look to Mona. "Thanks for having us to dinner. It smells amazing. You wouldn't believe how the quality of food has gone down at Annum Hall in the last few months."

Mona laughs politely, but Ariel slams his fork on the table. "Yes, that's what we should all be focusing on. The fact that the food is bad, not that the entire organization is so corrupt that no amount of investigation or rehabilitation will ever revive it."

"She was making a joke, Grandpa," Abe says.

"It's not a joking matter, Abraham."

"You know," Abe says, and now it's my turn to tense. No good has ever come from Abe starting a conversation with those two words. Those are his fighting words. "Just because you couldn't hack it in the Guard is no reason to take it out on me."

"Abe!" I gasp.

Ariel shoves back his chair. Then his finger is in Abe's face. "Two things," he says. "One. You were not raised to say those things to me, and don't you forget your manners just because I happen to disagree with your choices. And two. *Hacking it* has nothing to do with my leaving the Guard. *Nothing.*" He turns to his wife, and immediately his body relaxes and his eyes soften. "This smells delicious, my darling, but I fear I've lost my appetite for the time being." And then he walks down the hallway toward his office. The door slams shut soon after.

"I'm not hungry either. Sorry, Gran." Abe stands and goes out the back door onto the porch.

I bite my bottom lip. "I'm so sorry, Mona."

She waves her hand in the air. "Don't be sorry. Serve yourself the brisket. I didn't spend all day cooking this damn meal for no one to eat it."

I smile, then load my plate with the meat and a few potatoes. I tip the platter toward Mona, although I know she'll decline. Her appetite is next to nothing these days.

I pick up my fork, but I can't stop looking at the back door. At where Abe is probably sitting on the wicker bench on the porch, pouting. Or down the hallway to where Ariel is probably sitting at his desk. Stewing.

I finish eating and stand to take my plate to the sink, but Mona waves and takes it from me. "Go talk some sense into him," she says.

"Which one?"

Mona's brown eyes sparkle with life. "The one you came to see."

I nod, but then I hesitate outside Ariel's door. I can't believe how much things have changed in less than six months. Since I discovered that my boyfriend's grandfather was the mastermind behind a top-secret, time-traveling government agency.

I knock to be polite, but I've already opened the door. Ariel sits at his desk with his back to me, looking out over the yard. I wonder if he's looking at Abe. The tiny office is crammed with shelves of books. Books piled haphazardly on top of one another. Books lying on their sides on top of books standing up straight. Books stacked like dominoes on the floor.

I step over a pile. "Hi."

"Hello, Amanda." Ariel doesn't turn.

"Thank you," I say, and he does turn. "For calling me Amanda. It makes me feel normal."

Ariel doesn't say anything. Finally he sighs and his shoulders slump. "I'm not mad at you. Or Abraham, for that matter. But I don't know what the two of you want from me. I'm never going to be happy that Annum Guard exists."

I choose my words carefully. This is the calmest, most even-tempered that Ariel has been in months. "And I guess I'm having a hard time figuring out why."

Ariel takes off his glasses and rubs the bridge of his nose. "Time is a dangerous game. Back when I was young and naive, I thought changing the past for the better was the right thing to do. I've borne witness to a great number of horrors in my lifetime." He pauses, and I know why. He was born in Berlin. His father took a professorship at Harvard when Ariel was a child, before the Nazis banned German Jews from traveling, but the rest of his family wasn't so lucky. His mother was from Poland. Ariel grew up without a single cousin, not one uncle or aunt, no grandparents.

Ariel goes on. "But the organization that I helped found is so different from the one that exists today. It used to have a purpose."

"It still has a purpose."

"And what's that? Profiteering?"

"No," I say, standing straighter. "We improve people's lives. I mean, I saved half a billion dollars worth of art a few months ago—"

"Art! That's the example you're going to give me? Art! A few splashes of color on canvas, hanging on a wall somewhere, all so a gaggle of pretentious phonies can make self-important statements about how living a cultured life makes them *feel*. You're going to have to do better than that, Amanda."

My teeth tug at my bottom lip. I swore I'd never tell Ariel about how I saved Mona. Swore it up and down. I decided that wasn't the kind of news I'd ever want to know. But maybe I should tell him now, to make him see things my way.

No. No, I shouldn't. *Stick to why you came here.*

But before I can say anything, Ariel tells me, "I'm sorry. I shouldn't take my anger out on you." Then he gestures. "Shut the door." His voice is different. The veiled hostility is gone, and I see a glimpse of the man I know and admire. The man who welcomed me into his home and his family.

I do as I'm told, then sit on a leather ottoman tucked away beside a stack of books.

"Do you know why Annum Guard was founded?" he asks.

"I . . . I don't."

"Okay, then tell me what you know about the Cuban Missile Crisis."

"Well . . ."

Ariel sighs. "Honestly, kids these days." Before I can protest that I know the basics, he's speaking again. "In 1959, Fidel Castro assumed power of Cuba. Castro was a good friend of the Soviets, which was alarming given how close Cuba is to the US. In 1961, the US embarrassed itself in a disastrous failed attempt to remove Castro from power. The Bay of Pigs Invasion."

I nod because this much is familiar. But I'm not about to tell Ariel that I only know about all of this because of a song that came out before I was even born.

"All that failure did was strengthen the relationship between Castro and Soviet leader Nikita Khrushchev. Khrushchev convinced Castro to place nuclear missiles on his island, aimed at the US, and when we found out about it, we had an international crisis."

I nod again. "And then Kennedy was able to avert the crisis," I say. I remember covering this for like five minutes at the tail end of my eighth-grade American history class. We seemed to spend like two months memorizing the names of the governors of the colonies, and then we flew through the next three hundred years at a breakneck pace. American Revolution . . . blink . . . Civil War . . . blink . . . Industrial Revolution . . . Great Depression . . . FDR . . . a jumbled mess of everything that's happened since then. And my classes at Peel focused more on current events than historical ones.

"Wrong," Ariel says.

My head snaps up. "What do you mean, wrong?"

"I mean," Ariel says slowly, "that the crisis was not averted."

I press my lips together and say nothing.

"On October 27, 1962, in response to the shooting down of an American reconnaissance airplane over Cuba, the US launched a series of long-range nuclear missiles from Turkey that completely obliterated Moscow. The Soviets responded by launching their own weapons at our capital, and by October 28, the island of Cuba, all of DC, and most of northern Virginia and southern Maryland were no more."

I'm dizzy.

"The world spent all of early November plunged into an economic depression. Several European economies were on the verge of bankruptcy. And let's not talk about what happened in the US. Some one million Americans lost their lives. Six million Soviets. Nearly eight million Cubans. Men, women, children. The elderly, the infirm, babes in the womb—none were spared. Some died in the blast; some died of radiation poisoning in the days and weeks that followed."

My brain can't process this. The magnitude of what he's telling me is our *real* history. Fifteen *million* people. I . . . I can't. I stare at Ariel. I forget to blink. I think I forget to breathe.

"And on November 11, 1962, I got a phone call that changed my life. A phone call from President Kennedy himself. Washington had already been aware that I was developing a device that would allow man to travel through time." I nod. I know this. I first visited Ariel in March of 1962, and that's when he told me the Department of Defense was interested in the Annum watches. "And exactly one month later, I went on the very first Annum Guard mission, two and a half years before Annum Guard was officially founded."

"You changed the past," I whispered.

"You're damn right I did. I saved all of those lives. I saved *Earth*, if you want to know the direction the crisis was headed. The world would not have recovered."

"Why don't I know about this?"

"Why would you expect that to be common knowledge? The only other people who knew at the time were John Kennedy and Robert Kennedy, and they've been gone a long time now."

I don't tell Ariel that JFK died only because my father helped kill him.

"So besides officials with the highest clearance levels, you and I are the only ones who know. Everyone else shifted into a parallel present the moment I returned from averting the crisis. No one has any idea how close we all came to being wiped off the face of the earth."

"How did you do it?" I hear the awe in my voice.

"Does it matter?" Ariel shoots back.

"Sorry. It's just . . . that's the most amazing thing I've ever heard."

Ariel pauses. "This is extremely classified. This entire conversation is classified."

I nod. "Of course."

He takes another breath. "I infiltrated NASA. I went back months before the bombing and was hired by NASA in the communications department. I—"

"Hang on, you *stayed* in the past? For months? How much time did you lose in the present?"

Ariel waves his hand at me. "Thirty-seven days. A minor sacrifice. I didn't go back far, Amanda, so I lost less time. I assume you know how that works.

"I planted an encrypted telegram supposedly addressed to James Webb, NASA's administrator at the time, that I said was sent by Khrushchev through the Soviet space program. A back channel communication meant to fly under the radar screen for political purposes. I basically said that I—Khrushchev—wasn't advancing any further hostilities but couldn't say so publicly. Webb and I had known each other for a while—we'd both served on the Draper Committee in '58—so he trusted me to hand-deliver the telegram to the White House, and we never dropped the first bomb."

"Why are you telling me all of this now?"

"Because *that* is why I founded Annum Guard. Saving humanity. Reversing the true horrors that threaten our very existence. Not bailing out a museum from its embarrassing lack of security."

I feel stupid for even bringing up the Gardner heist. That mission was completely insignificant in comparison.

"Now ask me whatever it is you came to ask me."

"What?"

"You came here for a reason. What is it?"

"Oh, right." I shake my head, try to shake everything Ariel just told me out of my brain, but it doesn't work. "Have you ever heard of something called Operation Blackout? Something that has to do with Annum Guard?"

"No, I've never heard the term, but whatever it is, I doubt I'd support it."

I agree. I think. I don't know.

"I believe it has something to do with taking out Annum Guard members. Capture, kill, we don't know. Zeta hasn't been heard from in months, and Orange disappeared a couple of days ago. His tracker just went off. Can you think of any reason a tracker would just deactivate like that?"

Ariel raises an eyebrow. "Death."

"Besides that?"

"I don't know anything about the new trackers, Amanda. I don't know anything about the old trackers. I never used one. They started second generation. And I really wish you would stop telling me these things. I have a hard enough time knowing you and Abraham are out there—*projecting*—putting your lives in danger. Now to know someone might be trying to silence you? I don't want to hear about it."

"Okay," I say. But there's one more question I have to ask. "You don't know anything about an XP, do you?"

Ariel's eyebrows creep up again. "A what? Expy? What's that?"

"No. XP. Like initials. Maybe for a person or a project? Or the Greek letters chi rho?"

He shakes his head. "I don't know anything, Amanda. My involvement with this organization has been minimal for quite some time now."

There's nothing more I can say. So I stand up and give Ariel an awkward hug, which he returns with an even more awkward pat on the back.

I leave the office and find Mona sitting in the living room with a crocheted shawl wrapped around her. She looks at me with hollowed eyes and opens her mouth, like she wants to ask how everything went, but in the end she must decide it's too much effort, so she just nods.

"I'm sorry," I whisper.

Mona doesn't respond. I show myself out the back door to find Abe. He's slouched on the wicker bench, his head resting on the back and his arms crossed over his chest.

"Let's go," I say.

Abe opens his eyes. "Did he tell you anything?"

Tons.

"Nothing about a blackout or XP. He's never heard of either."

"Shocking. He probably knows exactly what they are but isn't telling out of spite." He pushes off the bench and walks toward the side of the house.

"He doesn't know, Abe— Where are you going?"

Abe lifts the latch on the fence gate. "We're leaving."

"But . . . You didn't say good-bye to Mona."

Abe shrugs. "She'll figure out we left."

I inhale sharply. "What are you doing, Abe? This isn't you. She's your *grandmother*, and she's sick. Tell her good-bye."

He hesitates, and I get angry.

"Do you even know how good you have it? Your life is a damned family values ad that runs during every election season— mom, dad, kids, and grandparents, huddled around a professionally decorated birthday cake while some blowhard politician talks about 'the way things used to be.' I would *kill* for this." I point toward the back door.

Abe is silent.

I shake my head, just once. "Do you know how much I wish my biggest family problem was a stupid fight with my grandfather?"

And then Abe yells at me. It's the first time he's ever done it. "Can you let me know how much longer I have to feel sorry for you and your crappy home life before you'll finally acknowledge that other people have real problems, too?"

"I . . . what?" His words land a sucker punch in my gut.

Neither of us says anything for a moment. Then Abe mutters, "I'm sorry. I shouldn't have said that. And you're right. I'll go say good-bye." He disappears inside the house, but his absence doesn't get rid of the pain I feel, mostly because he has a point.

The back door opens and shuts, and Abe's at my side again. "I'm sorry," he says. "Really."

"Me, too. I don't like fighting with you, Abe."

"Me either."

"Can we just . . . call a truce for now? There's so much else we have to focus on."

"Truce." Abe weaves his fingers through mine as we walk back to the car, and I try to ignore the fact that his are cold.

CHAPTER 10

I linger in the hallway outside Sit Room One the next morning. It's a few minutes before eight, the typical time that a small, weekend breakfast spread is set out in the dining room. I take a breath, then step into the room.

Red shuffles a bunch of papers into a folder, then looks up at me. "You do realize you get Saturdays off, right?"

I shut the door behind me and take a breath to calm my nerves, which doesn't help. So much is riding on this. I glance back to make sure the door is fully closed and that Bonner isn't hanging around outside, then I look at him. Red's at least six inches taller than me, and he has a way of standing and staring that makes me uncomfortable, that oozes authority.

"If I were to say the word blackout to you, how would you respond?"

"How about you cut the bullshit and tell me what you're doing here?"

Okay then. So much for that approach. I begin again. "I know there's more to Orange's disappearance than you're letting on."

"Excuse me?"

"I trust you, Red, and I want to tell you what I know— everything I know," I say without hesitation. If I hesitate, I'll lose my resolve. "So please just let me tell you, and then we can talk about what it all means afterward."

I'm met with silence, so I jump back in.

"I recently became aware of three things, and I don't know how much you know about them."

"Try me."

"First. You know about XP." I say it as a statement because it is a statement.

All I get in return is a blank stare and the tension ratcheted a degree. I'm suddenly reminded that Red isn't just another team-mate. He's a superior.

Red clears his throat. "And?"

"Right." Forget my nerves. I just have to do it. Like ripping off a Band-Aid. "I have a hunch about what happened to Orange."

Red raises an eyebrow.

I walk farther into the room and rest my palm against the edge of a table. "I have it on good authority that there might be a secret operation taking place inside Annum Guard. An operation that's responsible for making people disappear."

"A blackout," Red says.

"You've heard of it?"

"No, that's what you just told me. Where did you hear this from?"

"I'd rather not say."

"Uh-uh, wrong answer." Red crosses his arms over his chest. "That's one hell of a revelation, accusation, whatever label you want to slap on it. And you're going to tell me right now where you heard this."

This makes me hesitate. Because what I did was illegal, and I don't want to admit that to my boss. Or to the guy who would have been my boss had Bonner not come along.

"*Now,* Iris."

I clasp both hands in front of me. "I read it in some Senate testimony."

"Whose testimony?"

"Zeta's."

Red cocks his head. "And how did you come across this testimony?"

"Is that really important?"

"You know it is."

"I accidentally"—I hold up my hands to deflect Red's look—"I swear, it was accidental. I found his testimony on top of a stack of papers when I was meeting with the vice president."

"And, what, you accidentally read it while she was in the bathroom?"

"No, I very deliberately took pictures of all the pages I could while she was on a phone call."

Red's brow furrows and his skin reddens. But then, he composes himself. "Show me."

"I can't. I deleted the images from my phone, then scrubbed it. They're gone."

"What exactly did they say?"

"Just that there's some sort of covert operation team inside Annum Guard assembled for Operation Blackout. We've been trying to put two and two together ever since."

"We? Who's *we*? I swear, if you've told every other Guardian about this . . ." And then understanding dawns on his face. "You have, haven't you? You've told every other Guardian about this."

"We just want answers, Red."

"I am pretty damn annoyed with you right now. With all of you. You're lucky I don't have much authority these days."

"I'm sorry," I mumble. Then I stand tall. "No, I take it back. I'm not sorry. I want to know what the truth is. And I want you to help me. I *need* you to help me. We all do."

"Give me one reason why I should."

"That's the second thing." I pause. "What do you know about the reasons that Annum Guard was started, Red? About its very first mission?"

"That's classified, you know that. Way above my clearance level."

"Well, what would you say if I told you I know what the very first mission was?"

"Should I even ask how you know this?"

"Ariel Stender told me." I need to word this next bit carefully. I need to be resolute, but I don't want to come off sounding insensitive. And that's such a fine line. I reach out and touch Red's forearm. He's wearing a long-sleeved shirt, but I remember that glimpse of a tattoo peeking out under his sleeve all those months ago at Peel. The tattoo of two flags intertwined. Two national identities. The United States flag and one other. "It's above my clearance level. Yours, too. And I was told it in the strictest of confidences."

Red looks at my hand on his arm, then looks at me. I can see the struggle in his eyes. I know the business side of him wants to tell me to keep the mission to myself, but the personal side is curious.

Ariel told me this in confidence. But don't we all have a right to know our origin? What Annum Guard's original purpose really was?

"The Cuban Missile Crisis," I say. "That was the first mission. It really happened. In 1962, the Soviets and the US launched missiles at each other, and DC and Moscow both crumbled and burned. Fifteen million people were killed. Our economy was toppled. And Cuba was wiped off the map. Just . . . gone." I tap his arm once, right where the tattoo is under his sleeve, before I pull my hand away.

I don't know when Red's parents came to America, whether it was before 1962 or after, and I'm not about to ask. But I see Red struggling to put together the reality of the situation.

"The very first Annum Guard mission was to stop the bombing. To avert the crisis," I say.

Now Red looks angry. "And you know I'm a Cuban-American so you're trying to play to my sensitivities? You want me to weep for my homeland and give you whatever you want? You're out of line, and you clearly don't know me."

I take a step back and hold up both hands. Damn, I did this wrong.

"No, Red. All I'm trying to do is get you to see that Annum Guard needs help. Your help. We need to stop going on missions that don't matter, stop poring over tens of thousands of irrelevant documents, and we need to get back to what's important—finding XP, ridding ourselves of the bacteria that's infesting our ranks, and taking sight of our true purpose again. Changing the past to improve our present."

"You do know the 'enhancement, not alteration' thing is total BS, right?"

"But it doesn't have to be. Look, we've all decided we're going to dig."

"I'm pretty sure the first rule of going undercover isn't to tell your superior what you're doing."

"Help us, Red. We're getting back to the *old* Annum Guard. The one that existed before any of us were even born. The one with a purpose. The one that you *thought* you joined."

Red's quiet for a moment. Then he squeezes the bridge of his nose. "What exactly are you hoping I'll do?"

My heart lifts. "You have access to information we don't."

"I don't know what any of the XP missions are. That's in the realm of the Defense Department." But the way he says it—in a rushed voice just a smidge higher than his normal tone—tells me that this too is a half-truth. I don't know what he's hiding, but Red's never given me even the smallest indication that he can't be trusted. He's come through for me every time I've ever needed him.

"Only the DoD has seen Alpha's notebook," Red continues. "Or what's left of it." Most of the notebook was destroyed in an explosion back at Peel. That notebook detailed every mission Alpha ever sold, to whom, and for how much.

"The notebook! Red, what if I project back to that day at Peel? To before the notebook was burned and its remnants turned over to the DoD?"

Red draws himself up to his full height. "Are you joking? You are *not* asking me to authorize a mission where you'd go back in time and steal something from *yourself*. Do you have any idea how dangerous that is? What would you do if another version of you walked through the door right now and tried to take something from you?"

Fair point. "Well, then, another Guardian could do it. Like Green or—Oh! Abe! I mean Blue. I promise, I wouldn't have found it weird if he asked me for the notebook that day. And I would have given it to him."

Red shakes his head. "Nope. All of you were there that day at Peel. That would mean a double version of one of you. No, Iris. The notebook is off the table. What else do you have?"

Is that an invitation? He's staring at me. I can't tell if he's thinking about how he can help—about telling me what he knows—or whether he's going to make sure I get fired tomorrow.

"Okay, then, we start small," I say. "We'll look for any little trail we can find that might lead us to XP, and that's the direction we'll take." I tap the base of my neck, where my new tracker is. "You also control these, right?"

Red doesn't answer.

"And what's the third thing?" he says.

"The what?"

"You said there were three things."

"Oh. Right. Our interns. It's a pretty big coincidence that Orange went missing right after they started."

"You think we have a mole."

"I think we should try to find out."

He's quiet again.

"So now it's your turn, Red. Am I on the right track with any of this? What was Orange really doing when he disappeared?"

Red kicks a chair out from behind the table, and I sit quickly.

"What I've told you is the truth. I don't know who XP is, and I don't know what any of the XP missions are. But believe me that I share your frustrations with our current administration. Bonner is leading us on one wild goose chase after another, and don't for one second think I haven't asked myself why."

He opens the top drawer of the file cabinet in the corner and pulls out a plain tan folder. He slaps it onto the table in front of me, and I flip it open. A picture of Orange is clipped to the left side. This is Orange's personal file.

I scan it. Orange's real name is Jeremy Greer. He's twenty-seven. His mother—my breath catches—his mother is Epsilon. I think back to my very first day at Annum Guard. To the woman in the wheelchair with the broken, mangled body. A warning against the havoc that time travel can wreak on humans.

I look over the rest of the page. Orange grew up in Arlington, just across the river. Both of his parents still live there. There's a handwritten note at the bottom of the page, and I immediately recognize Alpha's handwriting. The note is dated nine years ago. It must have been written right after Orange joined. The note says that, at Orange's request, 30 percent of his salary is to be withheld and put in a special needs trust for Epsilon.

And with that, I flip the file shut. This is too much. Too personal.

"He's my friend," Red says quietly. "He's been my friend for a very long time. Yellow, Green, and Blue—Old Blue—didn't join the Guard until two years ago, and Indigo and Violet the year after that. For seven years, third generation was only me and Orange. He's my *friend*."

"What happened to him?" My voice is soft, too.

"I found something buried in a file. A note about how Eta referred to the election mission as 'The Cannonball Mission.' That's not how we name missions, and she was talking about a Massachusetts governor's election. Why would she call it that? It had nothing to do with a cannonball. So I dug and I searched and I dug and I searched. For weeks. And then I found a tree native to Central and South American rainforests nicknamed the cannonball tree."

I nod politely. What in the world is he talking about?

"Its scientific name is couroupita guianensis, so by a stroke of luck, I decided to do a search for that, and when I did, I discovered something called *morphnus* guianensis. The scientific name for the crested eagle. Eta probably thought she was being smart, that no one would ever be able to reverse engineer the scientific name of the bird back to a cannonball."

I sit up straight. Crested Eagle was the code name of my Peel headmaster—Vaughn—who was working for XP.

"So you thought the election mission might have something to do with XP?"

"It was a strong hunch, one that proved to be correct. Orange knew what he was doing. I told him about Cannonball not five minutes after I found it. He knew the real mission was to look for any signs of George Vaughn or XP. But neither of us were expecting that they'd be waiting. It was an ambush."

"We're going to find him, Red." I meet his gaze. "We are. But the only way we're going to do it is to keep digging."

Red looks past me to the clock. It's nearly eight thirty.

"Hope you're not very hungry," he says. "We need to plan."

CHAPTER 11

Phase One of our plan is to sniff out the interns.

Okay, actually, phase one of the plan is to put Yellow in charge of sniffing out the interns. Yellow may look like a helpless gazelle grazing in the savanna, but that's part of her charm. The truth is that girl is a cheetah through and through.

"Here's what we're doing," Yellow says as she pushes next to me on the stairs after the six thirty a.m. Monday briefing. She glances at the door to make sure Bonner isn't right behind us. "Tonight, you, me, and our potential moles are going out."

"Going out where?"

"Someplace fun. You're going to love it."

But she can't fool me. I can see the stress lines creeping across her forehead, the dark circles under her eyes from sleepless nights. She holds the door open for me, and I squeeze her shoulder as I walk into the common room.

"Why are you being intentionally vague?" I ask.

The interns are already in the library. Paige and Mike are sitting at desks, going through documents. Colton has plopped himself in an armchair and is scrolling through his phone.

"Bring socks."

"Socks? You're . . . you're not talking about bowling are you? Please tell me you're not talking about bowling."

Yellow's face lights up with a huge, exaggerated smile, and she turns toward the library. "I need to get out. I feel like I'm just constantly stuck here." She's talking loudly, and Colton directs his attention from his phone. Yellow grabs my arm. "Hey, we should do something fun tonight."

"Like . . . bowling?" I say in a flat voice.

Yellow gasps. "Yes, like bowling! Who's up for Lucky Strike tonight?"

Paige and Mike exchange a confused glance, as if they're not sure whether Yellow is talking to them. Colton looks at Yellow in a way that makes my stomach turn. He sees her as a conquest, which I know is playing right into her plan, but it makes me want to kick him in the nuts.

"I'm game," Colton says.

"Sweet." Yellow looks to the others. "And what about you guys?"

"Are you going, Iris?" Mike asks. His tone is casual, and I can't tell if he's being friendly or if there's something more there.

Yellow jostles my shoulder, and I say, "Of course."

"Then count me in," Mike says.

"Excellent," Yellow says. "And Paige?"

Paige brushes a strand of curly red hair behind her ear. "I don't know. I'm in the lottery for a fall semester Gov 94 seminar, and I'm really hoping I get my first choice—political economy. I want to get a leg up, so I think I should just stay home and read some more Iversen and Soskice tonight."

"That's the saddest thing I've ever heard," Yellow says, which makes Colton snort. "I won't take no for an answer."

There's a shuffle of footsteps behind us as Violet and Indigo walk into the library, making small talk about some MTV show I'll probably never watch. Abe's right behind them, looking down at his scrambler.

"Hey, Vi, you up for Lucky Strike tonight?" Yellow asks. "We're doing a night with the interns. You, me, and Iris."

Violet stops talking midsentence and says something to Yellow, but I don't hear. Because I'm looking right at Abe. He looks from Colton to Mike to me and back to Mike. It's subtle, but his expression sours.

Later, I mouth to him, and he nods and looks down.

Yellow links her arm with Violet's and pulls her over to the stacks of banker's boxes lining the far wall. "It's a date then."

But as soon as her back is to the interns, Yellow's facade crumbles. Her shoulders slump and her head drops to her chest.

There's a knock on my door a little after eight thirty that night. I hop off the bed to open it, but then Yellow barges in, Violet right behind her. Yellow hugs her makeup bag to her chest.

"Your turn," she announces. "I just finished Violet."

Violet holds her hands to her face, framing it. "I'm stripped-down, nineties Naomi Campbell."

"I have no idea what that means." I'm underdressed in jeans and a Yoda T-shirt. Violet has on white cropped pants and a flowy, lavender tank top. Her short hair has deep-purple lowlights at the nape of her neck. Yellow's paired a denim blazer with a black-and-white striped dress that's so short, I'm not sure how she's supposed to sit in it. Her blonde hair is pulled back into a high bun, and she has on thick black eyeliner, light-pink blush, and mauve lipstick. Her eyebrows somehow look darker and thicker.

"And I went with Audrey Hepburn in *Breakfast at Tiffany's*," she announces. "Sit. We're all going vintage tonight, and you're finally going to let me do Liz Taylor. A cat eye would look absolutely amazing on you."

"I'm already wearing makeup."

Yellow squints and leans in so she's about two inches from my face. "Where? I know you're not talking about that nude eye shadow and"—she sniffs—"cherry lip balm."

"Yellow," I say softly. "You can drop the act around us. I know this investigation is really hard on you."

Violet doesn't say anything. She picks at a chip in her nail polish.

"I don't know what you're talking about," Yellow says. She won't look at me.

"It's really hard to watch you put on this show day after day when—"

"When the only thing I can think about is whether I'll ever see my dad again? Yeah, I know." She hugs her makeup bag tighter, like someone's trying to steal it. "Because you're right. It is all I can think about. It's on my mind as soon as I wake up in the morning, and it's with me the entire day. *All day, every day, Iris.* And especially at night. When the sun goes down, all I can think is that my dad's not just being held somewhere. He's being tortured in a dark, dank cell, or he's already decomposing in a shallow grave with a bullet in his head.

"And the only thing that's keeping me from having a complete mental breakdown is this act, or whatever you called it. Makeup, clothes, stupid gossip. It's all meaningless crap, and it's what I need right now. Okay?"

"I'm so sorry, Yellow. I . . . yes. Okay."

"Now sit down and let me do a damn cat eye."

Everyone's silent for a moment, but then Violet breaks the tension. She lets out a giggle that's completely inappropriate but also so perfect.

I sidestep Yellow and grab my favorite khaki messenger bag, then sling it over my head. "Sorry. Put your liquid liner away for another day. We're going to be late."

It's a few minutes after nine when we walk into Lucky Strike. The place is packed for a Monday night, but Colton is easy to spot. There's a tall Secret Service agent hovering by the bar, and a gaggle of college-age girls a few feet away. Sure enough, we find Colton standing in the middle of them, dressed in designer jeans, leather loafers, and a shirt that I assume cost more than an average mortgage payment.

"Oh, hey," he says, his eyes trained on Yellow. The music is so loud that he has to yell. He pushes away from his groupies and sidles up next to her. It's like he doesn't even see me or Violet.

"Where's everyone else?" Violet yells.

Colton jerks his head toward the bowling lanes and grabs ahold of Yellow's wrist. "Come on, I have a table." He leads her toward a curved leather booth, and she lets herself be led. She looks back at me and winks. I know that going undercover involves playing along, which sometimes means making yourself seem weak and submissive. But damn if I don't have a hard time with that. Especially when Colton Caldwell is involved.

Mike catches my eye and waves. He and Paige are set up on the far left lane. *Perfect.* Away from the crowd a bit. There are red paper lanterns and blue lights hanging over the lanes, and thankfully the music is a little lower over in this corner.

"Hey!" Mike calls. He's changed into jeans and a T-shirt and already has on red-and-blue bowling shoes.

"I'll get us shoes," Violet says. "Eight, right?"

"Yep." I pull my bag over my head and set it next to Paige, who hasn't changed since this morning. Her white dress shirt is perfectly unwrinkled, as if she ran home after work to iron it. She nods a polite hello at me.

"How's it going?" Mike asks, and that's when I notice his shirt. It's dark gray with white lettering that reads "Whenever You're Having a Bad Day, Just Imagine a T. rex Making a Bed" and has a picture in the middle of a T. rex facedown on a mattress.

"So what's with you and T. rexes?" I ask.

He looks down at his shirt and smiles. "I just think it's hilarious. They're supposed to be these ferocious killers, right? But then they have these tiny little baby arms that make them seem as adorable as kittens. I mean, try to imagine a T. rex using a fork and knife." He pulls his arms close to his chest and mimics it. "Hilarious."

I laugh. And not just a polite laugh, but a full laugh that makes my stomach hurt. The kind of laugh normally reserved for adventure bodywash, which makes me stop.

"So, are you any good at bowling?" I ask.

"Nope. You?"

"Nope."

Paige takes the seat at the computer and starts typing in our names. "Are we playing or what?"

Violet comes back with the shoes and gravitates toward Paige. It's part of our game plan. We each get one of the interns alone and try to see what we can find out. Mike is my assignment, but it's not like I can just come out and ask him if he's disclosing our secrets to anyone, so I figure natural conversation is the best bet. Still, I have to keep reminding myself I'm here to do a job. Talking with Mike is just so . . . easy. So *natural*.

"Good one," he says after I make my seventh gutter ball in a row. He jostles my shoulder with his, like Abe would do.

The mole, I repeat in my head. *You're here to find out if he's supplying information to his defense secretary grandfather.*

"So tell me a little bit about your family," I blurt, then cringe. *Smooth*.

Mike sits down next to me. Paige and Violet are lined up at the ball return. "Well," he says, "you know who my grandfather is, and I'm pretty sure you know I have two moms." I nod. "And my résumé told you I grew up in Manhattan, so what else do you want to know?"

I shrug and tell myself to play it cool. "I just like getting to know the people I work with. So tell me something I don't know."

He leans back. "Something you don't know . . . Hmm. Do you know why my last name is Baxter?"

I nod. "After one of your moms. The one who works in finance." Layla Baxter, the one Bonner referred to as a renowned venture capitalist. I looked her up after Bonner told me that.

Turns out she's one of the only high-powered, female venture capitalists in the world. She's worth more than a billion dollars, 99 percent of which she's already pledged to charity. His other mother works for a nonprofit that provides vaccines in third-world countries.

"After both of my moms, actually," Mike says. "Back when they had a commitment ceremony—almost thirty years ago—they decided that they both would change their name. Partly because they wanted the same name and neither of them wanted to hyphenate, and partly for professional reasons. My mom Victoria is the pacifist, hippie type, and the Howe name doesn't get you far in that crowd. My other mom, Layla?" He pauses. "When she was just starting out in the financial world, things were different. Women in general had a hard time breaking in, but a woman with an ethnic last name like Teremun? Forget it. So they picked a new name."

"Like . . . out of the phone book?"

A grin spreads across his face. "Nope. It was the name of a shelter dog they'd adopted and recently lost to cancer. A mutt who was already named Baxter when they got him."

"Huh" is all I can think of to say. None of this was in the article I read.

Mike laughs. "Yep, I'm named after a dog. Bet that's something you didn't know. I don't think that story's common knowledge because, you know, it's a little weird."

"I think it's sweet," I say. And that's the truth. It's a sweet story, *and* it's making me feel a little weird because I doubt it's the kind of story Mike tells a lot of people. It feels personal. Intimate.

"What about you? Any pets?" he asks.

"Yeah, one. A dog. Dos."

"Dose? Like medicine?"

"No, *dos*, like the number two in Spanish. It's . . ." I'm not sure how much to disclose. "The dog's name is actually Malarkey the Second, hence the *dos*."

"What happened to Malarkey the First?"

"Malarkey was my dad's dog," I say before I can stop myself. "He died a few years after my dad died, and my mom rushed out the very next day and went to, like, four different shelters until she found a dog that looked exactly like Malarkey. Then she brought him home and gave him the same name." And then I do stop myself. I don't have a memory of this—I was too young—but it's still bringing back feelings I don't want right now. Sadness and bitterness, and a whole bunch of things I'd like to avoid. Besides, these days, the dog lives with our neighbor, Mrs. McNamara, most of the time.

Mike's leg brushes mine. I look down. He's moved closer to me. "I didn't know your dad died. When?"

"I was a baby." My stomach tightens.

"What—"

"He was a Navy SEAL." The lie slips off my tongue. "Working overseas. I don't have too many details. It's pretty classified."

Mike's knee inches closer, and his hand grazes my wrist, and this is wrong. All wrong. I look up and catch Yellow's eye at the bar. Her eyebrows have shot to the sky, and she jerks her head toward the restroom.

I spring up. "I'll be right back." Then I look over at Violet. "Bathroom?"

She drops her purple ball onto the rack. "Definitely."

When we're firmly entrenched inside the ladies' room, Yellow grabs onto my arm. "Sorry, are we interrupting your date?"

"My . . . what?"

"Oh, come on, I've watched you flirt with him for the past twenty minutes."

I cross my arms over my chest. "I was not flirting with him. I was getting to know him, which, you know, is the whole point of this thing."

Violet smooths a few strands of hair while looking in the mirror. "Oh, please. I was standing right there. You were absolutely flirting with him."

"I have a boyfriend. I was *not* flirting. And besides"—I shoot a glance in Yellow's direction—"pot calling the kettle black, much?"

Yellow pulls out a tube of lipstick and dabs light pink on her lips. "Oh, I definitely was flirting with Colton. The difference is, I was doing it intentionally and with zero feeling behind it."

"There's no feeling behind what I was doing either!" As I say it, I know that's not the hundred percent truth, and I don't know how I feel about that. Guilty? Not guilty? Somewhere in between?

"So you admit you were flirting then? Finally," Yellow says with a smirk, and Violet shakes her head with a telling smile on her face.

I grab both of their arms and guide them toward the door. "Can we focus, please? XP. Chances are, one of the three people out there is related to someone who knows more than they're letting on. So let's focus."

"I'm not the one who's lacking focus," Yellow says. "But I think it's a good idea for us to switch targets. I'll take Paige."

Violet nods. "I guess I'm with Mike, then."

Ugh. Colton.

When we return, Mike is still down at the lane, but Paige has joined Colton at the table. I take a breath and slide in next to Colton while Yellow scoots next to Paige. Colton doesn't take his eyes off Yellow.

"So tell me something, Colton. How is it that you haven't wound up on the front page of the newspapers yet?"

Colton's head snaps to me. "Huh?"

I plant the biggest smile I can muster on my face as I tilt my head toward the Heineken bottle he's holding. "Vice President's Son Arrested for Underage Drinking at Local Bar."

He laughs, even though it wasn't really a joke. "Yeah, well, last I checked, you had to be eighteen to get in here, so looks like I'm not the only one with a fake ID in this place."

I make myself keep smiling. "The only difference is, the *government* issued mine."

"Can I see it?"

"Not a chance."

And then neither of us say anything. Yellow and Paige are talking about the University of Pennsylvania for some reason, and I'm trying to think of how to ply Colton for information. He's not even looking at me. He's scanning the bar behind us, staring at all the pretty girls and winking at them. Really. Actually *winking* at them.

"Look, I know you don't like me, so I'm not even sure why you're over here."

I sit up straight. "Excuse me?" I have to shout to be heard over the music.

Colton turns to me. He really is attractive, which annoys me to no end. He has a strong jawline and chiseled cheekbones, and honey-brown eyes that twinkle. But it's also obvious that he knows just how attractive he is.

"I said, I know you don't like me. So tell me, what did I ever do to you?" The soft Texas drawl comes out.

"Honestly?" I glance at Yellow across the table, and she slowly shakes her head. "It's not that I don't like you, Colton. It's that you're not exactly taking your job seriously this summer, so I'm not quite sure what to think of you."

"Taking my job seriously? For real? It's a BS job. I thought you would understand that." He huffs. "Look, I know that my mom got me the internship as a résumé builder, and I know that the entire organization is annoyed that we're there. Hell, you probably think we're spying on you or something."

The comment knocks me over like a rogue wave, but I don't change my expression.

"But really, I don't want to have anything to do with politics. I grew up in politics. I know it's not for me. I don't *want* any of this on my résumé. Just like I know you don't want any of us there this summer. I figured I'd just stay out of your way, and when the summer is over, we'll never have to see each other again."

I'm silent for a moment, and the sound of pins knocking against wooden lanes fills my ears. What Colton said actually makes sense, and I hate to admit it. "So what do you want to do, then, if not politics?"

He shrugs. "I really like music, so I figured maybe I'd get a job at *Rolling Stone*."

"Yeah, and I really like photography, so I figured I'd go get a job at *National Geographic*."

Yellow snorts across the table, but Colton misses it. "Ah, cool, you like photography? I have a Mark III my dad got me last Christmas that I have no idea how to use, so maybe you could show me—"

I hold up a hand. "I don't know anything about photography. It was a joke. You're just . . . the most entitled person I've ever met, and I don't think you even realize it. You just assume that because you like music you could get a job at the most influential music magazine in the world?"

Colton shrugs and stretches his arm up over the back of the booth, over my shoulders. I think he does it to make me feel small. "You're probably right. I *am* entitled. But I'm also extremely well connected."

Yellow kicks me under the table. *XP,* she mouths.

"Speaking of being well connected," I say, knocking Colton's arm off the booth, "let's talk about your mom a little bit."

"Ugh. Let's not." Colton picks up the beer bottle and swigs the last sip, then sets it down with a *clunk*. He pushes me out of the booth as he slides past me. "I'm tired." He nods to the Secret Service agent, still lingering at the bar, who nods back. "See you in the morning. Paige, you hanging around?"

Paige sets down the water she's sipping. "No. I have so much reading to do." Yellow stands up to let her by and then looks at me with a frown.

"Baxter!" Colton shouts over the music. "Let's bounce!"

Yellow and I scoot out of the booth, and in a few seconds, Mike is at my side. He starts to lean down, like he's going to hug me, so I step back and shoot my arm forward. He stops, a horrified look on his face. "Oh, um, sorry. Yeah. Good night." Then he shakes my hand and follows Colton and Paige out the door.

I drop down into the booth. Yellow and Violet follow suit. "So, anyone know who XP is now?" I ask.

"Nope," Violet says. "I got nothing. Only that Paige is from outside Philadelphia, went to some ritzy private school, and wants to be the president someday. And that Baxter likes a good T. rex joke."

There's that weird feeling again. I ignore it.

"I got that Colton is a pretentious jackass and Mike is, well, kinda normal," I say.

Yellow groans. "So I guess it's safe to call Phase One a wash at this point?"

I sigh. Let's just hope Phase Two is more successful.

CHAPTER 12

At the briefing the next morning, Bonner's voice sounds a little more monotonous than usual. Or maybe it's just my foggy head. My head keeps bobbing forward and my eyes keep closing. I couldn't sleep last night.

Abe waited up for me—just to say a quick "good night"— which made me feel worse, and I don't know why. It's not like Mike and I ever crossed any sort of line. When I tried to fall asleep, I kept seeing an image of Dos running to greet me, which made me think of my mom, and as much as I tried to block her out, I couldn't.

The image of my mom cracking the canvas over her knee in Dr. Netsky's office flooded my mind. Like when a football player blows out his ACL in a game, and the network loops the footage over and over and *over* again. *Crack.* My mom still hasn't returned my calls. *Crack.* I bet anything she's back in Vermont, going about her life like nothing happened. *Crack.* I mean, she changed her voice mail greeting yesterday, so at least I know she's alive. *Crack.*

Screw her.

Or pity her. I don't know.

My head falls to my chest one more time, and I snap it back up. The Narc's looking right at me, but she doesn't stop talking. She's speaking about the corporate tax records of Iberia Holdings, the company my dad met about at McSorley's in 1939. Shocker, it doesn't seem to have anything to do with Eagle. I stifle a yawn, then reach for my now-cold Styrofoam cup of cinnamon cookie–flavored coffee. I gag as I swallow it. Who in their right mind wants to *drink* a cookie? Just say to hell with the calories and eat the real thing if you want it.

Bonner smiles. "So on to the next one?" No one responds. "Yellow, Green, Blue, and Violet, you'll join me in the library after this. A new shipment of boxes is due to arrive later this morning, and we'll need all the help we can get to go through them."

No one groans, but Violet rolls her eyes, while Green slouches in his seat. Yellow, being Yellow, sits up straight and smiles back at Bonner. Abe doesn't flinch. It's almost as if he isn't listening. He's seated on the other side of the room. We're continuing to dance around our relationship. Doing the choreography but not really feeling the beat.

I force myself to look away from him and shoot my hand into the air. I don't wait to get called on. "And what will the interns and I be doing today?"

Bonner gathers the papers on her lectern into a neat pile. "The interns will be assisting me this morning. Indigo and Iris, you're with Red. He'll help you with historical prep."

Indigo and I exchange a glance, then we both look back at Bonner.

Indigo half raises his hand. "But we only do historical prep when—"

"When you're about to go on a mission, yes." Bonner places both hands on the lectern. "I've authorized a list of acceptable missions, and Red has selected two of them. You will meet with him after this briefing."

I lean back in my seat and look at Red. He has to feel my gaze lingering on him, but he doesn't turn to me. This is really happening! We're going to track down XP. A million questions fly through my mind. Did the DoD tell Bonner what the XP missions are? Did Red break into her office and track them down? Am I going on one of those missions? Will I be able to crack this thing today?

Also: *No more paperwork today!*

After the briefing, Indigo and I follow Red up to his office. It's like being in a ghost town. Zeta's old office is across the hall, and the door is shut and locked. The plaque with his name on it has been pulled from the wall. We pass Bonner's office. The code Alpha used to lock it pops right back into my head—940211— and I wince.

Red raises both hands. He uses one to block the keypad as he enters his code with the other. But I still catch it. 126512. That's easy to remember.

Red swings open the door. "Just so you know, I'm changing that as soon as you leave."

"I didn't look," I say.

"Of course you did." And then he flashes me the quickest of grins. "I would be highly disappointed if you hadn't."

He shuts the door behind us, scoops two papers off the desk, and hands one to me and one to Indigo. I look at mine. A mission summary. I scan it. Almost six years ago, Eta—Violet's mother—met with a Massachusetts Highway Department official to discuss a kickback for using a certain contractor during the Big Dig.

I flip the paper over. What is this? A state highway department? That doesn't seem to have anything to do with XP. I mean, it's *state* government, not federal.

That's another thing I learned about Alpha. Annum Guard is a federal agency. We're not supposed to go anywhere near state governments. But Alpha had his hands in the cookie jars of at least twenty statehouses. It's a freaking mess.

I look over at Indigo. He's nodding. "The Treaty of Portsmouth. Very cool. I've always wanted to see Teddy Roosevelt in person."

"Red, what is this?" I wave my paper at him. "The I-93 tunnel. What can this possibly have to do with XP?"

"Nothing."

Indigo's eyes get big. "Wait, what? XP?"

I shake my head. "But I don't understand—"

"We're not going after XP quite yet. First we're figuring out this blackout thing. Look at the date, Iris. Six years ago. That's right around the time Yellow saw the blackout memo in Zeta's office, correct?"

I draw in a slow breath. "I'm not going to this highway meeting, am I?"

"Nope," Red says. "You're going to break into Zeta's house."

Indigo drops his paper onto Red's desk. "Whoa, whoa, what? Why aren't Yellow and I going on this mission? I mean, wouldn't it make sense for us to do it? We know the place."

Red sighs a long, exaggerated sigh. "Why do I have to keep explaining to you guys the danger of going on missions where you could run into *yourselves*? Honestly." Then he points at a chair. "Indigo, sit and start talking. Tell us everything we need to know."

He does. Yellow and Indigo grew up in Brookline, in what Indigo calls a "normal house," which, based on what I know about the Masters family, I'm sure is modest code for "huge-ass mansion." Indigo says it's been in their family for generations, so that's clue number one it's not, in fact, a "normal house." Zeta is a security nut, which doesn't surprise me. There are motion detectors and security cameras, but nothing I can't handle. There are also two Dobermans that might pose a problem, as well as a full-time housekeeper named Inez who's been with the family for more than twenty years.

"Am I going to run into an eleven-year-old version of you?" I ask Indigo. "Because that's going to be really weird."

"What's the date of the mission?"

"August 19."

"I don't know," he says. "Yell and I always went to summer camp, but that's really close to the start of the new school year. We might be there."

I really hope not. I hope it's just me and Inez. I can handle that. Oh wait, there are still the Dobermans . . .

"You need to pretend to research the Big Dig for a little while," Red tells me. "A few hours in the library with Bonner watching you. She has to buy this thing."

"Are you going to deactivate my tracker?"

"No. No one is going to be watching the trackers but me. Bonner won't know when you take a detour."

"That seems like a dangerous gamble."

Red sets down his paper. "And since when are you afraid of a little danger?"

He has a point.

"What about me?" Indigo asks. "What does the Treaty of Portsmouth have to do with the blackout?"

"Nothing," Red says. "That's a real mission. We have to keep an air of legitimacy."

I spend the rest of the morning in the library reading up on the Big Dig. The colossal highway improvement project in downtown Boston was supposed to cost $2.8 billion, but wound up taking *ten years* longer than scheduled to the tune of $14-plus billion. The whole project was plagued with design flaws, leaks, corruption, and death.

What Annum Guard should have done was go back and actually fix this project. Put it back on schedule, hire the right engineers, save the government twelve billion dollars.

Twelve billion dollars. I can't even wrap my head around that much money. But instead, Annum Guard just went back in time and became part of the problem. They probably screwed it up even worse.

Bonner's cell phone chirps, so she bolts out of the library. At once, the room lets out a collective sigh of relief. Violet drops a stack of papers and lowers her head to her desk for a moment's rest. Green wads up a piece of paper and sends it flying across the room, where it hits Abe in the back of the head. He whips around.

"Seriously?" he says.

The interns are seated at desks in the middle of the library. Colton doesn't stop smacking his gum as he bobs along to his music. Paige and Mike keep going through documents like nothing's changed.

Yellow jumps out of her chair over to me. "Indigo told me what you're planning."

I raise my eyebrows and give a half-glance in the direction of the interns.

She drops her voice lower. "And I just . . . want to apologize to you. For Dallas."

Dallas. Where my dad died. "I . . . what?"

"When you were tempted by the idea of saving your dad the day he died. I was kind of rude to you, but now I see that I just didn't get it." She blinks. Once. Twice. Three times, and I know she's trying to hold back a tear. "It's taking every ounce of self-restraint I have not to tell you—to beg you—to figure out a way to get my dad a message, to warn him. I . . . I'm sorry."

"Yellow, you don't have anything to apologize for."

And then she throws herself forward, wrapping her arms around me in a hug. I pat her back awkwardly. "Be careful," she whispers in my ear before pulling away. "And try to make sure I don't see you. I'm going to be seriously annoyed if all of a sudden I have the memory of you breaking into my house."

I smile. "That's not actually how it works, Yellow. You'd always have that memory."

"I'm just saying."

"I'll be careful. Really, really careful. I won't go snooping through your thirteen-year-old diary or anything."

Yellow cringes. "That's another thing. If you do happen to see me . . . don't judge me."

"What does that mean?"

"Just remember that I'm thirteen and I really have no idea who I am yet, so don't hold it against me for the rest of my life."

"You do realize you're making me want to go out of my way to find you in the past?"

"Just . . . be nice."

I glance over toward Mike. He's staring at me, and he immediately looks down. I catch Abe's eye, and he looks from me to Mike, then he looks away.

The door opens and Bonner walks in. Yellow heads back to her desk, and I stand. Enough. I need to get out of this room, away from the present.

"I'm ready for the mission, ma'am," I say.

"It's only noon," Bonner says. "I don't think that's enough time to prepare, do you?"

"I don't need to do historical prep. I'm only going back six years. And I've read up on what I need to do."

Indigo is in one of the velvet armchairs. He snaps his book shut. "I'm ready, too. This is the fourth mission I've gone on during Teddy Roosevelt's presidency, so I'm very well aware of the time period."

"And the actual mission?" Bonner says. "A few hours is certainly not enough time to prepare for that."

"No offense, ma'am," Indigo says, "but the only missions we go on these days are reconnaissance. A circus monkey could go on these missions."

I bite my tongue to keep from laughing. I would have left out the circus monkey part, but recon missions *are* simple. The goal is to blend into the background and observe. You don't need to know more than the basics.

Bonner narrows her eyes at us, but I can see her thinking about it. "Very well. I'll have Red meet you downstairs in ten minutes." She pulls the security token out of her pocket as Indigo and I fly out the door.

"I can't believe she agreed to that," I whisper.

"I know. I thought for sure we'd have to wait until tomorrow, which I think would kill me. Is it weird to say I'm really excited that you're breaking into my house?"

"About as weird as it is to admit I'm really excited to break into your house."

Indigo races up the stairs to change, but I don't bother. My Bonner-mandated outfit will make me look like all the other working drones milling about the highway department. If I was going to the highway department, that is. Besides, these pants are comfortable, and it's easier to break into a house wearing comfortable pants.

Indigo returns wearing ivory pants, a burgundy vest, and a black sport coat, and we go downstairs together. He has a black hat in his hands. Red is waiting for us outside the gravity chamber with two silver cases. He holds out a tablet, and Indigo hesitates.

"Look," Red says, "I know it's really you and not an impostor, but stop stalling. I can't open the cases until you've been ID'd."

Indigo places his hand on top of the tablet.

"Masters, Nicholas. Code name: Indigo. Annum Guard employee number 0020," a robotic voice says. The token stops on a number; Indigo plugs the token into the case, types the number, and waits for the lock to click open. He takes out his Annum watch and clips it to his vest. Then it's my turn.

"Obermann, Amanda. Code name: Iris. Annum Guard employee number 0022."

I slip my watch over my head and open the face. I click the year dial back five turns, then adjust the month and day dials backward as well. I wait for Indigo to finish.

"Ladies first," he says, gesturing to the open chamber.

I look at Red nervously. Can I do this? I have to do this. I think of Orange, how he disappeared on a mission, and that doesn't do anything to calm me.

"Good luck," Red says. We always say that to each other before we project. A throwaway line, like "Break a leg!" or "Have a good trip!" But not this time. This time, I know Red really is wishing me luck. And I'll need it.

"Thanks," I say. And then I step into the gravity chamber and shut the watch.

CHAPTER 13

I fall for a few seconds before I land on my feet. I'm standing in the broom closet—the place we always land when using the chamber—and I barely even wobble. I've gotten good at this.

I need to hightail it to the Park Street T stop, across Beacon Hill. I jog. I'd break into a full sprint, but that would attract attention. So I keep to an "I'm late for a doctor's appointment" pace—or maybe a "meeting a friend for lunch in ten" pace.

There's a C-line train pulling in just as I drop a token into the slot and slip through the metal turnstile. I'm thinking about how I should pick up a couple of tokens as souvenirs—in the present, they've been replaced with cards—as I hop onto the train and take a seat by the window. The train is half empty.

It's a quick ride aboveground to the St. Mary's stop, and then an even quicker walk to the house. I memorized the directions. A right on Carlston Street, a left on Ivy, and there's the house. And then I laugh because, just as I suspected, this is not a "normal house."

It's a massive, three-story, redbrick home that stretches nearly half a block. There are four chimneys that I can see, and I don't even want to guess how many bathrooms there are. It baffles me that people actually grow up in houses like this. Houses where there are maids and nannies and chefs. Being around wealth has always made me uncomfortable. There was plenty of that at Peel. It's so completely opposite to everything I know.

I decide my best bet is to go around to the back. The yard has a black iron fence, but I hop over it with ease. I pause, listening for those two Dobermans that I'm very sure would like to rip me to shreds. I don't hear anything. I'm walking toward the house when I hear it: barking and the rumble of eight legs charging toward me. I freeze. I have pepper spray and a couple of tranquilizer darts in my back pocket, but I'd really rather not. *Really.* All I can think of is Dos running to greet me, and how I'd want to murder anyone who pepper-sprayed my dog.

The dogs round the corner and I make myself relax. I even smile at them and hold out my hands. The dogs stop short in front of me.

"Shadow and Raven." I say their names in a low, slow voice, and their ears perk up. "Hi, puppies. I'm not here to hurt you. I'm a friend."

The bigger of the two approaches me first. This must be Shadow. He sniffs my hand, so I open it. There's a dog biscuit inside, and he snatches it out of my hand. Raven nudges her way forward, and I let her sniff the treat in my other hand before giving it to her. And then I reach out and gently put my hand on her head. She lets me, so I slide my hand down and scratch her ears.

I'm hit with a pang of sadness. Before I left, Indigo told me that Raven died last year.

"You guys have a scary reputation, but I know you're just sweet little pups."

I pull away and walk toward the back door, and the dogs let me go. Obstacle one, out of the way. I glance up at the camera hanging over the door. Obstacle two.

According to Indigo, there are no cameras inside the house, which makes sense. Can you imagine growing up in a house where a *camera* tracked your every move? He also said there's another one over the front door and half a dozen others guarding the first-floor windows. But if I come in the back, this is the only one I need to contend with.

I scoot around so I'm behind the camera and look in the window. I see a sunroom. Behind that is the kitchen. I nod my head, close my eyes, and map my location. There's a dining room and a formal living room and a parlor—whatever the hell that is—on this floor. The second floor has Zeta's bedroom and, more importantly, his office. Yellow and Indigo have bedrooms on the third floor.

I peer into the window again. There's no one in the kitchen. This is my chance.

I reach into my bag and pull out a pair of black gloves, which I know look very suspicious in the middle of August, but I yank them on my hands. Then I sling the bag over my shoulder, put my hands on the window ledge, and hoist myself up. The window box heaves a creaky sigh, and I silently pray it doesn't crack and break off. I scoot along the edge until I'm close to the door.

I keep one hand against the window for balance and with the other pull out a can of spray paint from my bag. I use my chin as leverage to get the cap off, then I shake the can and spray the camera lens black.

Obstacle two, conquered. I jump off the window box, put the spray paint back in my bag, and dust myself off. I try the doorknob, but it doesn't turn. Of course. I pull out the lock kit I have tucked into my front pocket. The simple hook pick should do it, so I slide it out of the leather pouch and into the lock. A few jimmies to the left and it *clicks* unlocked.

And now for obstacle three.

I turn the knob, and the alarm immediately blares. A series of loud, one-second-long beeps fill the house. I shut the door behind me, beeline through the sunroom and kitchen, and make my way to the stairs, to the door on the side of the staircase that Indigo told me about. I swing it open and hurl myself inside, settling behind a vacuum cleaner as the alarm continues to wail.

Footsteps thunder down the stairs over my head.

"Nicholas!" a woman shouts. "I told you that you weren't to leave this house until you've finished unpacking your camp bag!"

Inez.

I hold my breath as I strain to listen. Between the beeps, I hear a series of softer ones. Inez entering the alarm code. Sure enough, the house falls silent. I hear the back door swing open.

"Nicholas!" Inez shouts into the backyard. Then the door shuts, and I hear a gentler, "That boy!"

And then I remember to take a breath. Indigo told me that Inez wouldn't bother to check the security cameras—that she thinks Zeta is a little crazy for having them in the first place. But

I don't move an inch from my spot behind the vacuum. I close my eyes and listen. Waiting for some cue that it's safe to come out.

I hear it. In the kitchen, the faucet turns on, and there's the splashing of dishes being washed. I open the door and peer my head out. I don't see Inez. I step out and shut the door softly. Then I round the corner, grab the banister, and head up the stairs on my tiptoes.

On the second floor, there's a door that's shut and locked just to the right of the staircase, so I pull out my hook pick again, and a few seconds later, I'm in Zeta's office.

I rest my back against the door for a moment. I keep forgetting to breathe.

Zeta's office is the opposite of Ariel's. Nothing's out of place in here. Actually, nothing's *in* place. The desk is empty, except for a boxy computer monitor and one picture frame. I pick up the frame. It's a photo of Yellow and Indigo, and I smile. Yellow can't be more than six. She has white-blonde pigtails tied with pink ribbon and she's grinning at the camera. A front tooth is missing. Indigo's blond hair has flopped in front of his left eye, and he has his arm thrown around his older sister. This picture was taken somewhere on the beach, and there's the outline of another huge house in the background. I wonder if Zeta has a beach house on Martha's Vineyard or the Cape. That wouldn't be surprising.

I set the frame down. I'm wasting time.

Yellow told me the blackout memo was in a file cabinet to the left of the desk. I use my lock pick for the third time and slide the drawer open. *Damn.* There have to be fifty files in here. I don't know what I was hoping, that I'd open the drawer and the memo would be sitting there on top, waiting for me?

I scan the tabs on the folders. *Bank, Insurance, Investments*—no, no, no—*Warranties, Medical Info, Chilmark*—no, no, no, come on! And then I see it. *AG.*

Annum Guard.

I flip open the folder. I'm not here to snoop, I remind myself. No matter how much I want to pull out this file and read every word that's inside it, I won't. I'm looking for the blackout memo and the blackout memo *only*.

The first paper is a memo, and my heart leaps. I scan the first few lines. The word Delta jumps out at me. Delta—my dad. I close my eyes for a second before scanning the rest of the page. I don't see anything about a blackout, so I flip to the next paper. At this point, I don't think I even want to know anything more about my dad. He's not the man I built up in my mind, and finding out more about the man he really is—was—just makes me lose focus.

I flip past mission ledgers, forms, and contracts. But there's nothing about a blackout. I broke into Zeta's house for nothing. There are only a few papers left.

But then there it is.

A confidential memo. Subject line: BLACKOUT EXPERIMENT. I yank it out of the drawer. I'm going to read it, memorize it, then tuck it back into the file and bolt. But before I get a chance, I hear feet pounding down the stairs and shouting.

"Where are you going, Nick?" a young female voice shouts.

Yellow.

"It's gotta be in Dad's office!" Indigo's voice. He's on the landing, and he's heading here.

I'm trapped. I fly to the window, but it's not an escape. There's no tree or bush or anything to soften a fall. Plus, there are alarm wires running the entire length of the window.

"You know you're not supposed to go in there!" Yellow says. Her voice is outside the door.

I don't think. I leap into the closet, pull the door shut, and hope that whatever Indigo wants isn't in here.

"Yeah, well, Dad's not here right now," Indigo says as he opens the office door. "And besides, that's never stopped *you*."

I reach into my shirt and pull out my Annum watch. Should I project now? I press on the top knob—the one that automatically sends me back to the present—and listen as the hands spin around the face. I start to press the face shut and then stop myself. What if I project back to the present, only to find Inez dusting the office windowsills? And let's not forget that Zeta would certainly realize this memo is missing.

Not yet.

Yellow and Indigo are in the room. "Dad's going to kill you," she says.

"Shut up, Lizzie." *Lizzie.* It's so weird to hear Yellow called that. Hell, it's still weird to know that her real name is Elizabeth. "Go listen to some more of that whiny crap you won't stop playing." Indigo must be at the desk. I hear a drawer slide open, then another one, and then— "Look, Dad left the file cabinet open. It's like he wants me to find it."

Uh-oh.

"Dad *never* leaves the file cabinet open," Yellow says. Oh, not good. Not good at all.

There are footsteps. A loud *stomp-stomp* from whatever shoes Yellow must be wearing, which makes me wonder. In the present, Yellow is not a *stomp-stomp* kind of girl. She's a *click-clack* all the way. The footsteps head toward the closet. My fingers find the watch lid. Do I stay and let her find me, or do I run and face the unknown?

"Here it is!"

Yellow's footsteps fall silent, and I allow myself a quick breath. There's a ripping sound, like the opening of an envelope, and then an unfurling of paper.

Indigo sucks in his breath. "Yep, this is it. 'Dear Mr. Masters, we regret to inform you that Nicholas will not be welcomed back at Bretton Pines next year'—like I want to go back—'due to his extreme insubordination toward the Bretton Pines counselors.' Insubordination. What's that mean?"

There's a crumpling noise, and I assume that Yellow's grabbed the paper out of her brother's hands. "It means you're a huge jerk who won't follow rules."

"Fair enough," Indigo says. "But Cody's the jerk, not me. He only hates me because he hates Jack's dad because Jack's dad—"

Yellow gasps. "They talk about me, too," she says. "'I also must mention that I'm worried by Elizabeth's sudden mood change. I've gotten to know her over the past two summers, and thus you can understand that her appearance and attitude were surprising this year. I tried to engage Elizabeth in conversation but found her to be extremely withdrawn and sullen all summer'—yeah, because I don't want to be there—'and I can't help but wonder if her relationship with her mother might be the root of the problem.'" Yellow laughs. "Dude, she mentioned Mom. Just leave the letter there for Dad to read. He'll flip that they brought her up like that. There's no way he's sending us back there next year. He'll be so mad, he won't even care about your *insubordination*. Just keep playing the Mom angle—Cody wouldn't shut up about Mom, and that's why you never listened to him."

"Except that's not true."

"Whatever." Her tone is angry. It's very different from the sunshine Yellow she is today. Well, under normal circumstances. I have to physically restrain myself from opening the closet door and peeking out. "Come on, you did what you need to do. Now let's go."

Yes. Go.

"I'm taking the letter with me."

"Stop being a pansy," she snaps. "Leave it!"

There are footsteps against the wood floor, and the sound of the office door opening, and then I really can't help myself. I crack the closet door open an inch. My mouth drops open. Yellow—who is normally a walking J.Crew ad—is dressed head to toe in black. Black, sheer lace top with a black tank top over it. Layered black miniskirt. Ripped black tights. Black Doc Martens. Her hair is streaked with pink and purple, and I'd bet you anything that if she turned around, I'd see her eyes outlined in kohl like a raccoon.

I pull the closet door shut. So, Yellow went through a goth phase. *Fascinating.* And by fascinating, I mean hilarious. I'm dying to rifle through her bedroom, but I remind myself again why I'm here. The piece of paper I'm holding. I wait another minute to make sure they're not coming back, then I open the closet once more and slip out. I crouch low and slide underneath Zeta's desk to give myself a fighting chance in case anyone else comes in. Then I look at the memo. It's short. One quick, little paragraph.

My eyes widen. Zeta *wrote* the memo. The recipient was the defense secretary. And there's a CC: to A. Cairo. It's dated only a few weeks ago. I start reading.

It is my recommendation that the blackout experiment be regarded as a failure. We do not at present have the time or resources to police another layer of Annum Guard, and the Justice Department has quite unsurprisingly affirmed my opinion that there are serious constitutional, due process concerns in adding a punitive team to our existing ranks. While I commend your enthusiasm for the project, I regret that I must withdraw my support.

And that's it. Two phrases jump out at me. *Another layer of Annum Guard. A punitive team.* What does that mean? The defense secretary wanted to add more members to the Guard? Members that would . . . punish people? Who? I have more questions than answers. I know who the defense secretary was six years ago—I mean, today, in the past. And I do mean *was.* It was all over the news when he had a heart attack and died while still serving his post. But I have no idea who A. Cairo is.

And then I gasp. Loudly. I hope no one heard that. Because it's all adding up. XP really is Chi Rho. Chi Rho. Cairo. It has to be the same person. Does that mean Zeta *knows*—knew?—who XP is? Is that why he was taken—blacked out?

My hands are shaking.

I need to get back to the present. Now. I need to find Zeta, and I need to get some answers.

I read the memo two more times, then I repeat every word back in my head. I got it. I tuck it back in the drawer and slide it shut. There are voices in the hall.

"I don't care what you say, I'm not just leaving it!" Indigo shouts. The doorknob turns. I don't have time to hide. The door swings open. Indigo's head is turned toward Yellow, who's charging down the stairs in those big black boots of hers.

My necklace is still open. I slam my forefinger onto the top knob that will take me to the present, and shut the lid. It *clicks*, and the last thing I see is Indigo's head turning toward the sound. I'm shot up, and my heart is beating so fast that I don't even feel the pain of projecting.

I land in the same spot I left, but the office door is shut and the house is quiet. I strain to hear a sound—any sound—but there's only silence. I remember to breathe, and the breath makes me dizzy. I take a step toward the door, then stop myself. What am I doing? This is the perfect chance to see if there are any clues about what happened to Zeta.

I backtrack to the file cabinet. It's locked, but I break it in a matter of seconds. The door slides open easily. It's empty. Not one folder, not one slip of paper. I open all the drawers on the desk. Same thing. No pens, no memo pads, no paper clips. Nothing. There is no trace of Zeta in this room at all. It's . . . eerie.

I slip out of the office into the hallway. I pause and listen. Nothing. So I slink over to the staircase, pause and listen again. Still nothing. I wish I had some sign of whether anyone else is home. Inez, she's the wild card.

I walk down the steps very gently, my gloved hand gripping the railing. I don't want to risk a creaky stair, even though I'd be shocked to find one in this house. Zeta strikes me as the kind of guy who'd rip out the entire staircase at the first tiny creak and replace it with some state-of-the-art design that never makes a sound.

The only sound I hear on the first floor is my own breathing. The front door is right there, and I wonder if I should slip out that way. It's been six years since I arrived. I assume someone noticed the spray-painted camera in the backyard at some point and replaced it.

But I still think the back door is my best bet. I already have that route mapped out.

I creep down the hall. I'm almost to the kitchen.

Then there's a *click* behind me that stops my heart. I slowly raise my hands over my head and turn.

Inez is about ten feet away. Her right hand trembles as she holds a .357 aimed at my head. It's a small gun, but it looks enormous in her hands. I need her to move closer if I have any chance of disarming her.

"Who are you?" she demands. She looks up at my hands—at my black gloves. The kind of gloves you only wear when you're doing something very, very bad.

"I work with Ze—*Noah*. And I'm a friend of . . . Elizabeth's. And Nick's."

"I've never seen you before." Her voice shakes. I'm not sure how much she knows about Zeta and what he really does for a living.

"I know."

"Where is Mr. Masters?" Now she sounds almost pained, like a mother who's lost her child in a crowded shopping mall.

I shake my head. "I don't know. I'm trying to find that out, I promise." I take a step toward Inez, and she reaches up her other hand to cradle the gun.

"Don't move, or I will shoot you." Her voice and body language are telling me it's a bluff, but still I stop.

"Listen, I swear I'm only trying to help. I'm sure I frightened you"—her face relaxes just a little—"and I'm sorry about that"—I keep one hand in the air and lower the other so it's reaching forward for the gun—"but right now I'd really like for you to drop that gun." I take one step.

And then Inez pulls the trigger. A bullet flies over my head and into the wall. Inez rocks backward, thrown off balance by the shot.

"Holy shit!" I scream. I rush toward Inez, who's swaying on her feet. I instinctively slam my elbow into her chin, grab the gun, and twist it out of her hands. "I'm sorry!" I yell as she moans in pain. I jump back, unload the bullets, and throw the gun behind me.

Then I turn to Inez. "What was that?"

She's shaking. Convulsing, almost. She thrusts her hands in the air. "Don't hurt me. I have children. Grandchildren."

"I'm not going to hurt you! I told you that. I'm a friend. I know you've never met me before, but I'm a *friend*."

It's like she doesn't even hear me. "I don't know where Mr. Masters is. Please don't hurt me."

"I—" There are a million things I'd like to ask her. When was the last time she saw Zeta. Whether there was anything unusual in his behavior in the weeks before he disappeared. But Inez is a basket case right now. She's on her knees, muttering in Spanish, praying to *Dios*. Tears stream down her face.

So I just turn and bolt out the back door. I keep my head ducked as I run past the camera, even though I don't think Inez is going to call the cops. She knows they can't help. And Yellow and Indigo can make sure this all goes away.

I toss the bullets and my gloves into a trash can next to the T stop, and only then does it hit me.

I just came within a foot of getting my face blown off. I suddenly don't know up from down. I sway, and a guy in a suit and tie shouts, "Whoa!" as he hooks his arms around my waist to steady me.

"Easy there," the man says. Then he chuckles as I hold out my arms to keep my balance. "Rough day, eh? It's a bit early to be tossing back a drink, but I won't judge."

What? What is he talking about?

"Shut up," I mumble as a train rings a warning bell and pulls up to the aboveground stop. I push onto the train, plop onto a seat, and look down at my hands. They're still shaking.

CHAPTER 14

"It's a good thing your maid is a lousy shot," I hiss to Yellow as soon as I arrive back. She and Red are waiting for me. The Narc is nowhere to be seen, but still Yellow looks over her shoulder as I slip the Annum necklace over my head and hand it to Red.

"What are you talking about?" Yellow asks.

"She fired a gun at my head. *At my head.*"

Yellow's hand flies to her mouth. "No."

I nod.

"No freaking way. Inez has never touched a gun in her life. She wouldn't know what to do with one."

"Well, thank god for that." I sigh and put my hand on the wall to steady myself. I'm still shaky from my near-assassination, and it doesn't help that the projection turned my knees into blobs of gelatin. "Is Indigo back yet?"

"No," Red says in a hushed tone. "He went back much farther than you did. He's not due back until tomorrow morning at the earliest." Then he reaches out and touches my shoulder. "Seriously, are you okay?"

Oh great, it's the concerned voice. No, thank you.

I push off the wall. "I'm fine. And I found the memo."

I tell Yellow and Red word-for-word what it said. Both are silent when I'm done.

"My dad knew about a secret arm of Annum Guard." Yellow says it very matter-of-factly, but I know inside she's trying to come to grips with the whole situation. "I don't understand. That's a really dangerous thing to be playing with. Why would he do that to us?"

Red shakes his head. "Not important right now. Let's focus on the facts. We've gotten our first bread crumb, but we're still a ways off from knowing the *what*. We also need to figure out the *who*—Cairo—and the *why*. Iris, what are you thinking?"

"Um . . ." I try to focus. Try to think of Red as my boss, because, let's face it, that's what he is now. I've trusted him with this, and now I have to let him lead. I concentrate on examining what I know. "I'm thinking that our three prime suspects are related to the people sitting upstairs going through boxes of our sensitive information."

"Exactly," Red says. He looks from me to Yellow. "We're going back to Phase One. I want the two of you to find out everything you can about our interns. Their pasts, their families, their political connections. There has to be a lead we can follow." He looks back to me. "If I can distract Bonner tonight, do you think Blue can hack into the personnel files and access the background checks we had to run on them?"

"Of course he can."

Red nods. "The vice president, the secretary of defense, a senator. One of them has to be behind this. I don't think I need to tell you both to tread very, very carefully. I still don't know exactly what this blackout team entails, but I think you're right, Iris. I think the team is alive and operational and highly uncomfortable with the fact we're getting closer to XP. And I think it's very suspicious that Bonner knows about XP and isn't following any leads. I'm not saying she's a mole—*the* mole, if there is one—but I am saying that for now, she's not to be trusted."

And then we hear it. The sound of boxy heels stomping down a concrete stairwell.

I exchange a look with Yellow, then all of us whip around to see the Narc rounding the corner. Did she hear us?

"You're back," Bonner says in a flat tone. If she overheard us, she's not giving it away.

"As of about thirty seconds ago, yes," I say. I hope my voice is cool and collected.

"And? The DOT meeting?"

"It was a wash. I wasn't able to gain access to the meeting. It was held behind closed doors, and I couldn't come up with a cover that would let me inside. I failed. I'm sorry."

"That's disappointing. I'll see to it this is noted in your file."

I don't respond. Getting a bad grade on my report card is the least of my worries right now.

"Well, now that you're back, we could use the extra pair of hands on the new boxes that arrived this morning. You, too, Yellow."

"Of course," Yellow and I say at the same time, although her voice is way more chipper than mine.

She and Red exchange a glance, and then we leave Red in the hallway and follow Bonner up the stairs.

"Was my dad there?" Yellow whispers. "In the past?"

"No."

Both of us are quiet as Bonner holds open the door. I can see into the library. Abe sits at one of the desks and gives me a quick wave. More of a "hi" than a "welcome back."

Yellow slows down next to me as Bonner enters the library. "And what about me? You didn't see me, right?"

Those big black boots flash in my mind. The *years* of relentless teasing I could milk from this. But then I look at Yellow's bloodshot eyes. I remember how she gave up months of her life to help me when I ran from Alpha. She's the closest thing to a best friend I've ever had.

"Nope. You guys must have still been at camp."

Bonner clears her throat from inside the library. She's staring right at me.

"Sorry!" Yellow calls. "Coming!" She brushes past me. I haven't seen her look so relieved in months.

That night, we're all sitting around the dining room table—all of us except for Indigo and the interns—when Bonner's cell phone chirps on the table. She's the only one exempt from the no-phones-at-meals rule she set up when she arrived. Red is sitting next to her, and his eyes glance over at the screen, but Bonner grabs it out of view.

"Have to take this," she says as she hurries out the door.

I'm still looking at Red. He puts a finger to his lips and stabs a green bean with his fork.

And then Bonner is back. "I'm sorry, I have to run out for an hour or so. Let's try to make some more headway on those boxes before I get back, yes?" Technically it's a question, but her tone leaves no doubt it's a command.

In another second, she's gone. Out of the room, out the front door, out into the night. Red doesn't waste any time. He sets down his fork and stands. "You three"—he looks from me to Abe to Yellow—"go. I haven't bought you much time."

"What's going on?" Green demands, his fork still dangling a few inches from his mouth.

"Yeah, what is this?" Violet asks.

"I'm designing new missions for you," Red says. "For all of you. We have our top suspects, and I'm working on putting together missions that occurred when the three suspects were in Boston. I have a feeling that any blackout information is going to be found here, locally. Hopefully I'll have the missions ready to go when Indigo gets back. We can't delay on this."

"I don't understand what's going on," Green says, finally dropping his fork.

Red waves his hand in the air. "I'll fill you in." Then he looks at me. "What are you waiting for?"

I spring up. Abe and Yellow do the same. We rush into the living room, then stop. Abe's shoulder brushes mine. He gives me the smallest, thin-lipped smile. I smile back. *Trust your gut.* That's my motto. And right now, in this moment, my gut is telling me that Abe and I are meant to be.

We'll fix us. We will.

Yellow jerks her chin toward the library. "The computers in there?"

Abe shakes his head. "Nope, let's go straight to the source."

Yellow and I follow him to Bonner's office. Abe reaches into his pocket and takes out the rectangular metal box he's been tinkering with for weeks. The scrambler. He holds it to Bonner's keypad, and the lock clicks open. I guess he finally perfected it.

"Remind me that I need to loop over the security tape when we're done," he says as he swings the door open, looking up to the camera aimed right at the door. He holds the door for Yellow and me, and as I pass, his fingers graze my knuckles. It sends electricity jolting through my entire body, and I flash back to freshman year—to the spark I'd feel every time he touched me. That spark has since settled into a flame, but it's still burning.

We'll fix us.

Abe shuts the door.

"What's our game plan?" I ask. "There are three of us, so we each take an intern and start digging?"

Yellow picks the lock on the file cabinet in under five seconds. Honestly, why do people bother with them, especially here?

"Sounds good," Yellow says as she takes out three files and plops one on the desk. "I'll take Paige."

"Colton!" I claim. Mostly because my curiosity is getting the better of me. I would love to go digging for Colton's dirty little secrets. Yellow hands me the file.

Abe flicks on Bonner's computer and sits in her chair. "You sure you don't want to take Baxter?" he throws at me.

"Excuse me?"

"Oh, come on. I've seen the way you look at each other."

My hands clench into fists. I look over at Yellow. She looks down at the file.

"Look, I don't know what you think is going on, but I assure you there is nothing between me and *anyone*." I take a breath. "And for the record, petty jealousy isn't a good color for you." And then I stare at him, daring him to contradict me.

Abe reaches up and rubs his temple. "I'm sorry. I just . . . I'm sorry." He looks down and flips open his folder while he's waiting for the computer to start up, and his brow instantly furrows. I guess that's the best apology I'm going to get.

So all this time—all this stupid fighting—was it because Abe was *jealous*? He's so not the jealous type. He never has been.

I don't know what's gotten into him lately.

I open Colton's file. It's pretty slim. Looks like we're going to have to go deep into our country's classified files to find anything worth reading. But still, I read page one.

"Huh," Abe says behind me. I glance over and see he's on a search engine, not in a government directory. I turn back to the file.

Colton is two years older than me. His dad—Joe—was born in New England but his family moved to Texas when he was three. He met the future VP at the University of Texas. They married, then moved to Cambridge so she could get a master's degree in political science from Harvard, blah blah blah, who cares? I flip the paper over and smile.

Colton's freshman year GPA at Harvard was a whopping 1.8. Do they even let you stay at the school with a D-plus average, or did some money exchange hands? I bet it's the latter. There was an arrest when Colton was sixteen for underage drinking and disorderly conduct but it was quickly hushed up—shocker. A few parking tickets, a bunch of speeding tickets, but nothing that links Colton to XP or the blackout team.

"You guys," Abe whispers. "You can stop. I think it's Baxter."

I actually feel dizzy for a second and ground myself by putting both palms flat on the desk.

"What?" I finally say. "Are you just saying that because—"

"Of course not." He takes a heavy breath, and I'm not sure if it's out of frustration. "The first thing I saw"—he nods toward the file—"is that his middle name is Teremun."

"Yeah, I knew that. It's a family name. The maiden name of one of his moms." And then I instantly feel foolish. I know something's coming. Something big. Something that I should have caught, based on the way Abe's staring at me.

"It struck me as interesting, so I looked it up. It's Egyptian."

"Egyptian?" Yellow says, then she gasps. "Like—"

"Cairo," Abe finishes. He turns the computer screen toward us. "Mike's mom Layla was born there. Her family immigrated to America when she was young, but I guess they still have ties there. And big ones, it looks like. That venture capital firm she started? Guess who its biggest investor is? An Egyptian engineering and construction firm whose CEO was educated here. At Yale. Where both of Mike's mothers went. This is too big a coincidence to ignore."

I shake my head. "It can't be Baxter. He's the most normal of all of them." I think of T. rexes and it makes me smile—again.

But the smile disappears when I look at Abe. "It's usually the ones you'd least expect," Abe says.

I wait a second to react. I can't worry about this right now. About Abe. About whether I'll be invited to Rosh Hashanah dinner at his parents' house in September. About the framed *Night of the Living Dead* film cell I found on eBay that I'd planned on buying him for our third anniversary. Maybe Abe is right. Maybe we do need a break.

"That's such a cliché. You took the same profiling classes I did at Peel. It's usually the ones you'd most expect. You know that."

"Does any of that matter right now?" Yellow asks. She shuts Paige's file. "Mike Baxter is the best lead we have." She nods at the computer. "We need to determine how the secretary of defense figures into all of this."

Abe's gaze lingers on mine before he swivels back around. "I tried," he says. He pulls up a search engine with the United States seal in the upper left corner; his fingers dance across the keyboard, and in a few seconds, the screen goes black.

ACCESS DENIED

"But just as I suspected, all info on the secretary is hidden behind another firewall. It's going to take *days* to crack it."

"That's time we don't have," I say.

We're all quiet for a few moments. Then I flip Colton's file shut and toss it on top of Paige's. "Okay. For now, we focus on Mike Baxter. Let's find out everything from the information we *can* access. That's the best we're going to do for now."

"Agreed," Yellow says. She stuffs the folder back in the cabinet and locks it.

Abe erases our presence from the security footage in about thirty seconds, then rolls Bonner's chair to where it was. He doesn't look at me on the way out.

And I'm too annoyed to care.

CHAPTER 15

The next morning, Red pokes his head into the library. "I need Iris and Yellow for a minute."

Yellow and I don't move. Instead we look to Bonner, who sets down the stack of papers she's thumbing through and glares at Red. "Why?"

"I want to start historical prep for Yellow on the Hartford mission—"

"I thought we decided that mission wasn't to take place until next week at the earliest," Bonner interrupts. "We're already so behind on the boxes we do have. It's not wise to add another layer of documentation just yet."

"I know," Red says, "but it's a time period Yellow is unfamiliar with. I want to make sure we give her plenty of time to prep. We can't afford another failure." He jerks his head in my direction, and even though I know he's saying it just for Bonner, it still kind of stings. "And I found a few discrepancies in Iris's DOT report. I'd like to do another debriefing."

Bonner looks around the room and sighs. "It's going to be more work for everyone else, but fine."

Really? She has Green, Violet, Abe, and our three interns. How much more help does she need?

Yellow and I scramble up. I don't look at anyone on the way out, especially not Abe or Mike. Abe was quiet and distant all night. Stewing. He's always been the pot slowly simmering on the stove, while I'm the pressure cooker ready to explode at a moment's notice. Some things never change.

Yellow and I follow Red downstairs to one of the briefing rooms. We drop into seats, and I pick up a pencil.

"Don't take notes," Red says. I let the pencil fall to the table. "No paper trail on this, understand?"

I nod. Yellow does the same.

"The vice president has made a number of stops in Boston in the last few years. A dozen or so. But based on what you guys and Blue found out about Baxter, I think we need to shift the focus to the defense secretary for the immediate future. Agreed?"

"Yes," Yellow says, sitting up straight and folding her hands on the table.

"Yeah, sure," I mumble.

"Secretary Howe has made only two official visits to Boston in the last six years. As you no doubt know, he's been the secretary of defense only for the past three years. What you may not know is before that, he was CEO of National Defense."

I do know that. We found it out last night with a simple Internet search. National Defense manufactures war goods. Exactly the kind of thing Eagle does. National Defense also has a mercenary soldier wing. Private soldiers the US can rent when it needs military help.

"In addition, Senator Wharton made a highly unusual trip to Boston six years ago, around the time the blackout memo was authored. The senator was not here on official government business, and his travel log seems to be deliberately vague. He came in on a morning flight, had a lunch meeting, and flew out again the same day. I know we should be focusing on Howe, but there's something about the visit that seems off. I think we should investigate."

Yellow and I nod in agreement.

Red crosses his arms over his chest. "That's one mission. The other two involve Secretary Howe. His first visit was just recently. An anniversary celebration for the USS *Constitution*. The secretary was in town for that and, it appears, happened to take a detour to meet with a few of his old friends from National Defense. Definitely worth following up on.

"And the second is the jackpot. Six years ago, there was a fundraiser at the Back Bay brownstone of John Leighton."

He pauses like we should know who that is.

"Of Leighton Capital."

Another pause.

None of this is ringing a bell. I look over at Yellow, and even though she's nodding along, she's doing that wrinkled nose thing she does when she's confused.

"It's one of the largest real-estate investment firms in the country," Red says in his mildly annoyed tone. "Leighton made headlines last year when he tried—and failed—to buy the Red Sox."

"Oh, okay." I remember reading about that.

"Anyway, Leighton held a private party at his home to benefit the reelection campaign of Congresswoman Barbara Trabandt." He shakes his head. "That's unimportant. What's key is that Howe, Wharton, *and* Caroline Caldwell were all in attendance."

"Wow," Yellow says.

"She wasn't the vice president yet," Red points out. "She was a senator who was probably already looking ahead to the next presidential election, although nothing official had been announced. But yes, all three of our prime suspects were under one roof for one evening."

"Wow," I echo.

"That's clearly our most important mission, so I really want to focus on that one. I want three people covering it. Iris, I need you on this. I'm going to send Blue and Green with you, but you're most familiar with the situation, so you're leading it."

I nod, but Abe and Green? Really? One person who's barely speaking to me and another who isn't going to like me leading.

"And I'm going to put two people on Howe's National Defense meeting. I'm thinking Indigo and Violet. Yellow"—Red turns to look at her—"that means you'd have to fly solo on the Wharton mission. I'm really hesitant to send anyone alone because of the blackout team—whatever it is—floating out there somewhere."

"I can handle it," Yellow says.

"I know you can," Red says. "You're the most senior Guardian now. That's why I'm choosing you. But be careful." And then he reaches over and gives her hand this little squeeze that's really toeing the line between personal and professional, but Yellow doesn't flinch. In fact, she kind of relaxes into his touch. I pretend not to notice, but Yellow and I are going to have a serious conversation later.

"When are we doing this?" I ask.

Red pulls his hand away and clears his throat. "Tonight. Indigo's due back from the Treaty of Portsmouth mission around four this afternoon, so we'll just have to throw him back in."

Yellow's eyes get big. "Whoa. Tonight? Seriously?"

"How is that going to work with Bonner?" I ask.

"You guys aren't going back very far. Just six years. There won't be a lot of catch-up time. You'll lose maybe twenty minutes. If I send you all back at one a.m., even if it takes you hours, you'll return by five. Bonner will be asleep the whole time. I have the codes to wipe your trackers from the log. We should be fine."

I raise an eyebrow. "And if we're not?"

Red sighs. But it's not a sigh of frustration. It's more like resignation. "Then I take the fall. I orchestrated this."

"But you didn't," I protest. "If anyone should get the blame, it should be me."

"Let's not worry about that now. For now, let's focus only on success." Red slides a piece of paper and a lighter toward me. "The address of the catering company that John Leighton hired for the fundraiser. This is your ticket in. Memorize it and burn it. Yellow, your meeting takes place at L'Espalier. I assume you know it?"

"Of course," Yellow says, and I'm not surprised that she's familiar with one of the most expensive restaurants in Boston.

"Good," Red says. "And good luck."

It's hard to concentrate on the boxes upon boxes of documents after that. I spend most of the afternoon mindlessly glancing over them. For every twenty pages I flip through, I maybe read one. I scribble down a few notes that are probably completely irrelevant. Because all I'm thinking about is tonight.

After dinner, I lie on top of my bed and stare at the clock. 11:00. 11:30. 12:00. 12:30. 12:45. 12:50.

Close enough.

I slip on jeans and a light jacket and head downstairs to find that I'm not the only one who's antsy to get started. I'm the last one to arrive besides Red. Everyone has the same look of nervous energy, except Indigo, who has bags under his eyes and his chin tucked into his chest.

I pause at his seat. "How are you doing?"

His head jerks up. "I have never wanted to take a nap so badly in my life. Bonner made me start on my mission report right after I got back, and it took flipping forever."

I've never seen Indigo look worse. His eyes are bright red and watery, and his pupils are dilated. He's looking in my direction but through me, and he's swaying in his seat.

I touch his arm. "Indigo, are you okay to do this? Violet could probably handle the Howe mission alone, or I could lose Green on mine if—"

"I'm fine," he interrupts.

"You don't look fine. I don't want you to put yourself in any extra danger."

"Iris. I'm fine."

The door opens behind us, and Red walks into the Sit Room. He scowls. "I said one o'clock, people." Then he sighs. "Whatever. Let's do this."

One by one, we follow Red to the gravity chamber.

"Be careful," he says. "We don't know who or what is waiting for us out there, but it would be naive to think we're not being monitored on some level."

"Someone wants to black us out," I say. We're all thinking it.

"Maybe," Red says. "Yellow, you first." He hands her a necklace, and in a flash, Yellow is gone. "Indigo and Violet." I hold my breath as Indigo projects—and then only Abe, Green, and I are left. Red doesn't say a word as we slip our necklaces over our heads and step into the chamber. He doesn't have to. We already know this mission is do or die.

Green lingers behind, and I turn to Abe. "Hey. We need to be a team today. Deal?"

Abe's face softens, and I see so much going on behind his eyes. Thoughts and hopes and everything I *need* to see. "We're always a team," he says.

He gestures to let me go first. I close my eyes, shut my watch, and I plummet.

CHAPTER 16

I land inside the broom closet six years in the past.

Six years.

That means Alpha is upstairs. He's probably sitting in his office scheming how to make more money off of missions. All it would take to end this thing would be a quick trip upstairs and one shot. But I would never. First, it's *wrong*. And second, like Ariel said, time is too dangerous to just mess with it like that. If Alpha dies when I'm eleven, Peel might not have recruited me three years later. And if I don't go to Peel, I don't meet Abe. And that's a life I won't imagine, even now.

There are two loud *zips*, one right after the other, and I snap myself out of it as Green and Abe land next to me.

Abe looks uncomfortable. He still hasn't gotten used to the projections. But then he relaxes his shoulders and shrugs it off. Green powers out the door like we're wasting time.

"All right," Green says, as he holds open the door for us. He taps his foot against the old brick road of Joy Street. "First order of business—"

I hold up a hand. "Nope. First and only order of business is to listen to me. I'm leading this one."

I pause to see if he'll test me. I can tell he wants to—his mouth opens and he sucks in his breath—but then he stops himself. He simply says, "Okay."

This is the biggest victory I've had in weeks, which is completely pathetic, but I'll take what I can get. "We're going to Hub Catering, where we're going to steal uniforms and set up shop at John Leighton's house. He owns a whole brownstone on Commonwealth Ave., in between Berkeley and Clarendon."

"Nice chunk of real estate," Abe notes.

"No kidding," I say. "He got it in 2002 for the bargain price of fourteen million."

"Damn. We're in the wrong line of work."

Green huffs. "Where's Hub Catering?"

"The office is downtown. We can walk."

And so we do. It's a quick stroll across the Common. The midafternoon sun shines on the park. A guy tosses a Frisbee to his dog, not-so-subtly checking out the two college-aged girls lying on the grass nearby in tiny shorts and bikini tops. We pass a number of office workers eating a late lunch on the benches outside the T stop, then cross the street and head to a brick building on Summer Street.

"Plan of attack?" Green asks as we step out of view of the front window.

"You and Abe go in and ask to see sample menus and a rate chart. I'll slip in, grab a few uniforms, and we'll get out."

"And how exactly are three randoms going to blend in with a bunch of employees who probably all know each other?" Green asks.

I narrow my eyes just enough to let Green know he shouldn't underestimate me. "Do you know how much turnover large catering companies have? This place isn't exactly a mom-and-pop setup." I gesture to the three floors of the building. "Besides, there are easily fifty people staffing this thing tonight. Chefs, bartenders, servers. We're going to be fine."

Green waves his right hand in the air, like this is 1890 and he's dismissing a servant. "Fine. Yeah, let's go."

I'm about to snap back at him, but then Abe puts his hand to the small of my back. It's a *let it go* gesture. I've gotten it a lot from him in the past few years—whenever our Practical Studies professor would ride me for blowing a cover or messing up a tail, whenever a sparring partner tried to carry the fight off the mat, and, these days, whenever Bonner so much as glances in my direction. For some reason, his touch right now annoys me. It feels like I'm being undermined. I shrug away because I don't want to say or do something I'll regret.

"What are you guys waiting for?" I say.

I hang back and let Green and Abe go inside. A few minutes later, I peek in the window. Green is gesturing wildly while a woman at a desk is bent over, rifling through a filing cabinet. Abe catches my eye and motions for me to enter. I do and slip past the desk into the back. The woman doesn't notice a thing. That was ridiculously easy.

I make a left and find a woman with short, spiky blonde hair standing in an industrial kitchen. Nearly everything in here is stainless steel—appliances, countertops, a giant mixer. The woman is piping icing onto a wedding cake. She has a full sleeve of colorful tattoos on her left arm.

"Oh, hey," I say casually. "I'm a new hire. I was told to pick up a uniform?"

"You need Alberto," she says without looking up. "Second floor."

"Thanks." I sprint up the stairs. On the second floor, I pass several people: two older women arguing about brie; a guy with headphones on, bobbing his head as he rolls silverware into napkins; a man loading dingy white tablecloths into the largest washing machine I've ever seen.

And then I see a closed door with a sign marked "Linens" next to it on the wall. *Maybe this?* I rap my knuckles against the door, preparing my cover story. But no one answers. I try the handle. The door swings open, revealing a small room, dark and empty. Even better.

I'm inside in a second and shut the door quietly behind me. I flip the light switch, and then I'm faced with a sea of color. There are floor-to-ceiling shelves neatly organized with tablecloths, napkins, and chair covers in every color you could dream of. I keep looking.

And then, there it is. The last shelf—naturally—is lined with uniforms, but I'm not sure what to do. The chefs' jackets are easy to recognize, and I skip over those, but what are waiters supposed to wear? There are shirts and vests and pants and bow ties, and I'm so confused. I grab a bunch of stuff, then slip out the door and head back down the stairs.

I pause before the door that leads to the front office, straining to hear what's going on in there. Waltzing in with an armload of stolen uniforms might not be the best idea.

"Hey!"

I whirl around. It's the woman with the spiky hair. She's now adding tiny pink cherry blossoms to the base of each cake layer.

"We don't go out that way." She jerks the hand holding the piping bag toward the opposite end of the building, back behind the staircase. "Service entrance for employees."

I breathe a sigh of relief. A service entrance. That's a million times better. "Thank you," I tell her, and I mean it. I squeeze the uniforms tighter and disappear out the door into the warm spring sun.

Abe and Green find me outside. One quick change later, and we're on our way to the fundraiser. I didn't do such a great job at eyeballing sizes. Abe could fit two people in his vest, while Green can barely get his shirt buttoned. My pants are a little short, but I sling them low on my hips and it's passable. I use my ponytail holder to gather Abe's vest in the back. That's going to have to do.

We duck behind a group of similarly dressed people heading into the back of the house from an alley off Comm. Ave. A guy in his early twenties swivels around. "New?"

"Yep," I say. "Our first event."

His eyebrows shoot for the sky. "They gave you *this* as your first event?" Then he laughs and turns back to the group. "Can you believe that? Throwing baby cubs to the wolves like that?"

I roll my eyes at his back because, seriously, dude, a catering job is hardly the most difficult thing I've done in my life. And "baby cubs" is a totally superfluous expression. But correcting someone's grammar is completely Bonner-esque. Plus, there's no sense in making enemies.

We shuffle inside the house, where we enter . . . a room. I don't really know what it is. A parlor? Some other type of room that only rich people have? There's burgundy carpeting, silk drapes, and a bunch of tables and chairs. I have no idea how you're supposed to use this room. From the looks of it, no one else does either.

There are three coordinators for the event, and each of them has a clipboard with a list of names. Green, Abe, and I duck into the kitchen next door. It's way bigger than my kitchen in Vermont, which is a glorified closet with seventies-era appliances. This kitchen is even bigger than the one at Annum Hall. There are professional-grade appliances like the ones at Hub Catering, stone countertops, and what I assume is the finest cutlery on the market.

Abe nudges me, then looks toward the coffered ceiling. "And I'm willing to bet this is only the catering kitchen."

Catering kitchen? As in there's more than one kitchen in this house? *How do people afford this stuff?* "Okay," I whisper to my teammates. "I think we should split up and each tail one of the suspects. Abe—Blue—you take Senator Wharton. Green, you take the vice president. I've got Howe."

"Apps are ready to start going out!" one of the younger chefs yells.

Abe, Green, and I each grab a platter, keep our heads ducked, and follow the line of waiters heading up the stairs to the second floor. When we get to the top, I halt. Green bumps into me and has to use two hands to steady his tray.

"Watch it!" he growls.

But I can't stop staring. Because I'm in a ballroom. The entire second floor of this house is a *ballroom*. The ceilings have to be at least twenty feet high, and there are grand, sweeping drapes that fall all the way to the parquet floors. The whole room is painted a light blue, and portraits of very important-looking people line the walls.

The party must have just started because there aren't many people here yet. There are easily more waiters than guests. I make the rounds, keeping my eyes peeled for the defense secretary.

Senator Wharton is the first of our suspects to arrive, half an hour later. Abe nods at me, then sets off in his direction. The room is growing more crowded. In no time, I can barely move through the people. It's almost suffocating. I've completely lost track of Green and Abe. Unless I climb up the drapes to get a better visual, I don't think I'm even going to notice when Howe arrives.

But no sooner do I think that than I see him walk in. He's over in the corner, shaking hands with the congresswoman running for reelection. He says something I can't hear, then turns to head in another direction. I have to follow.

"Hold on a second!" someone says.

I spin around to find a man wearing a very ill-fitting suit waving greasy fingers at my tray of spanakopita. I glance back toward Howe. He's heading for the front windows. I look back at the man. He's trying to squeeze about seven spanakopitas next to a lump of meatballs on a tiny appetizer plate.

"Seriously?" I mutter. I've lost sight of Howe.

"What was that?" the man asks.

No, there he is! Talking to a woman with long, wavy brown hair swept into a low side ponytail. She's wearing a tailored black dress that stops at her knees and black, pointy-toed stilettoes. The woman turns her head to the side, and I gasp.

"Take the tray." I thrust it into the man's hands. He fumbles and nearly drops his plate but I don't turn to help him.

I keep walking toward the spot where the future secretary of defense is speaking to a much younger, much different version of Jane Bonner.

CHAPTER 17

I squeeze past Abe on my way across the room. He's keeping an eye on Wharton, who's talking to someone I don't recognize.

"Forget Wharton," I whisper to him. "New target." Then I jerk my head in the direction of Howe and Bonner.

"No way," Abe whispers back.

The two of us make our way through the crowd. We slide past men in suits and women in black dresses and blazers. Tall, white, powerful. That's a good way to describe this room. Or just about any high-level political fundraiser, I guess.

I have my eyes trained on Bonner. Howe leans down and whispers something in her ear. His expression is flat, annoyed even. But Bonner lights up with a smile, something I've never seen before. Bonner rests her hand on Howe's elbow. He looks down, and his glare makes her move it. Then he turns and continues toward the front of the room, not glancing back.

I grab on to Abe's sleeve. "You follow Howe. I'm going after Bonner." Abe nods once and takes off.

I hang back as Bonner weaves through the crowd. I brush past Green, and he touches my arm.

"Whoa," he says. "What is she doing here?"

Green shoves his tray at me. It's about three-quarters full of some sort of raw salmon and avocado thing. "Take it. You look too conspicuous walking around without a tray. I can get another. Don't take your eyes off Bonner."

"Obviously." I snatch the tray and leave Green where he is.

I push my way past a woman who is clearly overdressed in a floor-length, emerald-green, satin evening gown, and watch as Bonner talks to a doughy man in an expensive suit, then a man who's shorter than I am, and then a man with silver hair and a weak chin. Each time, it's the same deal. A touch on the arm that's borderline inappropriate, followed by a girlish giggle. Who *is* this woman?

"Caroline!" Bonner calls, raising a hand. My gaze follows, and I see the moment the future vice president realizes it's Bonner who's calling her. There's a fleeting look of disgust, followed by an almost immediate smile that's sweet as saccharine—and just as artificial.

I push my way closer, ignoring the hands reaching for my tray. I beeline for a group standing about five feet from Caroline Caldwell and hold the tray out to them while glancing over my shoulder. Bonner and Caroline do a double cheek kiss, and the future VP looks like she's about to vomit.

"Well, howdy, little lady. What do we have here?"

It's a voice I know. A voice that makes me squeeze the handles of the tray. I turn, and Joe Caldwell is staring at me. I open my mouth, but no sound comes out. I'm violating the first rule of reconnaissance, which is to not be seen by anyone you know.

Breathe, I tell myself. *He's not going to remember a waiter at one of the countless political fundraisers he's been to over the years. Don't draw attention to yourself, and he'll have no reason to remember you.*

"Sorry?" I say.

Joe points to the tray. "What is it?"

"Oh!" I look down. "Salmon and avocado. It's a chef specialty." Maybe that's true.

"Don't mind if I do!" he says as he takes one, and he's talking so loudly I can't hear what his wife is saying to Bonner. And then there are more reaching hands. Almost a dozen of them, and everyone is chattering, and I'm missing the whole freaking conversation that I need to be eavesdropping on!

"Deeeee-lish!" Joe takes the last one and pops it into his mouth. "My favorite of the night. Hey, sweetheart, why don't you go back down to the kitchen and grab another tray of those." He plops an empty glass onto my tray. "And while you're at it, get me another of these. Three fingers of Scotch, a splash of soda, two ice cubes." He pulls out a dollar and shoves it into the top of my vest. His hand lingers a second longer than necessary. Then he flashes me a grin. "For your troubles."

A dollar. *A dollar.* Are you kidding me, a dollar? I have to bite my tongue—literally bite down on it to hold back the words I want to say. I settle on a simple, "Yes, sir."

Joe claps the man next to him on the back. I'm already forgotten. So I return my attention to Caroline. Senator Wharton has now joined the conversation. I find Green in the crowd, and he shakes his head at me, like he's disappointed in me for the momentary attention lapse. I look away.

"Well, it was lovely to see you," Caroline says to Bonner, "but if you'd please excuse us, Senator Wharton and I have a few matters of business we need to discuss."

The smile vanishes from Bonner's face. "Um, of course. It was lovely to see you again, Caroline."

"Mm-hmm."

And then Bonner leaves. She passes right by Joe, and his head turns to gaze at her ass for a few steps.

"Who's that?" Wharton asks.

"That," Caroline says with a sigh, "is Marie Quail."

I'm not ready for that answer. I fumble the tray in my hands and have to grab onto the sides to steady it. Joe's glass tips over but doesn't fall off. Wharton and Caroline both look at me.

I clear my throat. "Do either of you have any glasses for me to take?" As soon as the words are out of my mouth, I realize what a dumb question it is. Wharton's holding a full glass of amber liquid. Caroline's hands are empty. She looks at me like I'm a complete moron and doesn't even acknowledge the question. I duck my head and turn to the side.

"She works in Washington," Caroline continues. "She probably knows half the men in this room." It's clear from her tone what that means. It's also clear the conversation about Bonner—Marie—whatever the hell her name really is—is over. "Listen, where are we on the energy vote?"

Wharton starts talking about this senator and that senator and what they expect the vote to be, and I don't care. Green meets my eyes and jerks his head back, a "come here" gesture.

"Don't ever beckon me again," I say as I sidle up to Green. "Did you hear what Caldwell said?"

Green stares at me for a second before he nods. "Who in the sweet hell is Marie Quail?"

And then Senators Wharton and Caldwell are shaking hands, and Caroline taps her husband on the shoulder. "We've made our appearances. I'm ready to leave."

"Sure," Joe says, and I turn my back as they walk past, but neither of them pay me a second glance.

Abe finds us in the thinning crowd. "Howe left about five minutes ago."

"Anything about XP?" I whisper.

He shakes his head.

I sigh. "So should we call this thing? Wharton's the only one left, and I don't think it's him."

"It's definitely not Wharton," Green says. "He doesn't have the air. I actually think he's trying to be a genuine lawmaker and stay away from the nasty underside of politics." He snorts. "Good luck with that."

"I say we head back and have a very serious conversation with Marie Quail."

"Who?" Abe says.

I explain to Abe on the walk back to Annum Hall. As we climb into the closet, I'm thinking about how I'm going to do it. I'm just going to come out and tell Bonner that I know she's hiding something. I'm going to demand answers.

But as soon as we get back, all that is forgotten. Because there's an alarm going off. The same alarm we heard when Orange went missing.

Someone else has been blacked out.

CHAPTER 18

Yellow, Indigo, Violet. One of them didn't make it back.

My mind goes right to Yellow—the only one flying solo— as my hand finds Abe's. His fingers close around mine, and for the moment, every bit of tension, of awkwardness, between us is gone. Green pushes past us. "Red!" He's racing down the hallway now. "Who? Who's missing?" His voice is almost panicked.

Red steps out into the hall, and Yellow is behind him. I blow out the breath I didn't realize I'd been holding. Yellow is safe.

But there are tears streaming down her cheeks. Big black smudges of eyeliner and mascara drip down her face, and she doesn't raise a hand to wipe them away.

And then I know.

Indigo.

No. NO.

Abe throws his arm around my shoulder and hugs me tight.

"Who?" I whisper, as if daring Red to say the name.

Then there's a familiar *ziiiiip*, and all of us spin around to see Violet tear out of the gravity chamber. She's choking and stumbling and holding onto the wall.

"I tried!" she yells. "They got him! They tried to get me, too. I wanted to go back for Indigo, but I couldn't. I just . . . It was chaos and confusion, and I don't even know what happened."

She sinks to her knees and gasps for breath, and I feel like someone should go to her, hug her, reassure her. But no one does. We all stand there. My feet are anchored to the floor. *Indigo.* They were following Secretary Howe. And now Indigo is gone.

"How many of them were there, Violet?" Red asks.

Violet swallows. "Two. There were two."

"Describe them."

She's still trembling. "I don't know. I couldn't see their faces. They were wearing ski masks. They weren't that tall, not that muscular, but clearly male and trained in combat. They had these long metal poles that whirred and hissed and lit up. One of them grabbed me, one grabbed Indigo, and I just sort of lost him. I was too focused on freeing myself, and as soon as I did, I ran and ran and ran. I was going to project back from where I was, but I just kept running."

No one says anything.

"We have to do something!" Yellow wails.

Red reaches out and helps Violet off the floor. He has to hook his elbows under her armpits to get her to stand. "Violet, pull yourself together. What did they say? How far into the mission were you?"

"Neither of them said a single word the whole time." Her eyes fly to each of us. "We were hours into the mission. They just showed up at the end, right as—"

The door to the stairwell bangs open, and the Narc storms through it.

"What is this?" Her voice is loud and screechy. "What are you doing?" She stares at us individually, and when she gets to me, her expression sours.

And then she's in my face. "It was you! You did this!"

Red lets go of Violet and pushes between me and Bonner. "It wasn't Iris. It was me. It was all me. Indigo was taken."

Bonner throws back her shoulders. "Both of you, my office. Now!"

Abe squeezes my hand. Violet looks around nervously, while Yellow stares at me with pink, puffy eyes. I try to give her my best reassuring look, but I don't think it works.

Red and I follow Bonner upstairs to her office.

"You can leave Iris out of this," Red says once we're inside. "I authorized the missions."

It's like she doesn't even hear him. Bonner's finger flies in my face. "You've been undermining my authority ever since I got here, Iris. You have a real problem with me, and I'm done taking your attitude."

"Jane," Red says, "let's not—"

I hold up a hand to stop him. "You're partially right," I tell her. "I thought I had a huge problem with *Jane*. Funny thing, though, turns out my issue is with Marie."

Her face goes white.

I'm not done.

"And what I want to know is why Marie seems so intent to cover for XP."

"I ordered you to let that go. Let XP go."

"What is going on here?" Red asks.

"Why?" I shout at her. "There's a real threat and a real enemy, and you're not following the trail!" I turn to Red. "Her name isn't even Jane Bonner!"

"What?"

Then Bonner is on me. She grabs my arm—all five of her fingertips pressing into my bicep. "You have no idea the danger we're all in." Suddenly I stop fighting her grip. I hear the fear in her voice, see it lurking behind her eyes.

"You know who's behind the blackouts."

"I don't."

"Bullshit."

Bonner pushes me away as she lets go of my arm. "Give me your watch. It's going back in the lockbox, back in the safe, and it's never coming out again. You are on indefinite administrative leave."

I blink. "You're firing me?"

"Jane!" Red says. "I told you—"

"Give me your watch."

"No. Not until you tell me what you're doing here, *Marie*, and who you really are."

"I said *give me your watch*."

"And I said *no*! Who are you working for? Whose pocket are you in?" And then I smirk. "Or should I ask, whose pants are you in?"

Before I have time to move, her knuckles crack across my cheekbone, and light explodes behind my eyes. I stagger sideways and slam into the side of the desk. Red reaches to help me, but I shake him off.

I push off the desk and turn to Bonner, fists raised. No one has ever hit me like that before, and every instinct I have says *fight*.

But then Bonner raises her hands in submission. "I'm sorry." She drops into her chair and cradles her head in her palms. Her shoulders shake, and I can tell for sure now that Bonner—Marie Quail—is terrified.

"This is not supposed to be happening," she whispers.

I lean over the desk. "What's not supposed to be happening?"

Bonner looks up. "Believe it or not, I'm trying to protect you."

"From what?" I bang both fists on the desk. "I think you're just trying to get rid of me."

"Give me your watch. Please. *Please* give me your watch! This is the only way I can help you."

"No, it's not. You can tell me—"

"Your watch, Iris!" She holds out her hand, palm up. It's clear she's not going to tell me anything else.

And so I slip the watch over my head and hand it to her.

"You can stay at Annum Hall until the end of the week." She gestures to the door. This conversation is over.

Except that it's not. She can be scared and try to hide the truth, but I'm not giving up. Not when my teammates—my friends—are in danger.

As soon as I have my hand on the door, she adds, "I'm serious, Iris. Don't go digging for answers you don't want to know."

But I do want to know.

"Well, I'm not quite sure how you expect me to dig, given that you just fired me and all."

Bonner narrows her eyes. "Leave. And close the door behind you."

I don't look at Red on the way out. I should have known I'd take the fall for this, no matter what he said. And, as Bonner knows, without Annum Guard, I have no way to figure out who XP is.

CHAPTER 19

What happens next is a blur. I stumble past my teammates, past Abe. I mumble, "I got fired." There are gasps and protests, but I ignore them. I go out into the foyer and instinctively look toward the library, even though the interns aren't there. It's just after six in the morning. I go upstairs. I call my mom's cell. She doesn't answer. I call the house phone in Vermont. It's been disconnected. I try her cell again and leave a message. My third? Maybe fourth? I tell her I'm coming home. Even though I don't know if she's in Vermont.

When a manic period hits, she's a compulsive road tripper. Up and down the east coast, as far as her wallet will take her. I have good memories of riding the Ferris wheel at the Jersey Shore, of pretending to churn butter at Colonial Williamsburg.

And then not good memories of Mom's shouting matches with a security guard at the Met, after he asked her to keep it down and to stop screaming at everyone in the gallery that her work was better than Rothko's. I was thirteen. I remember how I felt being escorted out through a security entrance, the deep shame down to my toes.

I answer the door when I hear the knock because I know it's Abe. I don't say anything. He doesn't say anything. I tumble into bed, and Abe lies behind me, wrapping his arms around me like a blanket. I let myself melt into him.

For a second, I let myself imagine that I'm back at Peel, that I get a big do-over of my junior year. And then for another second, I imagine I'm not at Peel, not at Annum Guard. That I'm just a normal girl living a normal life, about to start my senior year of high school. I have a boyfriend, maybe even a summer job, and I'm starting to think about college. How nice would that be? To have my biggest problem in life be the SATs rather than bringing down a corrupt ring of time-traveling criminals.

And then I close my eyes.

Before I know it, I'm waking up. I'm alone, and I roll over to look at the clock. It's eight twenty-seven. I blink. Did I sleep the entire day?

I know the answer as I push myself off the bed. I feel drugged. Woozy. I always feel this way when I get too much sleep. It's definitely night. But still, I slide open the door and peek out the window in the hallway. The sky is a hazy, pinkish purple fading into a deep mauve along the horizon.

I look down at the floor. There's a silver tray with a sandwich wrapped in wax paper and a lidded glass bowl full of grapes sitting outside my door.

Abe. I bend over and pick up the tray. This has to be Abe.

I should go to him. Or to Yellow. Or to all of them. I should come up with a battle plan. I should let them know I'm not going to take this lying down. But instead I wolf down half a turkey sandwich, take a quick shower, and get back in bed.

Naturally, I'm not tired. Battle plan it is. I sit up and lean back against the headboard.

Options. I could force Bonner at gunpoint to open the safe and give me back my watch. But what good would that do? I'd still have no idea how to bring down XP—is it Secretary Howe? Maybe?—and let's not forget about the tracker in the base of my skull.

I could go to her and try begging, playing to her weaknesses. Maybe if I act brave enough, she'll want to help me. I laugh. Why am I even factoring her into this? She's a fraud. No, what I should be doing is finding out everything I can about XP before I'm cut off for good. That seems like an obvious step one.

I bolt into the hallway and knock on the door two down from mine. Abe answers right away.

"You okay?"

"Never better," I say as I push my way inside. His room is identical to mine. Single bed centered on the wall straight ahead, dresser to the left, closet and bathroom to the right. But his is painted a light blue while mine is lavender. "Thanks for the sandwich and grapes. I was starving."

"I figured."

I slide Abe's closet doors open. "I need some bugs. What do you have available?" I kick a pair of sneakers and a pair of dress shoes out of the way until I find the small metal safe in the back of the closet.

"Bugs?" Abe sounds confused, then he looks down at the safe. "Surveillance bugs? Who are you spying on?"

"I'm going to pay our interns a visit. Now. While I still have the chance."

"You do realize what you're talking about is illegal, right? You don't have a court order."

"What are they going to do if they find out? Fire me again?" I drop to my knees. "Is the combination still eleven-oh-three-twelve-seventeen?"

"Of course."

That gets my blood flowing. Abe picked that code freshman year. It's my birthdate, followed by his. I enter it into the keypad, and the light flashes green. I open the lid to the safe—to Abe's toolbox. "Do you have any ultrasonics in here?"

"Probably not." Abe reaches over, lifts the safe, and sets it on his bed. The two of us sit on either side. "I know I have at least one RF, though."

I scrunch my nose. RF bugs use radio frequency, so they're really easy to detect, but they're cheap, so that's a plus. Ultrasonics are my favorite. They take a sound and convert it into a signal way above what the human ear can hear; then you can intercept it and convert it back into a normal tone. They're much harder to trace. But they're also pricey.

Abe digs around and pulls out a smaller box, like the kind you get when you buy jewelry. He opens the lid and dumps a gold microchip the size of a fingernail into his palm. "Last one."

He holds it out, and I reach, but then his fingers close.

"You do realize that anything you hear on this isn't admissible in court?"

"I sat next to you in that Fourth Amendment seminar, Abe. I don't care about admissibility. All I care about is getting Zeta and Orange back." And then it's like I'm stabbed as the realization hits me again. "And Indigo."

Abe opens his fingers, and the bug falls into my outstretched palm. "Be careful. You're going to get arrested if you get caught." His voice is matter-of-fact. And rightly so. What I'm doing is highly illegal, not to mention unethical.

But screw that.

"I will." I close my fist around the bug, then I push up off the bed and head for the door. "Thanks for this."

"I . . ." He trails off. I turn around, waiting for him to say it. Waiting for him to tell me he loves me. "Good luck."

I try not to let my disappointment show. "Thank you." Then I shut the door.

I deactivate the alarm to the front door—I'm seriously surprised Bonner hasn't changed the code on me yet—and step out into a warm summer night. I walk a block west before I hail a cab. I'm not going to bother with the T. It's so unreliable at night. Even though I'm only going a few miles, to an off-campus apartment in Cambridge, it could take me forty minutes on the T. Hell no.

The driver drops me off in front of a four-story brick building just a few blocks from the edge of Harvard's campus. I push the bottom button, and a voice I recognize crackles through the speaker. "Hello?"

"Hey, Mike, it's Iris. Can I—" The door buzzes open, and I walk into the foyer. Mike's already in the hallway, standing outside the first door on the right. The door to the apartment he shares with Colton. There aren't any Secret Service agents loitering in the hall, so I have to assume Colton isn't here.

"Hi," he greets me. He has on a concert T-shirt and jeans, and he's standing in the hallway with no shoes on.

"Are you alone?" I ask. I know the question is giving him the wrong idea about my visit, but I don't have any time to waste.

"You mean is Colton here? No. He's barely ever here. He'll sleep here a few nights a week, but that's about it. It's pretty much like I live alone." He heads back into the apartment and holds the door open for me.

I step inside. The apartment has brick walls and exposed duct work. There's a twisted, wrought-iron staircase leading up to an open, second-story loft. There's no separation between the kitchen and the living room, and there are two doors to the right. One is shut, but the other isn't, so I can see it's a bedroom. The entire place is open and airy, which is a good thing—if I plant this bug in a central location, it can pick up the whole house— but also a bad thing—how am I supposed to plant it without Mike seeing?

My eye goes right to a large silver sculpture shaped like a C on a living-room end table. It looks like a giant sink faucet, but it's plugged into an outlet on the wall, so it has to be a lamp. That will work.

"So what can I do for you?" Mike asks, stepping close to me— too close. He smells good, like he just took a shower.

I step away. "I came to say good-bye, actually."

Mike's mouth drops open and his eyes soften like someone just told him his puppy died. "You're leaving? Or . . . wait. Are you here to fire me?"

"The former." I lift my messenger bag over the top of my head and drop it on a very modern, angular, white leather sofa that doesn't look at all comfortable. "I'm leaving Annum Guard effective immediately." I see no need to mention that it's not by choice. I look up at the loft space. There's a pool table in the middle of it, but the space is so open that it looks right down into the living room. Mike's bedroom is the one room with a door where I could distract him, but that's not going to happen.

"Can I ask why?" Mike asks, his voice low.

Oh, I don't know. But the fact that you're likely spying on us for your grandfather, who's actively trying to kill me and my friends, has something to do with it, maybe?

"I'm excited to explore new opportunities." I sound like an ousted politician giving a concession speech on TV.

"And you came all this way across the river just to say good-bye to someone you've only known for a couple of weeks?" He has a point. I'd be suspicious too if I were him.

"Can I get a glass of water?"

Mike looks at me for a second too long before turning away. I watch him open a cabinet drawer and grab a tall glass. Then he opens the refrigerator, and I whip the bug out of my pocket. This might be my only chance. I take a step toward the lamp.

"You're sure you just want water?" he calls. "I have a few beers in here."

"Just water, thanks."

He pulls out a pitcher, and I grab the lamp. It's much heavier than I was expecting. It wobbles in my hands, but I slap the bug on the bottom and set it back on the table. Under three seconds.

Mike turns around and walks toward me with the water. "So can I ask you a completely inappropriate question?"

My pulse is racing. "Go ahead."

He hands me the glass, and his fingers brush across mine. "I've been trying to figure out your ethnicity. I feel like such an ass asking that because it drives me crazy when people ask me, but I'm curious."

I take a sip of the water and a deliberate step away from the end table. "I'm actually a bit of a mutt. My dad's your standard American Caucasian—mixture of this and that. Some German, and maybe some Irish? But my mom's father was Moroccan."

"Moroccan, cool." Mike takes a step closer, and I eye the door. I did what I came to do, and now I need to get out without looking too suspicious. "I stayed at a *riad* in Marrakech a few summers back. Gorgeous place."

"I've never been." *Exit strategy. I need an exit strategy.* "Sorry, I probably shouldn't have come. I just didn't want to leave without saying good-bye, so . . . good-bye." I stick out my hand.

Mike takes it, then pulls me into him, and before I know it, his lips are on mine, kissing me with urgency. *He's a traitor!* my mind screams, but my lips part to find his tongue as yearning rips across my belly, spreading downward.

Mike holds me tight, pressing his body into mine, and I let out a moan. This feeling—the excitement, the danger—it's exactly what I felt the first time I kissed Abe.

And then I pull away.

Abe.

"I can't do this," I say. "I'm sorry. It was a mistake to come here."

"Iris, wait—"

But I've already opened the front door. I leave without looking back.

I'm the traitor. To Abe. To my missing teammates. To myself. I raise my hand to call a cab, and when it pulls to the curb, I put all my feelings to the side. I say good-bye to Mike.

At least until I have to testify against him.

CHAPTER 20

It's nearly midnight by the time I get back. I go straight to Abe's room and knock on the door. He opens it.

"Done," I say, not moving from the hallway. "Can you check it to make sure it's working?"

"I already did." I can't tell what he means. Whether he just checked it ten minutes ago or whether he was listening the whole time.

"Mike kissed me. I let him."

The truth hangs between us like a dense fog. I can barely see him and he can barely see me, even though we're so close.

"Okay," is all Abe says.

"Abe—"

He holds up a hand. "I really can't right now, Mandy. There's too much going on, and I don't want to get distracted. We'll work through it, but not now."

Now it's my turn to say "Okay."

"I'm tired," he says, and I see the exhaustion written on his face. "We'll talk in the morning."

"I love you," I say as he starts to shut the door.

"I know." He pauses. "And I love you, too." The door closes, and I wander down the hall to my room. What happened was wrong. And I let it happen.

Never again.

I plop myself on my bed, but unlike Abe, I'm not at all tired. The opposite, actually. I've never felt more awake. But Abe's right. I can't dwell on him and me right now; I can't dwell on Mike. My time here is limited. It's on to Bonner.

Game plan number two.

A while later, there's a knock on my door. It's 1:08 in the morning.

I push off the bed. "Abe?" I whisper. He can't hear me. I crack the door. It's not Abe.

The Narc's frizzy hair is pulled back into a messy ponytail. I can't tell if she has liner smudge under her eyes or if they're dark circles. She clutches a folded set of papers to her chest and looks at me with wild eyes. My mind panics as I glance over my shoulder to the spiral notebook on the bed. The notebook in which I've spent the last sixty minutes plotting her demise.

"Pack a bag."

"What? You said I had until the end of the week to get out."

She shoves the folded stack into my hands. I look down and unfurl it. Seven pages full of dates and addresses, in probably the smallest font size there is. I have to squint to read it.

"What is this?"

"Pack a bag and meet me downstairs. I'm telling them you went home to your mother. It's as much lead time as I can give you."

"Wait . . ." I struggle to put it together. I don't want to get my hopes up, but they're already hurtling out of the stratosphere. "Are you sending me after XP?" I look back down at the papers in my hands, which are now shaking. "Is this a list of every XP mission?" There have to be several hundred missions here.

"Don't be ridiculous," Bonner practically spits. "Those are all the Annum Guard missions. Every one of them. I don't know the XP missions. You have to find them."

My head is spinning. "How? By going back in time and stealing them from myself?" I think of Red's warning.

Bonner doesn't respond.

"Wait, seriously? That's what you want me to do?"

"We don't have much time. You have to get away from here." She starts for the stairs.

"Bonner!" My call is hushed.

She doesn't turn.

"Marie!"

Then she does. But she doesn't say anything.

"Who are you working for?"

She slowly shakes her head. "I don't even know. Just pack a bag and come downstairs. I'll tell you what I can."

"How do I know I can trust you?"

She shrugs. "You don't." And then she's gone.

I shut my door. The papers are still shaking in my hands. I set them on my dresser and stare at them. This could be a huge trap.

I could be walking into the middle of a blackout. Maybe they're downstairs right now waiting for me. Or maybe Bonner really is trying to help me.

There's only one way to find out. I grab a duffel bag from the bottom of my closet and start stuffing clothes into it. I don't bother with any of my things. I go straight for my historical wardrobe. A baby-blue, silk colonial gown; a simple, gray Victorian dress with a lace collar; a soft corset that isn't at all period appropriate; a tweed skirt suit that I think is from the thirties or forties; an orange polyester jumpsuit from the seventies. As much as will fit. Then I rip the pages out of the notebook and shove them in the bottom of the bag. I toss the mission ledger on top, zip up the bag, and sling it over my shoulder.

I linger in the hallway and glance at Abe's door. We're not going to have that conversation. At least not yet. I have to trust it'll be okay to wait.

Annum Hall is dark as I slip down the stairs. I'm on the landing between the first and second floors when there's a noise that makes me jump. A loud crack, then a bang as the front door is forced open. The alarm sounds for one quick second, then falls silent.

Did someone just break into Annum Hall?

I wait. No one is responding. They must not have heard the alarm, or maybe they mistook it for a faulty smoke detector. It was just a few beeps. I'm all alone on this.

I hurry down the stairs. I step off the last one and freeze. Bonner's office door is open, and there are two hushed voices coming from it.

The smart thing to do would be to haul upstairs and get help. Backup. But I don't always do the smart thing. I tiptoe down the hallway to Bonner's office.

"I don't know how many times I have to say it. You messed up, Marie." The voice is male.

I stop. I'm only a few feet from her open door. I don't recognize the voice. Nothing about the tone or inflection is even remotely familiar.

"This is not what I expected." That's Bonner. Her voice is rushed, frantic even. I flatten my palms against the wall behind me.

"No one pays you to expect *anything*. You do as you're told."

"If I'd known people were going to get hurt, I never would have agreed . . ." Her voice gets loud, and then she drops it back down to a whisper. "No one told me what they really wanted me to do."

I can't breathe.

"Well, darlin', that's part of being the lackey. No one's ever going to ask your opinion, cuz no one cares. You wanted to play with the big boys, and well . . . tag. You're it."

"*Please*," Bonner says, and the way she does twists my heart. She's scared of this man. And in a split second, I act. I move toward the door. There's a huge man standing with his back to me. He has a square-shaped head, a pudgy neck, and shoulders that stretch for miles. Bonner is in front of him, her face distorted in anguish.

And then she looks up and catches my eye. She jerks her head to the side—telling me to get the hell out of here in no uncertain terms—and looks away. And so I take another step, just to the other side of the doorway. I'm standing in front of Red's closed office door.

"Are you going to take me like you took the others?" Bonner's voice trembles.

"You're going somewhere, yes."

There's a gasp, then a gargle, then, "Sandline!"

My breath catches in my throat. She has to mean that for me?

"What the hell are you blabbering about?"

Is that a password? To what?

She says it again. "Sandline!"

"Aw, shut up, Marie."

There's a muffled slide and a cry and a *thunk*. Then another. And another. I feel nauseated. I clutch the edge of the doorframe, ready to pounce and help Bonner, but every rational thought in my brain is telling me to stand down. Not to blow my cover.

There are footsteps. A grunt. The sound of Bonner being hoisted up. And I'm standing right outside the door.

My hand flies to Red's keypad. *Please! Please, Red, tell me you didn't change your code!* I punch 126512 into the keypad, and the door silently clicks open. I slip inside. I keep my hand on the knob, making sure the door hovers a few millimeters from the frame. Closing it would make too much noise.

Footsteps pause out in the hall. Is he looking at the door? It's pitch-black in here. I can't see if Red has any weapons. But then the footsteps start again, fainter, then fainter still. The front door shuts a few seconds later.

What just happened here?

Where did that man take Bonner? And why?

My thoughts run together. I'm so dizzy. I wait. I don't know how long. I don't know whether I'm more afraid that the man might come back or of what I might find in the next office.

Finally, I open the door, one inch at a time.

Or is Bonner dead already?

No.

Her office is empty, but Bonner's computer is on. The security camera feed is up, each of the twenty-four boxes showing the same black-and-white static. My brain is static, too. Clouds rolling in on a harbor, and I can't see, can't think. But then there's a beacon. *Sandline.* That has to be a password. Something she wants me to know.

I should get someone. Red. Abe. I need help. *Bonner* needs help, and the sooner the better. But I don't want to involve anyone else in this mess. If these people know we're after them, they'll come for us first. I'm not losing anyone else. Not Abe, not Yellow . . . hell, not even Green.

No, *I'm* following this lead. Alone.

I grab a piece of notepaper from the desk.

Bonner was taken. I went after the people who did it. You have to trust me to do this alone. Please. —Iris

I place the note on the center of the desk and sprint toward the gravity chamber.

I'm halfway down the stairs when I realize I can't project without my watch, which is locked inside the safe. I screech to a halt. I do need Red. Dammit!

But then I realize . . .

Sandline

. . . could be the code to the safe?

I'm off and running again, tearing into Sit Room One. I drop the duffel bag to the floor and reach for the keypad to the safe, then stop. It's a numeric punch-pad. There are no letters.

I step back and make myself take a breath. Let my Peel training kick in. I need to let logic and levelheadedness take over.

All right, let's start with the obvious. A phone keypad. I visualize it in my mind. SANDLINE. That's 72635463.

The pad beeps, but the light on the bottom stays red.

I think about Bonner. She's smart, but she also knew how much danger she was in. My gut is telling me she wouldn't make the code too hard to crack in case she had to count on someone else to get into the safe.

Me.

It has to be easy, like . . . a letter-number cipher? The simplest cipher there is assigns a number to each letter of the alphabet. A is 1, B is 2, C is 3, and so on. I rush through the alphabet in my mind, counting on my fingers. *Sandline* translates to 19-1-14-4-12-9-14-5. Is that it?

I type in 191144129145. The light stays red.

No, maybe it's a standard eight-digit code. I have to break it down further so each letter has only one digit. S is 19. Add the 1 and 9 together and get 10. Add the 1 and the 0 together and I come up with 1.

S is 1.

A is 1.

1-1.

N is 14, which is 5. I go through the rest of the word, and then I have it.

1-1-5-4-3-9-5-5.

I cross my fingers with my left hand and type it into the keypad with my right. And then the light turns green.

The safe holds all sorts of goodies. I go straight for my watch. I enter the same code, and the robotic voice of the briefcase echoes throughout the room as the case clicks open. I mutter a "Hush!"

After the watch is around my neck, I go for the money box. It's all organized by decade. I have no idea what to take, so I just start opening the drawers and shoving fistfuls of cash into the duffel bag. Then I run down the hallway and step into the gravity chamber.

I have to go to Peel. To the day Alpha died. I know what Red said; I know about the dangers of running into myself. But that's the only date when I know I had Alpha's notebook on me, and that notebook is the only way I'll be able to find out the XP missions.

And so I shut the watch. Time to rendezvous with myself.

CHAPTER 21

It's a February morning when I land, and I instantly realize I didn't pack a coat. I'm wearing the old, olive-green hoodie and yoga pants I wore to Mike's, but that's not exactly winter weather gear. I have a coat hanging upstairs in my closet. A warm, puffy down one. But I was a wanted woman in February. I need to get out of Annum Hall. Now. So I open a door in the gravity chamber, the one that leads outside. An icy wind blows right through my hoodie, penetrating my skin.

I hunch my shoulders and tear across the Common to the Park Street T stop. I buy a new Charlie card, and soon I'm huddled inside the bus depot at South Station, my teeth chattering. An old woman sits on the bench across from mine. She looks at my hoodie, then frowns and hugs her oversized purse and bag of groceries closer, as if any second now I'll leap over the aisle at her. Do I really give off such a crazy vibe? Maybe I am my mother's daughter.

I'm grateful for the warmth on the bus. I sit next to a window and put my hands against the slatted heater. The metal burns, but I don't move my hands. It's a good pain.

A half hour later, the bus dumps me a short distance from Peel. I take the shortcut through the woods, then squeeze myself through the hole in the fence.

And I'm on campus. In just a few minutes, Alpha is going to be here. Then most of my team is going to project here from 1982, from when they found Yellow and me. Yellow will have been shot. Later, Abe and I will arrive. Then there will be helicopters and a SWAT team, and Alpha and I will go running across campus and into the science building. Where Alpha will die and I will cause an explosion.

I stare at the science building. At its plain brick exterior. It has none of the charm of the old New England prep schools. There are no notches in the bricks; there is no arched wooden door, no wall of ivy snaking up the side. No, this building is like every other building on Peel's campus. A big rectangle. Tilt walls hoisted up with a brick facade slapped on top. Efficiency and cost savings; that should be Peel's real motto.

In less than an hour, that building is going to be on fire.

I need a game plan, but I can't think of where to start. I can't be seen. Certainly not by my Annum Guard teammates, *definitely* not by myself, and really, not by anyone on campus. Peel doesn't have that many students. We all basically know one another. And that long-lost twin explanation only flies on soap operas.

This is a suicide mission. But before my brain can come up with another thought, there are footsteps pounding right toward me. I look up to see Alpha and Red running in my direction, and

I slip back through the bent bars of the fence and flatten myself against the hedge. I drop the duffel bag to the ground. My heart is hammering in my chest.

"They'll be back soon!" Alpha yells. "Capture immediately, and use any force you deem necessary."

Red doesn't say anything. I wonder if he's already suspecting that Alpha isn't being entirely truthful. After all, he's about to save my ass and call in SWAT after he learns the truth about Alpha.

Less than a minute later, there's a series of loud *zips*, followed by lots of screaming.

"My sister!" Indigo wails. "Help her! Help her!"

My entire body is shaking, and it's not from the cold. I don't even feel that anymore. I slide a branch out of the way and peek my head around. Yellow is on the ground. Indigo and Violet have crouched down next to her. Indigo's hands are covered in blood. Green is holding Blue—Tyler Fertig—with his hands clasped behind his back. Red rushes over to Yellow. He pushes Violet and Indigo out of the way and puts two fingers on her neck.

"Still breathing!" he yells to Alpha.

Alpha doesn't move.

Red keeps one hand on Yellow and puts the other to his ear. He bends his neck into his chest and says something into his earpiece. I take a step forward to try to hear.

A stick cracks and breaks beneath my feet.

Red's head whips up, and I let go of the branch and drop to the ground. No more peeking. I'm trapped here until the old me chases Alpha into the building. Making a move now is too risky.

And so I stay here, crouched on the ground, reliving one of the worst days of my life. An ambulance wails onto campus. More sirens follow. My teammates pile into cars. The tires squish in the mud, leaving a damp smell when they depart.

Now only Alpha and Red remain, and I take a slow breath. I close my eyes. I need to prepare for what's about to happen.

And then there are two *pops*. Abe and I are back. I hear my own anguished cry when I think Abe's been shot. I have to clasp my hands over my ears, but it doesn't block out the sound.

I'm trembling. A wave of nausea bubbles in my stomach, then rises up into my throat. I thought I was past this day, that I'd come to grips with everything. I haven't.

The old me is shouting at Alpha now, and in the distance, I hear the helicopters. There's another *buzz* as Alpha Tasers Red, and then I prop myself up and peek through the bushes again.

I watch myself chase after Alpha.

I have to follow.

I push through the bars and pull my hoodie strings tighter. I keep my head down and jog across campus.

"Is that Amanda Obermann?" someone gasps, and I think my heart stops.

But then I glance up to see Jackson Rybaks pointing to the old me who's just sprinted into the science building.

"What's going on?" Ashlee Chroma yells as I brush past her.

I don't look at her. I don't look at anyone. I slip inside the science building and head for the stairs.

"When are you going to give up?" I hear myself shout from the floor above.

I rub my temple and linger in the stairwell. Listening. Waiting.

"Don't do anything stupid," I hear myself say to Alpha.

I close my eyes, and a memory floods the blackness. Right now, Alpha has a gun pointed at my temple.

"I'd give you the same warning," Alpha tells me, "but it seems we're a bit late for that."

And then a door clicks closed.

I sprint down the hall, past the advanced chem lab where I'm locked in with Alpha, and into the biology lab next door. There's yelling in the next room. A scream from me. I think Alpha just held my hand in front of a Bunsen burner. I'm going to throw up. I put both hands on my stomach and bend over. And then the door to the chem lab opens and shuts as Headmaster Vaughn enters, and less than a minute later there's a shot that echoes throughout the entire floor.

Alpha is dead.

Again.

And I do throw up. I retch into a trash can next to the teacher's desk. I shouldn't have thrown in the towel after only one week of the counseling the government arranged for me. I'm not over this.

Shouts come from the hallway. The SWAT team is here. I only have about thirty seconds to make a move, and I'm blowing them!

I remember what they taught me, right here on this campus: how to compartmentalize. I close my eyes and isolate this day. This one day in my history. I allow myself to linger, to revisit, to continue *feeling*, for just a few more seconds. Then I visualize a filing cabinet. One of the big, gray metal ones. I mentally slide open the top drawer and slip this day inside. Then I shut it.

I open my eyes. We're back in business, and I'm about to cause an explosion next door. I slink to the window and open it, to try to minimize the—

BOOM!

I slam to the floor and put my hands over my head. The walls shake. Several of the stools fly across the room. Microscopes dance on the shelves and crash to the ground. Then there's silence.

I push myself up. The walls are swirling in front of me, and I wobble to the side. But I have to do this.

I climb out the window and swing myself into the one next door. The old me is lying unconscious in the hallway. Abe is beside me, yelling. A SWAT guy kneels down next to me. Headmaster Vaughn is in a crumpled heap by the trash can. And the notebook is smoldering right beside him. The notebook that details every mission Alpha sold and for how much.

I leap into the room, scoop up the notebook, then climb back out the window and into the next room.

"Evacuate the building!" SWAT yells from the hallway.

Not good.

I poke my head out the window. I'm three floors up. I can't project yet because SWAT has to find the notebook. And I can't very well leave it in this room because that would lead to questions no one could answer. I turn my head to the right. There's a drainpipe.

That will have to do. I'm out the window again. I grab onto the pipe. It creaks and snaps and pops away from the wall.

No!

I slide down as fast as I can. The pipe bends. No, no, no! I'm level with the second-floor windows. I peer into a lecture hall. Then the pipe breaks away from the wall. I tuck myself into a ball and crash into the bushes below. I land with a thud and groan. I roll my ankles and wrists a few times. Tenderness but no pain. I don't think anything is broken.

There's shouting from above and screaming echoing across campus. I crouch low in the bushes, open the notebook, and flip through. There's an XP entry a few pages in:

XP

150.00

A hundred and fifty grand. I memorize the date. There's another one after a few more pages. And then one more. And that's all I see. Three. *Only three.*

I don't have time to double-check. I ditch the notebook in the bushes, below the chem lab window, and I run off across campus.

No one pays me any attention. Everything is in chaos. Students run screaming to their dorms. Teachers try to usher everyone away from the buildings. I run toward the back corner of campus and squeeze myself through the fence. Then I grab the duffel bag and unzip it. I have to dig for the mission ledger. It's sandwiched behind a wad of cash and a dress that was in style more than a hundred years ago.

I repeat the XP dates out loud, then trace my finger down each of the pages as I look for them. I find all three and put little check marks next to them. And then I close the bag, project to the present—to June—and run toward the bus station.

Everything feels surreal, like I've just woken up and I'm remembering a dream. It's not until I'm on a bus, halfway back to Boston, that I even realize I got on a bus.

We pull into South Station, and I think about hopping in a cab, but instead I opt for the subway. It's more anonymous, and anonymity keeps me safe. I have to catch two trains, but soon I'm climbing the steps at Copley Square. The Boston Public Library is right across the street. I look both ways before I run across Boylston on a "Don't Walk" and in through the front doors.

I head for the computers and put the duffel bag on the empty seat next to me. *Breathe. Breathe.* I take a minute. Two minutes. I close my eyes and focus on my breath. It's what my training tells me to do. The only way I can think of to ground myself.

When I open my eyes, I feel only marginally better, but I'm not shaking anymore. I grab the mission ledger and find the first check mark. I type "511 Tenth Street NW, DC, April 14, 1865" into the search engine and chew on my bottom lip as I hit Enter, because that date sounds very familiar. When the results come up, I feel like I've been punched in the throat.

The Lincoln assassination.

XP had a hand in the Lincoln assassination.

I sit back in my chair. Five minutes ago, I was hot, sweaty, and jumpy from all the adrenaline. Now I feel like I'm sitting in a freezer. My hands tremble.

Eagle Industries assassinated two presidents? I want to know the answer to this question, but I'm also beginning to understand the term "ignorance is bliss."

I put Lincoln to the side for a minute and go on to the next mission. 426 Marlborough Street right here in Boston on August 25, 1962. I type it in.

Nothing comes up. A few real estate links, a few present-day, city government PDFs, but nothing like Lincoln. Nothing obvious. That's weird. I delete the street address and just type in the date and the city. The first page of results is for a Red Sox–Indians game, so maybe that's something? Fenway isn't that far away from Marlborough. But I keep scrolling. Page after page.

And then I get a really funny feeling in the pit of my stomach. On page five, there's an encyclopedia entry for the Boston Strangler. I click on it. A bunch of women were killed beginning in August of 1962. Is that related? Every instinct in my body is telling me this isn't about a baseball game. This has something to do with a serial killer.

And I don't like it. Not one little bit.

I keep reading and scroll down to the few paragraphs on the murders themselves. Fourteen single women, murdered in and around Boston, from 1962 to 1964. Each of them had willingly let the murderer into her house, only to be sexually assaulted and strangled, most often using her own nylon stockings. I shudder.

In October of 1964, a suspect was arrested. His name was Albert DeSalvo. He was convicted but, later, doubts began to swirl. It's now thought that the murders were the work of a number of killers, probably an original and one or more copycats.

I shudder again. Copycat killers. Those people are even more messed up than regular serial killers.

I look over the names and descriptions of the victims. They're all women who lived alone, but that's all they have in common.

The youngest was 19. The oldest was 85. They're different races, different ethnicities, different socioeconomic backgrounds. We spent only a semester at Peel studying FBI profiling techniques, but even I could tell you this is likely not the work of only one person.

Is XP . . . a serial killer? Is it a side hobby? What is this?

I move on to the last mission, and I pause. Because I know the address. A first grader could tell you the address.

1600 Pennsylvania Avenue.

The White House.

And then I look at the date. I know it, too. Ariel just told me about it.

October 27, 1962. Right smack in the middle of the Cuban Missile Crisis.

CHAPTER 22

I close the browser. What the hell does XP have to do with the Cuban Missile Crisis? With the very first Annum Guard mission?

Wait, what if XP is . . . Ariel? *No.* The thought has barely entered my mind before I realize how ridiculous it is. Ariel isn't XP. XP must have tampered with the mission later on. It's the only explanation.

I have to follow these leads. Location-wise, it would be much easier to go to the Boston mission first, then do both DC missions at once, but logic is telling me I should go to them in order, the way XP commissioned them. Like following a trail of breadcrumbs.

Lincoln it is.

I sling the duffel bag over my shoulder and jog down the stairs, toward the door. I pass the security guard.

"Hang on!" he says, slipping his fingers under his bulging stomach and into his belt loops. He hoists his pants up. "I need to check your bag."

I stare at the duffel. It's full of clothing and money from other eras, which is going to lead to a bunch of unnecessary questions. So I hug the bag to my chest and barrel through the door at a sprint.

"Hey!" the guard shouts. "Stop! Someone stop her!"

The guard certainly doesn't chase after me—no one does—but still I run. I slow down around Arlington Street. I need to find a place to project. I jog across the street, and before I know it, I'm approaching Annum Hall.

I didn't even realize I was coming back here.

Abe is inside. Yellow. Red.

My heart pangs. I haven't been gone very long, but . . . I miss them. All of them. Someone I've come to know as more than a leader. Someone who's become the closest thing to a best friend I've ever had. And someone who's my everything. For now, for always, no matter the bumps we hit. An image of Mike flashes in my mind, and anger erupts in my chest. I let him kiss me. What was I thinking?

I'm stupid for coming here. I whip out my watch and set it for four in the morning of April 13, 1865—almost forty-two hours before the Lincoln assassination. I pause. That's pretty far back. Every hour in 1865 is about twenty here. That's . . . whoa. That's thirty-five days. On one mission. I wish I could travel to DC in the present and project from there, but that's not as safe. They're going to be anticipating that. They won't count on me giving up more than a month of my life and taking a train the night before. But *damn*. Thirty-five days.

It is what it is. See you on the other side, July.

I shut the watch face. When I land, I'm in Civil War–era Boston.

I've been to the latter half of the nineteenth century before. Several times. It's starting to feel familiar. Not quite like *my* home, but maybe the home of an aunt we visit several times a year. I look at the carriages parked in front of brownstones the same way I'd look at an old, battered mailbox. They're comfortable. Comforting.

I could use some comfort right now.

Boston is asleep at this hour, so I grab the dark-gray dress out of the duffel bag and duck into a doorway on a side street. I put on the soft corset so the dress has some hopes of fitting, then slip the dress over my head and zip it up. It's designed to look like it buttons up in the back but has one very key modern convenience. Finally, I pull the shoes on my feet. They're stiff leather booties, not nearly as comfortable as my running shoes. But they draw less attention.

I cross Beacon Street and trot down the steps into the Common. The park is deserted. It's just me and my thoughts. Me and my thoughts. Me and the terrified voice of Jane Bonner, of Marie Quail. The ghost of Alpha. Memories I'd like to forget. More questions than answers.

I put my hand on the back of my neck, where the tracker is. As much as I want to—*need to*—follow this lead, I know it could end any second now. Red might send someone for me. He's going to want to know what happened to Bonner.

But something tells me if he hasn't come for me yet, he's not going to.

I'm heading toward South Station. I wander through the downtown district and pass by one closed shop after another. Then there's a bakery with light spilling from the window. I watch a baker pound dough on a butcher block. He catches me staring and frowns, then tilts his head as if to say "Move along."

I know what he's thinking. There's only one profession that would have a woman wandering the streets in the wee morning hours in 1865. And there's no point in correcting his assumptions, so I keep walking.

I've been to South Station a lot lately. It's easy to find, a massive brick building by the water that stretches an entire block. Still, making this walk so long ago is disorienting. There are no sidewalks on the cobblestone streets and no skyscrapers to help me find my bearings. And then I'm at the water.

Wait, what?

I spin around. There's no South Station. It should be there. Right there, where there's . . . nothing. A tract of land. *Oh, not good.*

"Excuse me!" A young man is loading bricks into the back of a horse-drawn cart. I rush over to him. He's dressed in dirty pants and a shabby black cap.

He turns to me. "Miss?" He's missing at least two teeth.

"I need to catch a train. Could you point me toward the station?"

"A train at this hour? Ain't no trains at this hour."

"I need to depart first thing," I say firmly.

"Where you heading?" I can't tell if he's being creepy or just curious, so I hesitate. I'm really not looking for trouble. But then he adds, "What station you need depends on where you goin'."

My shoulders relax. He's being helpful, that's all. "Oh. Washington."

The man's nose scrunches. "You do realize there's a war bein' fought right now."

"I . . . yes. I do." I clear my throat. "But it's important that I get to Washington immediately."

The man nods with a disbelieving look on his face. "You can try to catch a B&O train to Baltimore, and then try to find another one into Washington from there. The station's at Utica and Kneeland."

Utica and Kneeland. My mind maps it in the present day. "In Chinatown?"

The man laughs. "In what?"

I bite my lip. "Never mind. Thank you." And then I run.

The station is small and cramped, nestled in between a garment factory and an Irish grocery on a dirty, dingy street. The station's also closed. I sigh and lean against the side of the building.

As the sun rises, the streets fill. Horses clomp by, leaving an odor of manure and earthiness. There are carriages hauling lumber, dry goods, animals off to slaughter, and people covered in layers of grime. The whole place reeks with the scent of unwashed skin and soiled clothing. I grit my teeth and wait.

As soon as the station opens, I buy a ticket on the Baltimore and Ohio line. The train leaves at 10:30 a.m. and is due to arrive in Baltimore . . . sometime. That's as specific as the man at the ticket counter can get. He looks at me with a slack jaw and mumbles that we might be taken over and forced out so the Union army can transport goods. There's no twinkle in his eye, no humor in his voice, so apparently this is a very real possibility.

I splurge and buy a ticket in the most expensive compartment available because, if this becomes an overnight trip, I have no desire to sleep sitting up in a dining car. Plus, it turns out I took a crap load of money from the safe. Enough to probably *buy* my own train.

The train starts boarding at ten, six hours after I arrived in 1865. That's 120 hours—*five days*—in the present.

No.

Blackout. That's what I have to worry about now. "Traveling alone, miss?"

I jolt and turn around. There's a man standing behind me. He's well dressed in a dark-gray suit. He's taken off his top hat and is holding it close to his chest, along with a black walking stick with a marble top. No luggage. The man looks to be mid-forties, maybe? He has a soft, rounded face and a midsection to match. He smiles at me, and I know it's meant to be friendly, but still my hackles are raised. I'm probably reading too much into this. I know that a young woman traveling alone in the nineteenth century is an eye-raiser, especially with a war going on.

"Oh, no," I say, returning his smile. "My chaperone is already in our car. I just stepped out for a moment."

The man gives me a quick nod and another smile, and I'm probably reading too much into this, too, but it's not as friendly. And then his gaze travels down to the duffel bag in my hand. I squeeze the handles but don't hide it from view. That would raise even more suspicion.

"Have a good day, miss," the man says, before walking in the opposite direction.

I watch him slide open a door and disappear into the next compartment. New strategy: stay hidden in my car until we arrive in Baltimore.

I don't make eye contact with anyone as I find my car. I'm in a long compartment with two rows of paired benches, one facing forward and the other backward, and a center aisle. And that's it. No beds. What? I specifically asked for a sleeper car. I glance down at my ticket again to make sure I'm at the right car. I am.

A porter with dark-brown skin rushes forward and takes hold of my bag. I instinctively snatch it back, so hard that he stumbles. He looks at me with wide eyes.

I give a forced laugh to diffuse the tension. "I'm sorry; you startled me."

"I apologize, miss. Would you like me to stow . . . er"—he looks at the duffel—"your bag?" He holds out his hand for it, but I wave him off.

"I've got it." I'm sure this is not normal behavior for the time—a young woman fighting to keep her very odd-looking bag—but I'm not letting it out of my sight.

I can see him debating whether to argue, but ultimately he just nods and gestures to my ticket. He looks down at it, then indicates I'm in the third bench on the right.

Well, at least I'm facing forward. I drop into my seat. The train is half full at this point. Heading to my compartment are men in top hats and suits, and women in long dresses or long skirts and crisp white shirts with necks so high they could strangle you with one wrong turn. Heading to the back of the train are Union soldiers dressed in blue uniforms with hats that stand straight in the back and slouch in the front. I'm sure Yellow would know the correct term.

I keep my head down, glancing up only briefly whenever another passenger enters the car. I'm looking out for that man I met on the platform. But he's not here. I feel relieved.

The last passengers arrive, and I stare at the empty bench directly across from mine, facing me. And then I watch a very large, very gruff older woman deposit herself onto it.

"Will you be needing anything else at this moment, Mrs. Withers?" the porter asks her.

"When I need something, George, you'll know it."

Her tone is rude and dismissive. She doesn't even look at him. I give him a sympathetic smile.

"Don't smile at him like that," Mrs. Withers orders me. "You have no idea what his sort is capable of."

My mouth drops open because, one, *who says that?*, and two, *he's standing right there.* I want to tell this woman exactly what I think of her, but I can't. Blend in. That's my story right now.

The porter walks away without another word, and I look out the window.

"Are you traveling alone?" Mrs. Withers asks me. Unlike the man on the platform, there's no joviality in her voice. It's almost an accusation.

I guess I can't lie to her because it's going to be obvious that I'm alone. Sure enough, the train lurches forward on the tracks at that exact moment. We're off. Headed toward Worcester, then Hartford, then down to Baltimore.

I hope.

"Yes," I mutter as I look out the window.

"You're a rude little strumpet, aren't you? Look at me when I'm speaking to you."

I turn from the window and toward this toad of a woman. Wiry silver hair escapes a hat that looks like it's smooshing her bulbous head down into her neck. She narrows dark, beady eyes at me.

"I'm on my way to a funeral," I lie. "I apologize if I'm not in the mood for conversation." And then I turn away. I know I'm in an era where manners and niceties were everything, but that's as polite as she's going to get from me.

I can feel her staring. But if I don't give in and turn my attention to her, eventually she'll get bored and look away. *Rude little strumpet*. Whatever. If she thinks that's the worst insult I've ever heard in my life, she's mistaken. My mom's hurled some good ones at me during her down periods. Ones that involve four-letter words and would require some smelling salts to revive this woman.

I close my eyes. I bet you anything my mom did go back to Vermont, even if just to pack a bag. I should have called our neighbor, Mrs. McNamara, before I left. To tell her that there might not be any money in the mail this month but that I'd think of something soon, and to ask her to keep an eye out for Mom. Not that she really needs the reminder. She's been keeping an eye on both of us for years. Maybe Abe will have thought to call. No, not maybe. He definitely will have thought of it.

Abe.

He must know I'm gone by now. All of them must know. My tracker is still active, but no one's come for me yet. Red has to know that I went to Peel, so they must believe me, right? They must trust me.

Stop, I tell myself. *Stop thinking about them.* XP. That's why I'm here. To find out who XP is. And to avoid being taken out by a blackout squad in the meantime. They're going to get me for sure if I'm not at the top of my game.

I keep one eye trained on the window and the other on my surroundings. The blackout team might not know I'm on this train, but they're definitely going to be expecting me in Washington. XP was involved in the Lincoln assassination somehow. He isn't going to let something that huge go unguarded.

He or *she*, I chide myself. I don't know who's behind this.

Around noon, the porter comes by again. "Pardon me, ladies, I'd like to accompany you to the dining car, if I may."

"It's about time, George," Mrs. Withers says, swaying from side to side to get out of her seat. She grabs the porter's arm, almost yanking him down on top of her as she rises. Then she pushes past him so forcefully he bumps into the seat on the other side of the aisle.

"My apologies, sir," he says to the man whose shoulder he bumped. The man gives a curt smile, and the porter turns back to me and extends a hand.

"Thank you, George," I say, and he winces. *What did I do?*

"My name is Willie, ma'am," the porter says quietly.

"Then why—" But I cut myself off as I see Mrs. Withers glaring at Willie, irritated that he's taken so long to open the door for her. And suddenly I know. Well, I get the gist. George is an insult of some sort, and I'm going to guess it's based on the color of his skin.

"I'm so sorry," I whisper back. "I didn't know."

Willie's face softens, and he gives the smallest nod. Mrs. Withers clears her throat loudly and heads to the door.

"Miss, you can leave your bag here. Nothing will happen to it." Willie tips his head toward my hands.

"I'd rather take it with me, thank you." I grip the handles tighter.

Mrs. Withers clucks her tongue. "Am I supposed to open this door myself, George?"

"Of course not, ma'am," Willie calls up to her; then he turns back to me. "As you wish, miss." He lets me pass.

"It's as if no one cares about service anymore," Mrs. Withers says as Willie slides the door open. She shoves past him, and I slink through behind her. Willie brings up the rear.

We have to pass through three passenger cars before we get to the dining car. It's packed, but my eyes zero in on one person. I scoot around Mrs. Withers to get a better look, to make sure I'm right. My mouth goes dry.

"I'm not hungry," I say. "Willie, would you please escort me back to the car?"

But it's too late. Because the man from the platform has already looked up and caught my eye. He's sitting at a table only a few feet away with another man, whose back is to me. The man from the platform is pointing right at me.

The other man hands him several bills, which he shoves into his pocket. He stands and hightails it in the opposite direction, disappearing into another car. Then the man who's still seated turns to face me. And I realize he's not a man at all. He's only a couple of years older than I am.

It's Tyler Fertig.

And I *know*.

Old Blue is part of the blackout team.

And he's here for me.

CHAPTER 23

"Tyler!" I gasp. I'm not sure what I'm hoping for. That the murderous look on his face will melt into a smile? That some resemblance to the guy I used to know at Peel will peek through?

But the Tyler I know is gone. He's been gone for a while. He pushes his chair back and stands, then lets his napkin drop casually to the table.

"I told you I could wait," Tyler says, "but now I don't have to anymore."

Fear pricks the back of my neck. The Tyler I know is *long* gone. This Tyler is here to hurt me. Just like he hurt Orange and Indigo? Zeta?

I turn and run smack into Mrs. Withers, who's blocking the entire doorway. I look back. Tyler is taking his time. He knows I'm trapped.

"Move!" I bark. Mrs. Withers raises an eyebrow at me and I can see her anger rising higher, higher, higher. She opens her mouth to let it loose, but then she focuses on something—someone—behind me. On Tyler.

"Please move!" I hiss.

She does, and I push past her. I tear through one compartment, then another, and I hear laughter following me. He's laughing at me. Like this is some big joke.

He's close. I run into my compartment. It's empty. Everyone is in the dining car. Tyler slams the door shut behind him, and I shove my bag over my arm and keep running. I throw myself into the door at the other end and jiggle the handle. It won't turn. I flatten my back against the door.

"What do you want from me, Tyler?"

He smiles. "I think you already know the answer to that question."

He's not going to answer any of my questions, but I can't help but ask them. "Who sent you?"

He says calmly, "Oh, I think you already know the answer to that."

I do. XP.

"Where's the other man?"

He looks genuinely puzzled for a moment, but then he lets out a small laugh, like I just made a joke. "Oh, Iris, come on. You can't tell he's just someone I met on the platform and hired to watch out for a young woman with dark-brown hair, traveling alone? What were your grades like at Peel? Or are you letting your paranoia get the best of you?"

I don't want to fight Tyler, but I will. I bend my knees into a crouch. Tyler looks like he's packed on twenty pounds of muscle and grown several inches since I last saw him, but I know that's not possible. I *just* saw him.

The door on the other side of the car slides open. Mrs. Withers is standing there, hands on hips.

"What's this all about?" she asks.

"None of your business," Tyler says without turning. "Go back to the dining car."

Mrs. Withers looks at me, but I don't respond. No eye raise, no pleas for help. What can she possibly do besides make the situation worse?

"You leave that girl alone," she says. "She's on her way to a funeral."

Tyler snorts. "Yeah, her own."

And then terror seizes me. He wants to *kill* me. Are Orange and Indigo really dead? Zeta, too? I must be very close to the truth. I reach behind me and grab the handle again.

"I've already alerted the porter," Mrs. Withers says. "There will be twenty men in this car in less than a minute."

"Minute's too long. I won't need all that." Tyler reaches into his jacket pocket and takes out a small cylinder, and then with one flick of the wrist, he shakes it, and it expands into a long pole. It looks like what Violet described, the same weapon they used to get Indigo.

"What is that?" I demand as Tyler twirls it around like a baton.

"Makes dual projection a snap." He snaps the fingers of his other hand for emphasis.

Dual projection. How two Guardians can travel together to the same point in time. This is how Tyler is able to take us.

"And it jams the signal in your tracker. It's a twofer."

I'm a piglet trapped in the back of the pen, staring down a farmer with a butcher knife. But Mrs. Withers doesn't seem to see the danger. Or she doesn't care. She barrels down the aisle and throws a shoulder into Tyler.

"I told you, you're going to leave her alone!"

He whips around, his elbow raised. It connects with the side of the old woman's skull, and she crumples to the floor.

He doesn't even flinch. He walks toward me. I scan the car, looking for anything I can use as a weapon.

I lunge forward and grab a man's walking stick, lying across one of the benches. I slam it against Tyler's ear as he reaches for me. He howls and stumbles back. But only for a moment. Then he lurches at me. I raise the stick, and he raises a hand in anticipation, so at the last second I swing it low. It hits his leg with a *crunch*. He buckles in pain and lets out a scream, but I don't think I've broken his kneecap. I didn't use enough force. I've only bought myself a second or two.

That will have to do.

I leap onto the seat on my right and I pick up the edge of the dress and scramble over the back of the seat. Tyler tries to get to me, but I'm too fast. He grabs the sleeve of my dress, but I twist away and over the back of the next seat. Then I hop into the aisle and run.

I barrel over Mrs. Withers as she stirs on the floor and offer her a silent *thank you* for her momentary distraction.

Tyler shouts behind me. He's grunting. I push through the door, wedging my way between a group of men who've returned from the dining car.

I need to get off this train! I reach into my dress and pull my watch out. I can project and be safe in a second.

But I need to get to Washington, too. If I project now, my watch will never be able to come back to this date. It's a limit of our Annum watches—they can never return to the same date twice. Projecting would mean abandoning the Lincoln assassination, at least for now.

Dammit!

"There's nowhere to hide!" Tyler shouts behind me, and he's right. This train is a prison and a bull's-eye all at once. What am I going to do, keep running the aisles until we get to Baltimore?

No, I have only one option. I turn the knobs on my watch and meet Tyler's gaze. "Until next time," I say with a smile that's more nervous than confident. I slam the face shut.

I'm shot up. The pressure builds in the back of my throat, like I swallowed a rock, as I fly though time. I'm ripping through time, stretching, straining. Projecting without the protection of the gravity chamber is hell. I can't breathe. My bones are popping and cracking. I can't take this—

I land in the exact same spot, sixty-three years and four days later. I land on my feet but stumble and immediately go down. My knees crash into the wooden railroad ties. I allow myself one yell, then I roll off the tracks and down a short embankment. I push off the ground and stand. My dress is torn, one huge gash right at my knees.

It's . . . I do the math . . . 1928. And I have no idea where I am. Somewhere in between Boston and Worcester. Railroad tracks are the only thing I see in either direction. No towns. No streets. No buildings. There's nothing. I've gone and stranded myself in the middle of nowhere.

I rifle through the duffel bag. I don't have any clothes for 1928, and it looks like I skipped that part of the money drawer, too. We'd traveled about forty-five minutes. I assume that means I'm close to Worcester? Maybe? I kick at the ground and send a dying clump of grass and dirt into the air. Then I heave a sigh, sling the bag over my arm, and start walking back toward Boston.

I don't know what to do. I could always project back to a few days before the assassination, hop another train, and just wait. But then I'd be giving up way more than thirty-five days of my life. And my teammates can't wait that long.

Or I could call it a loss and move on to the Boston Strangler. Goose bumps dot my arms as I think of it. I really don't want to do the Strangler mission. Really *really* don't want to do it.

So I think about Tyler. XP got to Tyler. I shake my head. It's so obvious, I can't believe we didn't really consider it before. Each of our Annum watches costs something like twenty million dollars a pop. Tyler's watch only works with his DNA, so he's essentially free labor for XP. Plus, Tyler has a serious vendetta against our organization.

My mind races with questions. Violet said there were two people who snatched Indigo, so there's at least one other member of the blackout team. Who? Another Guardian? Is Tyler's tracker still active? If it's not, how will we ever find him? And how did Tyler get his watch back in the first place?

I look up. In the distance, a building rises into the sky, and I take off at a trot, then break into a run. I forgot how good it feels to sprint, to forget about everything and just focus on how fast you can go.

I also forgot how much sprinting takes out of you, especially in a stiff dress and booties. I stop and bend over, gasping for breath, then decide on a brisk walk. I find the main road and stick to the shoulder. Cars zoom past me, and I don't want to get hit. Well, "zoom" is a bit of an overstatement. They're topping out at like twenty-five miles per hour.

I'm getting stares. Lots of them. Mostly from the women, looking my weird dress up and down. I keep my eyes on the cars as they pass.

One creeps by at about ten miles an hour. A Ford Model T. There's a girl in the passenger seat who is about my age. She's laughing and shrieking at something and brushes a strand of bobbed hair from her face. She has both legs propped up on the dash and a bottle of clear liquid raised to her lips. Moonshine, most likely. I'm pretty sure we're still in the middle of Prohibition.

Her dress is a sleeveless silk number with a short hemline. It's obviously expensive. She makes eye contact with me for a brief second and winks. Not a friendly wink. A wink of superiority. I narrow my eyes at her. Yeah, go ahead and wink. You won't be winking a year from now when the stock market crashes and that little silk dress goes the way of your savings account.

That was mean.

I wish Abe was here. He'd tell me that was mean, and then I would admit that it was mean, and then we'd laugh about how it would take a week to drive from Boston to New York in that car.

I wait until the car is completely out of view, then I turn to make sure another isn't coming. There's a horse-drawn carriage half a mile down the road, but they shouldn't be able to see me. I drop the duffel bag, take hold of my right sleeve, and yank against the shoulder seam. It takes several pulls, but eventually it rips. I tear off the sleeve, then start on the left. Then I bend down, grab a handful of fabric right below where it's already ripped, and pull with all my might, trying to rip it as evenly as possible.

I stand up. I should have left well enough alone. I don't look like I fit in to 1928, I look like I just lost a fight with some old, rusty playground equipment. Threads of various lengths dangle down my arms, and my skirt goes from long to short to long again as it travels around my knees.

I'm going to be run out of this town on a rail.

But what's done is done.

About twenty minutes later, a sign welcomes me to Framingham. Framingham is twenty miles from Boston. That's as far as we got? I head for the building I saw in the distance and discover it's the town hall. The large brick building is held up by eight Corinthian columns that are each two stories high. The words "Framingham Memorial" are etched above. The building looks brand new.

There's a restaurant across the street, so I duck inside. Every head turns to look at me, and I grimace.

"Good lord, child," says a man with a rag, wiping off a table. He stops and stares at me. "What happened to you?"

"I . . ." I look around. "It's a long story. I'm trying to get back to Boston. Can you point me toward the train station?"

"I can show you," a voice says from the back of the room.

My duffel falls to the floor. I know that voice. I lock eyes on a guy plunking a few coins on a table. He grins.

It's Abe.

CHAPTER 24

I can count on one hand the number of times I've been so thoroughly and completely shocked that I forget how to speak. The first was when I was seven and I found my mom passed out cold on the bathroom floor. I stood there, staring, for what felt like hours, my little first-grade brain incapable of processing what was happening. The second was when the woman from Peel showed up unannounced on our doorstep the summer after eighth grade. She introduced herself and extended a hand, and all I did was look at it—this foreign hand offering me a way out. The third was just a few months ago, when I found out who my dad really was and how he died.

And now this is number four. My mouth drops open, and I gaze into eyes that are so familiar to me. Are they mad? Suspicious?

No. They're not. They're warm, hopeful.

I have to restrain myself from leaping at him. He walks up to me, and I stand there like a statue. He pulls a tweed cap out of his back pocket and plops it on his head.

He smiles at me and holds open the door. "Ma'am?"

I blink, then blink again, then walk out into the sunlight. And then I throw myself at him. I wrap my arms around his neck and inhale. The scent of adventure bodywash fills my nostrils and leads me back to Annum Hall, to Peel, to Ariel's house, to all of the places I've smelled it before. Everything is forgotten.

"What are you doing here?" I whisper into his neck. "Did everyone see my note?"

He reaches for my hand. "Everyone wants answers, but no one thinks you had anything to do with whatever happened to Bonner. Well, at least no one from Annum Guard."

"But that means . . . who?" A man loading chicken crates into a wooden-framed truck bed looks up at us, so I duck my head and pull Abe farther down the sidewalk.

"It's all being kept very hush-hush. No Boston PD, very limited number of feds. A special FBI task force made up of those with the highest clearance levels."

"And they think I had something to do with it?"

"They want to know where you are." He pauses. "Red has your back on this. He had me disable your tracker right after you projected here. He sent me to find you. I overrode my tracker, too."

Another Model T goes whizzing past at about ten miles an hour. I watch it for a few seconds, then turn back to Abe. "Does Red want me to come back?"

"The opposite. Red wants you—us—to keep digging. We're not going to get this opportunity again. With Bonner gone, Red has better access to old mission ledgers. He's got Yellow, Green, and Violet following up on a few more leads. And here"—he reaches into his back pocket again and pulls out two folded pieces of newspaper—"you have to see this."

I take the papers, then park myself on one of the steps leading up to Memorial Hall. There are all sorts of people around. Men wearing flat-brimmed straw hats rushing up the stairs, women with bobbed hair wearing shapeless dresses walking down the sidewalk. A few of them eye my dress, but only for a moment.

I look down at what Abe's given me. The first clipping is from the society pages, dated about ten years ago. Well, ten years ago from the present. The half-page spread is devoted to pictures from a charity golf event. I wrinkle my nose. "What is this?" But then I spot a picture of Secretary Howe. He's standing next to a man I've never seen before. The man is probably in his late fifties. He's wearing a golf shirt and light pants. I look down at the caption:

National Defense CEO Francis Howe
and National Defense COO Alexander Quail

Quail.

"Wait, is that . . . is that Bonner's *dad*?" I drop my voice lower as two older women on the sidewalk shoot disapproving glances in my direction. "Her dad was the chief operating officer of Howe's company?"

Abe nods, then juts his chin toward the picture. "And an old golf buddy."

"So her dad basically got her the job at Annum Guard?"

Abe nods again. "Yep."

"But that doesn't make any sense. Why? And that doesn't explain why she changed her name to Jane Bonner."

"There's something else. We found her file. Seems that after college, Marie bounced around jobs for a few years, but then eight years ago, she got a new position." He looks at me, like he wants me to say something.

"Um, okay . . ."

"Working on then–Senator Caldwell's reelection campaign."

"The vice president?" I practically shout, then duck my head. A group of boys playing a game with a stick and a thin wooden wheel are staring at me. And I don't know why I'm so surprised by this revelation. I mean, I saw at the party that the VP and Bonner have known each other a while, but I find it hard to believe that they worked together. Caroline Caldwell looked like she wanted to knife Bonner at Leighton's house. Then I remember how Joe Caldwell ogled her, and something clicks.

Was Bonner involved with Joe at some point? Hang on, is *that* why Caroline Caldwell asked me to exercise discretion? She thought there was a chance I'd find out about it, and she didn't want it going public?

"Vice President Caldwell ruined Bonner's reputation, didn't she?" I ask Abe.

"Obliterated it with the force of an atomic bomb is a more accurate description."

I look at the second clipping. It's a long article.

"Do you remember that big, campaign finance scandal when we were in, like, seventh grade?" Abe asks.

"No." What seventh grader remembers something like that? Besides Abe. He grew up in a family where CNN and PBS were the only TV stations allowed and where NPR was a constant on the car radio. We've played this "Do you remember . . . ?" game a lot. I always lose. My mom likes reality TV and old-school Madonna.

"Anyway, Marie took the fall. She admitted to taking money from corporations that had hidden their identities to give more than they're legally allowed. There was a special prosecutor assigned. Caldwell testified against Marie, and after that, Marie took a plea deal." He pauses. "She went to prison, Mandy."

My mouth falls open.

"Marie served eighteen months. When she got out she stayed low for a while, but then, like a year ago, she popped back up on the radar screen as Jane Bonner."

"How did she get the Annum Guard appointment with that kind of past?"

"Think about it. She's the perfect lackey to a corrupt government official. Someone on the straight and narrow isn't exactly going to be lining up for that job. Howe needed someone he could use, someone he could manipulate. Someone who wouldn't go digging into Eagle. Red thinks she must have panicked when we started disappearing and was going to turn on Howe, and that's why . . . well, they got to her."

It all makes sense, but something is still nagging me. "Howe is XP then?"

"All signs point to him, yeah."

"But I saw a man with Bonner. The man who took her. I only saw the back of him, but it wasn't Howe. This man was much bigger, much bulkier."

Abe shrugs. "It was probably someone who works for Howe."

I hand Abe the clippings and stand. "So now we need evidence."

"We need evidence," Abe echoes.

"Has the bug picked up anything on Mike?"

"Nothing much. A few things we're looking into, but so far, nothing we can use."

I pause for a second to gather my nerves. "And where are you and I on the Mike front?" I'm trying to keep things professional, but I know I probably just sound awkward.

He sighs. "Obviously, I don't like knowing that you kissed him—he kissed you—whatever. But unless you say otherwise, I'm going to assume that whatever you did, you did out of necessity in order to plant the bug."

"I'm not going to say otherwise." Even if the truth is somewhere on the gray spectrum.

"Then you and I are fine," Abe says.

I interlace my fingers in his, and this time he squeezes them back.

We start walking toward the train station in town. "I blew the first XP mission. Blackout was on the train."

Abe gasps. "And you got away?"

"Barely. It was only one person." I hesitate. "Tyler Fertig. One of us."

"We have to tell someone. We have to warn the others."

"I know."

"Let's go back now."

I shake my head. "I'm sure we're going to run into him again on the next XP mission . . . which is the Boston Strangler." I hear the edge in my voice. I don't know why this one is creeping me out so much. I've had plenty of training running around in dark warehouses at Peel, unsure of what dangers lurked ahead. I guess I've just always found the idea of killers who prey on victims like they're hunting animals to be horrifying. I had nightmares for a solid month when we studied serial killer patterns at Peel.

"We can take Tyler down on that mission, just us," I say.

"But what about the other blackout member? Violet said there were two."

"I think we can handle it. I just . . . I don't want to put anyone else at risk. You and I are the best trained to handle combat situations. Yellow would be useless right now. Violet is . . . not the best with these situations." I remember how she nearly chickened out on the Gardner mission, which now seems like a lifetime ago. "And I just don't trust Green enough to let him in on this. But you . . ." I reach out and squeeze his hand. "You, I trust."

Abe purses his lips together for a moment. "I think you're wrong, Mandy. And I think you're selling everyone else short. The smart thing is to go back now and get more help. Think with your head, not your heart."

A little voice nags me that Abe's right, that we'd be much better equipped to handle the blackout squad if we're at our full numbers. But then I think of losing Yellow or Violet or even Green . . . I can handle myself. Abe has a black belt.

"Abey, I really think it should just be us."

Abe is silent, but then he blows out a breath and nods. "Okay. We'll do it together. But what in the world does XP have to do with a serial killer?"

"I have no idea, but whatever it is, it can't be good. Especially considering the first mission—the one I abandoned—was the assassination of Abraham Lincoln."

What if XP is a murderer? And not like my old headmaster or—I hate that my mind goes there—like my dad. Not someone who kills for money. No, someone who stalks his prey. Someone who kills just to kill. Someone who gets off on the psychological mind games.

I shudder again.

"Since Vaughn worked for XP, that means XP killed *two* presidents?" Abe says.

"I don't know. I don't know if we'll ever know."

"What's the third mission? Do I even want to know?"

I run a hand through my messy hair. "Probably not. But the third mission is the Cuban Missile Crisis."

"Okay? Why are you saying it like that—like you know something I don't?"

"Because." I pause. "That night at your grandparents' house? Ariel told me about the very first mission he went on. Annum Guard's very first mission ever. It was the Cuban Missile Crisis. It wasn't just a crisis. We dropped a bomb. Moscow retaliated. Fifteen million people died. But Ariel—he stopped it. He saved all of us."

"What?" Abe's voice is barely a whisper.

"I'm sorry I didn't tell you before."

Abe shakes his head. "This doesn't make any sense. How is the third mission the Cuban Missile Crisis? If what you told me is true, then my grandfather was—in on it? No. Someone messed with it later? I don't understand." I can see him thinking, puzzling through the same things I am. Which is to say he has a jumble of thoughts running together in his head like a herd of sheep fleeing a dog. He shakes his head, like this will make all of the thoughts fly out of his brain.

"So, Boston then?" I say.

He nods silently.

There's a train heading back into the city, but neither Abe nor I have the correct money.

"We either steal, which is risky as well as illegal, or we project to 1962, which is where we have to go anyway," I say. "I've got plenty of money for 1962."

"Sounds like you've made up your mind there already, cowboy."

"Please don't ever call me cowboy again."

Abe laughs. It's warm, a beam of light that shines on me, on him, on us. We're okay. Just like I knew we would be. I interlace my fingers with his, and he squeezes my hand. "What's the date we're going to?"

"Hang on." I dig the printout from the bag and unfold it, then I let go of Abe's hand to flip to the second page. There's really not much to go on, just the date and location of the mission. "August 25, 1962. We're going to be in the Back Bay."

"What time of day?"

"Um"—I look again—"just after ten thirty p.m."

"So let's go back in the morning. That will give us plenty of time to get to Boston."

We duck inside the station bathrooms to project. I lock myself into the farthest stall and hold my breath. I pray for two things. One, that this is still a bathroom in 1962, and two, that I'm not about to project on top of some woman doing her business thirty-four years from now.

I slam my watch face shut and fly up. My limbs stretch and pop and burn, and I want to scream. A few seconds later, I land in the same spot and finally let out my breath and gasp for air.

I'm in a bathroom. An unoccupied bathroom. A lucky break. Of course, it is six in the morning. I take a second to contemplate changing into that hideous polyester jumpsuit from the seventies that's in my bag but decide against it. It's ten years from being in style. We'll deal with clothing in Boston.

The platform is outside, and there's a slight morning chill in the air, but I find it familiar and reassuring. Abe and I park ourselves on a bench. It's Saturday, so the train isn't running that often.

I scoot close to Abe so that our legs are touching. He doesn't tense or move away. "I have to warn you that I have no idea what we're in for. According to what I found online, there was no murder on August 25. At least not one attributed to the Strangler."

"So either XP murdered someone and hoped it would be pinned on the Strangler, or he . . . saved one of the victims?"

I shrug. "Those seem to be the only two options. I guess we'll find out."

There's a high-pitched wail of metal against metal as the commuter train locks its brakes and slides into the station. I stuff the printout back into the bag, then Abe and I climb aboard and find seats next to each other. It's not that hard. This early, there's only one other person on the train. An old woman so short her legs don't touch the floor. She has a blue kerchief tied around her head and two large shopping bags piled haphazardly on the seat next to her. She eyes my dress as Abe and I walk past her.

It's a short ride into Boston. They've made some improvements on train speed since 1865. The train drops us at the Back Bay station, which in true Boston fashion technically is in the South End, not the Back Bay. We need to get out of these clothes—people stare at us left and right—but it's still too early for any shops to be open. So we head for 426 Marlborough Street to scope it out. It's at the very far end of the Back Bay, just a hop, skip, and jump on the green line from the Mass. Ave. T stop. We stare at the three-story brownstone with shiny, black French doors. The building looks like the hundreds of others that line the streets of the Back Bay. We're at the less expensive end of a very expensive neighborhood. The street seems just a little dirtier down here, the brownstones not quite as stately. Even so, there's no way I could afford to live here. Like, ever. Not on my government salary. Well, former government salary.

We have a lot of time to waste and not much preparation to do for tonight's mission—I mean, how can we prepare for something when we have no idea what to expect?—so Abe and I wander the city.

As soon as the stores open, we head into Jordan Marsh, the same downtown department store where Yellow and I bought clothes during our last foray into this decade. Walking through the double glass doors into the cosmetics section—waving off a slender redhead armed with a spray perfume bottle—gives me a wicked sense of déjà vu.

The sixties are becoming familiar to me. I've spent a lot of time here now. But it's not a good familiarity. It's one that sets me on edge. Like a visit to a relative you don't really like. A trip you have to endure. This time period brings back memories of death and deceit, lies and corruption.

I pick out a knee-length, kelly-green, A-line dress with thin white stripes across the bodice. It costs nine dollars, which makes me laugh. Nine bucks will buy me a pair of socks and some hair ties in present-day Boston. I drop the duffel bag below the counter, out of the sales clerk's view, and dig through the stacks of twenties. I definitely took too much money.

I change in a dressing room and then find Abe, who's now in a blue striped shirt and light-brown pants that are way tighter than any he owns in the present. We venture outside and stroll around, mostly in a comfortable silence. We pass a woman dressed in black pants that end at her ankles, a cropped silver jacket, and oversize sunglasses. She has dark, wavy hair, just like my mom, and she has an artist's portfolio tucked under her arm. She slips into a gallery on Newbury Street.

She's like the artist mother I always dreamed of. The one with an organized studio and a stable life. Not the manipulative, irrational mess I wound up with.

I'm done.

I don't think I realized it until right this second, but I'm done. No more voice mails, no more begging. If my mom isn't going to change, when we both know she can, I have to walk away, for me.

You have to come first sometimes.

"What about this one?" Abe says.

"Huh?"

He points at a brownstone on the corner of Comm. Ave. and Clarendon Street. "We could live here someday. Top floor, maybe? Something with two bedrooms? Enough room for you and me and baby you-and-me?"

I snort. It's nice to hear Abe talk about the future, but this is the first time he's ever mentioned kids. "Yeah, I'm not having kids."

Abe blinks. "I wasn't talking about right now."

"I know. And I'm talking about ever."

"You don't want children . . . ever?"

"Nope," I say. I've never felt very motherly. When other little girls my age were tucking dolls into play cribs or feeding them with those weird bottles that drain into nothingness when you tip them over, I was busy on the monkey bars. I don't know if it's a nature or nurture thing. Both, I guess?

I refuse to let myself think of my mom anymore. I don't have time for that distraction. If she's not going to get the help she needs, I have to say good-bye. I've been stuck on a constant, loop-ing roller coaster, and it's time to get off, to plant my feet on solid ground.

Focus. It's time to focus. I look at Abe, and there's an ex-pression on his face I've never seen. It's not quite his mad face, not quite his disappointed face. "I'm just being honest," I say. "Besides, I can't see wanting to bring a child into this completely messed up world. And I don't exactly have the tools to teach that kid how to thrive. I'd mess up a kid worse than the world would."

Abe doesn't say anything for a while, and I start panicking a little. What if this is a deal breaker for him?

"There's still plenty of time for you to change your mind," he finally says, and I choose to let the conversation drop. It would take a lot for me ever to change my mind, but this isn't the time or the place for that debate. We have a job to do. We need to get into professional mode.

It's August in New England, so night doesn't begin to fall until around nine. That's one thing I've always loved about living here. The endless summer. Of course, the trade-off is that you're freezing in the winter, and it's dark by 3:45.

We hang around the city all afternoon, grabbing lunch and a quick nap under a tree in the Public Garden. Around nine, we make our way back to Marlborough and wait across the street, on the stoop of number 427. Just after 9:30, a young couple comes out the front door, and Abe hops up to grab the door behind them. They don't say anything as we slip inside, no question whom we're visiting in the building. I love when things are easy.

The door is made from heavy wood and painted black, but there are two windowed side panels. Abe and I each take one and squat down. We have a perfect view across the street, at number 426. And really, that's all we're here to do. Observe.

Well, observe and hide from Tyler, who's bound to show up any second now.

But he doesn't appear. There are a few people walking down the street, but not many, and definitely not Tyler.

"Where is he?" I whisper, even though we're inside and no one on the street can hear us.

"No idea," Abe whispers back. "I thought for sure he'd try to find us before the mission goes down."

"Maybe he isn't coming." But there's a blip of fear bubbling in the back of my throat that I can't ignore. At just after 10:30, the street is deserted. We are on the least populated section of Marlborough, which also happens to be the least trafficked street in the Back Bay. Most people stick to Boylston or Newbury, or even Comm. Ave. It's much more convenient to take any of those, especially when you hop off the T. You have to want to be on this stretch of Marlborough. I can see how some women living alone would find safety in that.

Me, I see it as being a sitting duck.

And sure enough, a few minutes later a lone man staggers down the street. He has dark hair, his jacket is zipped tight, and his hands are in his pockets. His chin is tucked into his chest. It's impossible to get a good look at him from this angle.

All of a sudden, the blip of fear rises into terror. A serial killer. Across the street from me. I look over at Abe. He's still crouched down, and he has his hands in front of him, as if he's waiting for the gun to start a hundred-yard dash.

I know what he's thinking. That we could take this guy out and stop the killer. Or one of them, at least.

"Abe."

He turns his head to me but keeps his eyes trained on the guy across the street, who's jogging up the steps of 426.

I shake my head at Abe, but I don't think he sees me. I turn back. There's a light illuminating the call box on the side of the building, and I see the man press the button that's second from the top.

Shouldn't one of the second-generation Guardians be here? Isn't one of them supposed to intervene soon? XP bought this mission from one of them. And then the thought hits me: *What if this confrontation goes down inside the building?*

Abe and I will miss it. I look over at him again, and I can tell he's just had the exact same thought.

The door across the street opens, and Abe and I stand in unison. We have to get inside somehow!

But just then, Beta—Green's dad—steps from a shadow in 426's vestibule, and Abe and I both freeze. Words are exchanged, then there's a flash of metal as Beta whips out a pocketknife. The killer raises his hands, then bolts down the steps and away from us. Beta flicks the knife closed and heads in the opposite direction, out of sight.

I remember to breathe. My fear is gone, and I feel sort of silly for having been afraid in the first place. That was like the least dangerous situation I've ever been in. Holy letdown.

"What was that?" I ask Abe. "That was the biggest waste of time ever."

Abe nods but keeps looking out the window. "Come on, I don't see anyone."

The two of us jog across the street to 426. Abe peers through the window in the front door while I keep a lookout. I hear the snap of a twig and I jump, but I don't see anyone. There's a rustling of tree branches but no other movement. Still, I can't help but feel that something is off.

"Abey, we need to move."

He's still looking in the window, and I turn to the call box. And then I stop breathing. Because there are names on the call box. Names handwritten by the tenants. There's one next to the second button from the top.

D. Callaway.

We're wrong. It's not Secretary Howe. It's not Mike Baxter.

Colton Callaway Caldwell. A family name, he said. His grand-mother. Yellow was right. XP isn't Cairo as in Egypt. It's Chi Rho as in Jesus Christ. Initials. JC.

Joe Caldwell.

The vice president's husband.

And maybe even the vice president herself.

"Abe!" I yell. "We have to get out of here. Now!"

CHAPTER 25

I grab Abe's hand and yank him off the stoop. "It's Caldwell! XP is Caldwell."

"Colton? But he's not nearly old enough to—"

"No, not Colton—Joe! Which means maybe the vice president knows, which means we need to get the hell out of 1962 *now*."

But then two people are standing there on the sidewalk, and I have no idea how they got there. Abe and I skid to a halt. He squeezes my hand.

Tyler is to our left. There's another guy on the right, dressed head to toe in black. Black combat boots, black cargo pants, long-sleeved black shirt, black vest. And a black ski mask so I can't see his face.

"Joe?" I say, taking a gamble. I'm showing my hand, but I have nothing to lose at this point.

Tyler laughs. "Come on, you don't really think he's here, do you? But good to see you again, Iris. And so soon!"

"So you're not going to deny that XP is Joe Caldwell?" I say.

"What I am going to do," he says as he takes that silver rod from his pocket and flicks it open, "is note how absolutely adorable it is that you two are holding hands. Like children afraid of the dark." He takes a step closer to us. "And trust me, you should be very, very afraid of our dark."

Before I know what's happening, Abe's flying through the air. He spins and lands a kick right across Tyler's jaw. Tyler staggers back and goes sprawling onto the sidewalk.

The other guy rushes me. I raise the bag and swing it into his nose. He stumbles backward, and I don't hesitate. I elbow him, then grab on to him and knee him in the groin. He screams as he sinks to the ground.

I reach into my dress and pull out my watch, then open the face and spin the dials backward. I don't know where I'm going, and it doesn't matter. I just need to grab Abe and project the both of us out of here.

But then the guy has me. He yanks my hand from the watch. "Don't even try." I know that condescending drawl. I reach up and yank off the ski mask, and I'm not surprised to find Colton staring at me with that cocky grin.

All right, prep-school Ivy League, let's see how you do against government training. I lunge forward and throw a punch, but Colton deflects it. He grabs my arm and twists it behind my back. I try to spin away again, but he holds me. He does have training.

I look over at Abe, and panic strikes. Tyler has him in a full nelson, Abe's hands wrapped behind his head. Tyler's got that long metal wand. He hits the top button.

"Abe!" I yell. "No! No!" I squirm, but Colton squeezes my arm and tears prick my eyes. I think he's going to break my wrist.

The silver wand starts to whir—a soft humming at first but then it builds and builds into a shriek, and I match it pitch for pitch.

"Abe!" I keep squirming. I don't care about my wrist anymore.

And then the wand erupts into an arc of light. It showers all of Marlborough in a white glow.

I squint. I can hear Abe shouting over the noise. "I love you, Amanda!" And then there's a scream and a click, and then darkness. Colton lets go of my arm, and I spring away. To where Abe and Tyler should be standing. But they no longer are.

"Where is he? What did you do to him?" I yell at Colton.

Colton shrugs. "Guess you're about to find out." He pulls out another metal wand and slams his palm into the top. It starts glowing and humming. Colton lunges for me, but this time I'm quicker. I sidestep him, sweep his leg out, and knock him to the ground. I kick the metal pole into the gutter.

"Tell me where he is!"

Colton just laughs. I grab my watch again, grab onto Colton's bicep, and slam the face shut.

Both of us are ripped through time. Pain shoots down my arms, threatening to tear my body in two. And then it goes to my legs, to my toes. I'm projecting for both of us, taking the pain for Colton. I try to push the pain out. I'm going to need my strength when we land.

And then we stop. I gasp for air, but instead water rushes into my lungs. I choke and swallow and gag and let go of Colton. I go into survival mode. I kick and find the surface. I spit out water and choke again. I flail and choke and flail and choke, and finally it all comes up. I vomit up a cheeseburger I bought for a dime in 1962 and barely even notice.

I'm under the water again. Two strong hands are pushing me down. I claw at them. Dig my nails in, but it's no use. I kick. I whip myself around, and my chin makes contact with Colton's arm. I open my mouth and sink my teeth in. I feel the skin break and taste blood. And then I'm released.

I come up for air.

"You bitch!" Colton screams. He's treading water and holding his arm. And then he propels himself at me again.

I dive under him and start kicking. I need to get to shore. I need to get Colton to shore. I kick and kick until I can't breathe anymore. I come up gasping. Colton's behind me, swimming quickly. I don't have time to process anything. I launch into a freestyle stroke and sprint toward the shore.

1810, I think. I set the watch for 1810. Because I am a complete moron. I knew the Back Bay wasn't filled until the middle of the nineteenth century. I *knew* this. And still I went and projected myself right into the middle of the damned Charles River.

I'm close to shore. Twenty yards maybe. Colton grabs my ankle and twists, but I take my other foot and smash it into his chest. I feel his grip release, and I swim like hell again. I launch myself onto the shore and, not a second later, Colton is on me.

He grabs my hair and yanks it. I scream, then slam my elbow into his temple. He lets go and staggers back.

"Who pulls hair?" I yell. "What are you, twelve?"

He flies at me again, and I duck, then raise another elbow. It catches him square in the chest, and he falls to the ground. I pounce on top of him. Both of us are yelling and cursing and panting. He tries to push me off, but I take hold of his head, lift it, and ram it into the ground. Once. Twice. Three times. His eyes roll back and he's out.

I check Colton to make sure he's breathing. Then I look up. A crowd is gaping at us in horror. I smile weakly. I don't know where I am. I turn my head and see Beacon Hill and the State House in the distance.

"Alert the authorities at once!" a man shouts. He pushes his way to the front and points at me. "Ma'am, raise your hands and step away from the young man."

I can't imagine what these people must think. A woman dressed in clothing that won't be popular for another hundred and fifty years, pummeling a man dressed all in black. Well, it's time to confuse them even more.

I open the watch face and for a moment I'm afraid that it won't work. But just for a moment. I assume that if the government is going to invest twenty million bucks in time-traveling technology, they'd make sure the damned thing is waterproof. Which they did. My watch is still ticking.

I spin the year dial forward one click, adjust the time so I'll land in the middle of the night, then grab on to Colton. We fly forward and I'm taking it for both of us, but the trip lasts only a few seconds. Then we're in the same spot.

Colton is still unconscious. I check him again. He's breathing. I grunt and roll off of him, then grab his wrist and take off his watch. I hold it up. In many ways, it's similar to my own. There are Y, M, and D dials, but there's no fancy script with the word Annum on the face. Instead there are two boxy letters: X and P.

Whoa. Joe Caldwell bought his own version of Annum Guard. When did he do this? And why?

I have no idea what to do. I have an unconscious Colton on the ground and it's 1811. I have no money. I have no *Abe*.

"I hate you," I whisper to Colton.

Wait. I'm looking at this the wrong way. I have a bargaining chip, right here passed out on the ground. I have the key to getting back Abe, and Zeta, Indigo, and Orange, too. Assuming they're still alive. Assuming all of them are still alive.

Answers, that's what I need.

I glance around. A full moon is high in the sky and the streets are deserted. So I hook my hands under Colton's arms and hoist him up. He's heavy. Maybe a hundred and sixty pounds. But I'm strong. It's been a few weeks since I actually got to the gym, but I can do this. I squat low, hoist Colton's torso over my shoulder, loop the handle of the duffel through my arm, then stand very slowly. I take a few steps to test my balance, then walk, carefully.

Yeah, I'm strong, but we're not going to make it very far, that's for sure. I need to get back to the gym.

A block or so later, there's a small shopping district. I pass a milliner's shop, a shoemaker, a tailor, a stationer. All of the shops are closed, obviously, and from the stink of the street and the grime on the windows, I can tell I'm not in a very wealthy area of Boston. I pass an empty storefront. "HUDSON'S DRAPERY" is written on the front in gold paint that's past its prime. I stop and peer in. There's a wooden mannequin in the middle of the room, which is creepy as hell, and the walls are lined with shelves, all empty save a few crumpled sheets of paper. I squint and stare into the back, where I can see a storeroom and a set of stairs leading to a second floor.

Perfect.

I squat again and let Colton slip off my shoulder onto the ground. My legs are going to kill me tomorrow. I look down the street one more time to make sure we're alone. Then I jiggle the handle. Locked. Of course.

I step back and eye the glass. I could easily toss a rock through, but that could wake the entire block, and at best would only buy us a couple of hours until morning dawns and the damage is discovered. I go to the door and drop to my knees.

This is an easy lock. I could get this open in a second with a credit card, if only I had one of those. Or a business card or anything useful. I look around on the stoop. There's dirt and crushed leaves and . . . some old, bent nails. I use my foot as leverage to bend one of the nails into a hook. I slide another nail into the lock, then use the hook-shaped one to catch the release.

It takes four tries, but then I'm in. I open the door gently, grab Colton's shoulders, and drag him past the mannequin, into the back room, and up the stairs.

The top floor is empty, too. I was hoping for a few abandoned bolts of fabric, something that would help me tie up Colton. But there's nothing like that. Colton is still out. He's not even beginning to stir.

It's damp in here. We're past the point of a small chill. My teeth are chattering. I now understand the expression "cold, wet, and miserable." I am all of these things.

I need to secure Colton. I can tie him to some of the spindles on the staircase railing, no problem, but I need something to tie him *with*. My dress is the only thing I can think of, and that's not happening, so instead I yank on Colton's sleeves until they give way. Then I tie both of his arms to the railing and yank to test the bindings. Colton isn't going anywhere. I rip off his vest, twist out the water, and use it as a gag.

I sink onto the floor. My arms are howling in pain. My legs are in agony. But it's my heart that hurts the most. I lost Abe. I look at Colton. He *stole* Abe.

And just as soon as Colton wakes up, he's going to give me some answers. I don't care what I have to do to get them.

CHAPTER 26

Colton stirs in the early dawn hours. His eyelids flutter and his shoulders drop back. His head rolls to one side, and I wait. Wait for the moment he remembers that he tried to drown me. And the moment he realizes I've got him.

It comes.

His eyes pop open, and his head whips down, then up, then to the side as he tries to look behind him. He thrashes against the railing, his wrists pulling at the bindings, but they don't budge. I know how to tie a knot—thank you, Peel. He tries to open his mouth, but the only sound that comes out is a muffled choke. Then he looks at me with wide, frightened eyes.

I smile at him. "Hello, Colton. I think it's time you and I had a little chat, don't you?"

Another muffled choke.

"Oh, sorry," I say. "Would you like me to get that for you?" I bend down, slip my hands behind his neck, and loosen the gag so that it slides down his chin.

"You have no idea what you're playing with," he spits.

I take a step back. "I know exactly what I'm playing with, Colton. Or should I say, *who*. And I also know that you've stolen three members of my team and one of its leaders, and I would like them back." I swallow the lump in my throat. I need to keep my voice flat and distant. Colton has to know how much losing Abe is affecting me—but I can't let him see it.

"I've stolen more than that," he says with a coy smile.

I clench my fists. "Start talking, Colton. Where are they? What did you do with them?"

"You'd like to know, wouldn't you?"

I squat down in front of him so that we're eye level. "Colton," I say in the calmest voice I can muster, "we can either do this the easy way or the hard way." And then there's a jolt to my system as I realize Alpha said almost these exact words to me the first time I met him, when he had me knocked out, strapped down, and implanted with a tracker. I push Alpha from my mind. "I think you and I would both prefer the former."

He winks at me. "Is this the part when you tell me you studied enhanced interrogation techniques or some other crap that's meant to scare me?"

I did, in fact, study such interrogation techniques. But I don't need to use them. Because I have something more effective.

I stand. "I'll tell you what I do have. This." I finger the Annum watch hanging from my neck. "And I'll tell you what you *don't* have." I pull his watch from my pocket and dangle it in front of his face.

His smug look is still there, but for the first time I see a hint of fear behind it.

"I'd like that back, please," he says.

"I bet you would. But we're not bargaining over that right now. No, first you're going to answer some of my questions."

"I don't know where they took your boyfriend."

"Really now?"

"Nope," he says.

"That's disappointing." I shake my head. "Let's try another then. How long has your dad been running Eagle Industries?"

"Never heard of it."

"Okay, Colton. Hard way it is." I put the gag back in his mouth and tie it so tightly it's straining at the corners. Then I turn the day knob of my Annum watch forward one click. "Why don't you think about things for a little while?" I shut the face.

I lurch toward the ceiling but only for a moment. Then I'm standing in the same spot. Colton is right where I left him, but he's slumped over, still tied to the railing. The gag is in place, but I can see the frayed edges where he tried to chew it away. There's a strong odor of urine, and I wrinkle my nose. He's asleep. I nudge him awake with my toe.

It takes him a second to stir. Then he looks right at me, and he pulls and strains against the bindings. I hold my breath as I get close enough to untie the gag.

"I could kill you," Colton gasps. His voice is raspy.

"I did offer you the easy way, and you turned me down."

"Water," he says. Then he says it again, louder. Like he's trying to shout but can't.

"It's still early, Colton. No one is around to hear you. And I will get you some water. But first you have to answer one of my questions. So either tell me where my team is or tell me about your father's connection to Eagle. One simple answer, Colton, and I'll get you what you want."

Colton's eyes roll back and he shuts them. I'm feeling more than a twinge of guilt. I'm feeling full-on regret and revulsion by causing such anguish. But I don't have any real choices here.

"Come on, Colton," I nudge.

He opens his eyes. "They're being detained."

"Who is? My team?"

He nods.

They're not dead. Abe is alive! "Where?"

"I answered your question."

"No, you didn't. Where is my team being held?"

Colton's head drops forward. He snaps it back up. "Dorchester. A private house."

"And *when* are they being held? What year?"

"No, I answered your question. Your question was where, not when. Give me some water."

I stare at him. He's totally defeated. And I do know that I am playing with fire. Colton is connected to highly important people. And there's also the fact that he's a human being, and he's suffering.

I tie the gag back in his mouth, and he whimpers and thrashes. "I'll be right back," I say. "I promised you water."

I slip out into the early Boston morning. The sun is just starting to think about rising. Water. Where am I going to find water? Then I see a wooden bucket sitting on a stoop a few doors down, outside the milliner's shop, and I grab it and walk toward the river.

I know you'd be stupid to drink from the Charles River in the present day. It's filthy and polluted, but I don't know when that started. It had to be okay at one point, right? And it's not like there's a 7-Eleven down the block where I can pick up a bottle. I dunk the bucket under the water, then carry it back to Colton. I slip the gag down once more.

"Open up," I say. He does. He doesn't hesitate, doesn't ask where I got it. The water spills over his face and into his mouth. He gasps for it, but after a second, I right the bucket.

"You want another sip, you give me another answer. *When* are they being held?"

"1832."

I do some quick math and realize that every hour they're there equals a day and a half in the present. A day and a half. Orange has been gone for more than a week. I close my eyes. That's . . . No. That can't be right.

I calculate it again and come to the same conclusion.

Orange has lost at least 250 days. *More than eight months.*

And Zeta.

He's been gone for two months. That's . . . almost six years. They're trapped in their tunnels, and we can meet them only at the end. I choke. "You're killing them! You're making sure they can never return to the present."

"Water. I answered you."

I raise the bucket to his lips and allow him another sip. He slurps it down like a dying man. Which I suppose is a fairly accurate description.

Six years. Yellow and Indigo won't have their dad back for six years, and that's assuming I find him *now*. And it's going to take Orange eight months to travel through the wormhole back to the present. It's June now. I won't see him until next February at the earliest. Indigo has been gone for only three days, but that's three and a half months. I've lost Abe only for a day and a half so far, but every second is ticking. Dual projection only works when you're traveling back in time; you can't do it to get to the present.

I need Abe back. I need them all back.

Ariel was right. He was so freaking right. Time is a dangerous and deadly game. It is not something to be messed with.

"Give me an exact date and an exact address, Colton."

And now Colton hesitates. He knows we've reached our first stalemate. I desperately need this information. He desperately needs to withhold it. But I have the upper hand.

I tap the bucket. "Tell me the exact date and address, and I'll let you have a three-second sip."

Colton looks at me with exhausted, red eyes. I don't have time to dwell on the ethics of this right now. Every second counts. Every click of the second hand on my watch damns four people I care about.

"The date and address," I repeat.

"May 2, 1832. Three hundred forty Seaver."

I memorize this before tipping the bucket over Colton's lips. I count to three, then lower it. And then Colton and I continue our dance. He tells me my teammates aren't being mistreated, which I want to believe, but there's a feeling deep inside telling me that it's probably not the whole truth. He claims he doesn't know how much Eagle has made off the scheme, which I believe. Colton doesn't strike me as a guy who'd have any idea what to do with a balance sheet. Then he tells me he has no idea what his father has to do with the Lincoln assassination, which I'm sure is a flat-out lie, but we can circle back to that one.

"Who is D. Callaway?"

His nose scrunches. "What?"

"D. Callaway. Back on Marlborough Street. Your dad saved her from the Strangler." I pause. This makes me uncomfortable. Somehow, acknowledging that act out loud is making Joe seem *human*. Like a normal person with a complex set of emotions, not the single-focused mastermind behind Eagle that I want him to be. "Who is she? Your dad's mother?"

Colton shakes his head. "His mother's sister. My great aunt Dorothy." Colton's voice catches, and he turns away.

I try a different approach.

"Tell me *why*, Colton. Why did your dad start Eagle?"

"My father is not a bad guy, *Iris*." He says my name with pure derision.

"Really? Because I'm pretty sure that murdering two presidents guarantees you a seat at the table in hell reserved for the VIPs."

"You don't know what you're talking about. You literally have *no idea* how far off base you are."

"So tell me. Why did your dad start Eagle?"

The grin disappears off his face, like he's just realized he's saying too much. "No clue."

"You're such a bad liar." I take a moment to think. There's only one reason that's popping into my mind—the most obvious answer there is. I pick up the bucket and hold it in front of Colton's face. "Money. It's that simple, isn't it? That's where all that oil money came from, right?"

Colton stares at the bucket, and his lips part in anticipation. I tip the bucket and let the smallest splash touch his tongue before I yank it away, to remind him we're still talking.

Colton pulls his head back. "If that's what you want to think." A half-laugh escapes his lips. "But it's true that political aspirations aren't cheap."

I drop the bucket to my side. "Wait—your mom *knows*?"

He stops laughing. He yanks his hands forward, but the bindings hold. "No, she doesn't know. And she can't *ever* know. That's rule number one."

"But she's spearheading the entire drive to bring down Eagle."

Colton clucks his tongue. "Life can be pretty ironic sometimes, huh?"

Caroline Caldwell is spending all this time—all this effort—trying to bring down her *husband*, whose stolen oil money is the only thing funding her political career. Talk about a snake eating its own tail. "Your dad had Marie Quail put at Annum Guard, didn't he? To make sure we didn't dig too deeply. And then . . . you." I think about my meeting with the vice president a few weeks ago. How she told me that keeping Colton in Boston was Joe's idea. And there's only one federal agency headquartered in Boston . . .

Colton just shrugs.

"Tell me about the missions you guys have been on."

"You know all of them," Colton says. The water is helping him recover. The color is returning to his face.

"The mission when you nabbed Orange, the one where you nabbed Indigo, the one on the train, the Strangler mission. What else?"

"That's all of them."

"*What else?*"

"I told you that's all of them!" His voice is coming back. "More water!"

"No. We're done with the water until you tell me everything. Then you can drink the whole damned bucket."

"That's not what you said earlier! You said a sip for every question and I've answered—"

"Well, the rules have changed. You answer all my questions, you get the bucket. Now tell me about the other missions!"

"I already told you!"

"Tell me about the Cuban Missile Crisis."

I see the fear flash in his eyes. Cuba is big. Cuba is important.

"We haven't gone on that one yet," he says. "Because *you* haven't gone on that one yet."

"You know something about the Cuban mission." It's not a question because it doesn't need to be. Colton's body language is giving everything away. I tap his foot with mine. It's not an outright kick but there's enough force to be threatening. "Tell me."

"Our mission was to stop you before you ever got to DC. *Is*. Is to stop you before you get there. You can't get to DC."

"Why?"

Colton doesn't answer, but it's obvious. "Your dad's there, isn't he? Or at least there's some solid proof that Joe Caldwell equals Eagle Industries. That's what's there."

Again, he doesn't answer, so I know I've hit the nail on the head. I need to get to DC in October of 1962. I need to see the evidence for myself. That's the only way to end this thing.

"How did your dad recruit Tyler?"

Colton raises both eyebrows. "*Recruit* Tyler? Are you joking? Tyler came to *us*."

His voice is firm, amused. He's telling the truth. Tyler is an even bigger threat than I thought. But I push him to the side for a moment.

"Okay, Colton, when did Eagle start? How long has it been going on?"

Colton's eyes flick down to his waist, then back up. I can tell he's trying to hide his fear, but his body is betraying him. His pulse is racing; I can see it throbbing on the side of his neck.

I stare at his midsection. "What's on your waist that you want to hide?"

"Nothing." He says it so fast that I barely hear him.

I take a step closer. "You've had some combat training, I'll give you that. But clearly no one's taught you how to lie." I crouch down and lift the side of Colton's shirt. There's a tattoo peeking out of the top of his waistband. I push down his waistband to see it.

HC1013LX3V

"You know, you really should be better about picking pass-words. You've shown me your hand twice now. So sloppy." I stand up and cross my arms over my chest. "What does it mean?"

Colton's head bobs forward, and he takes a long, ragged breath. I really think he's about to cry.

I tap him with my foot. It doesn't take me long to put it together. "It's a date, right?" 1013—October thirteenth? LX3V. Roman numerals . . . L is fifty, I think? X is ten. Three of them is thirty. V is five. Eighty-five altogether. "That's easy. So what's HC?"

"No. I'm done talking to you."

"Colton."

"I SAID I'M DONE!" And then he opens his mouth and lets out a scream so loud, I'm afraid he'll wake the entire city. I drop to my knees and force the gag into his mouth.

I have so many more questions. Logistics questions. Who created Colton's watch? How can he project? How long has he been projecting? What sensitive Annum Guard information has he given his father? How did Tyler find out about Joe? But Colton is clearly done talking.

I slip downstairs to the shelves and grab one of the rumpled papers. I straighten it as best I can. There's a pencil trapped in a crack at the very back of the shelf, and I wriggle it free. The point is dull. It's almost flat, more of a stick than a pencil. I try to whittle a point against the wall, but the pencil keeps slipping. I claw at it with my fingernails, but all I wind up doing is pierc-ing my nail beds with shards of wood. A dull point will have to do.

I bend over the counter and scribble down everything Colton just told me. Then I head back up the stairs.

"You need to sign this," I say as I slap the paper down by his hands. "It's your confession." I'm going to take it to Red. Right now. I don't know if it's enough, but it's a start.

He garbles something that I'm pretty sure is, "Screw you."

I look down at him. "Colton, do you want me to take out my watch again? You've had some water, so maybe we can try two days in the future this time? Three?" I hate myself for saying this, for doing this. But I need my teammates.

Colton rears back his head and screams into the gag. It comes out like a growl. Then he looks right up into my eyes with pure venom, and I know he's vowing to kill me for what I'm doing.

I put the pencil in Colton's hands, which are still tied to the rail. He hesitates, then scribbles something that looks like a straight line on the bottom of the paper. It probably doesn't look anything like his signature. It doesn't really matter. Nothing about this is legal. I'm taking Red something that could be in a textbook under "coerced confession." But I can't think about that now.

I shove the confession in my pocket. "Sorry, Colton, but for now you're staying put. You're the biggest bargaining chip I've ever had."

Then I stand, hit the top knob on my watch to take me to the present day, and shut the face.

CHAPTER 27

I land in someone's living room. There's a leather couch and a pair of armchairs, and I'm standing on a rug. I scan around and find a mantel clock. It's four in the morning.

It's four in the morning, and I'm an intruder in someone's apartment. I don't even want to breathe for fear of waking whoever is sleeping . . . somewhere. I try to get my bearings. The stairs where I left Colton tied in 1811 have been replaced by a door. Behind me, there's a tiny kitchen off to the side and a hallway that I assume leads back to a bedroom or two.

I tiptoe over to the door and unlock the deadbolt. It makes a *click*. I hold my breath and wait, but no one stirs. I open the door. There's a muted scraping sound against the carpet, so I only open it about a foot and slip through. I quietly shut the door behind me, then I tiptoe down the stairs.

The whole building has been converted into apartments. I was up in number 2, and there's a door on the ground floor with a bronze number 1 nailed to the center of it.

I slip out the building entrance and take off at a sprint. I go so fast that my lungs take in more air than they can expel. They're filling . . . more, more, more. More than they can hold. They're going to burst. But I don't slow down.

I tear up the steps to Annum Hall. The door is locked. I don't have a key, so I ring the bell. Once. Twice. Three times. I pound on the door. I keep pounding as I ring the bell for a fourth, fifth, sixth time. I don't know what day it is. I don't know how long I've been gone. I don't know if I'm going to find Red or another interim leader.

Then there are footsteps on the stairs and a hall light flicks on.

The door swings open, and Red stands before me, dressed in rumpled khakis and a button-down shirt with the sleeves rolled up. "Calm down. One ring would have done it. It's not like I'm sleeping much these days."

"Is it just you?" I'm out of breath.

"Yes."

I push past him. "It's Joe Caldwell. XP is Joe Caldwell."

"Are you sure?"

I nod. "And the blackout team is Colton Caldwell—"

"Colton?" He sounds shocked.

"And Tyler Fertig. *Tyler Fertig*, Red. He's a mercenary now, employed by Joe Caldwell."

"Are you absolutely sure?"

I slap Colton's confession into his chest. "It's all right there."

Red scans it.

"And I know where everyone is being held. *When* everyone is being held. Three forty Seaver Street in Dorchester. May 2, 1832. We have to go get them, now! They took Abe—Blue—too!"

Red's still reading.

"Is that enough? Can we go after Caldwell with that?"

Red looks up. "We need more, Iris. You have to know that." He waves the paper at me. "This is almost laughable."

My spirits crumble, but I knew that was coming. "I have two leads. There's one more XP mission. It's . . . the Cuban Missile Crisis. I'm pretty sure there's some concrete evidence there that links Caldwell to Eagle. And there's something else. Something about Eagle being formed in the first place. A meeting, maybe? I have a date. October 13. The year's in Roman numerals. LX3V. That's eighty-five, right?"

"LX3V," Red repeats. "You mean LXXXV? Yeah, that's eighty-five."

"October 13, 1985." It has to be 1985. That's the only '85 Joe's been alive for.

"Do you have a location?"

I shake my head. "HC—initials. That's all I have."

Red takes off down the hall toward his office. By the time I catch up he's already typing into a government database. "We need to find a reference to an HC that means something to Joe Caldwell."

"Colton goes to Harvard," I point out.

"Not in 1985."

"The vice president got a master's degree there, too."

Red shakes his head as he scrolls. "The grad schools are part of Harvard University, not Harvard College. Here's something. Joe owns a shipping facility in Haltom City, Texas, in between Dallas and Fort Worth. We can check the address."

"I don't think that's it. I think it's bigger than that." I remember how proud Joe was the first time he introduced me to Colton—practically beaming when he told me about Harvard. My gut is nagging me that I'm on the right track. I think. Harvard Campus. Harvard Cambridge. Harvard— I gasp.

"Harvard Club! Red, it's Harvard Club!" I've walked past the clubhouse building more times than I can count. It's a huge mansion on Comm. Ave., right in the heart of the Back Bay. I look at Red, and he nods at me.

I'm already out the door, but then I stop and turn around. "The others? Seaver Street?"

"Dorchester. I got it. I'll send Green and Violet now." He nods again as he stands. "You did good. We'll take care of it. We'll find them. You go get Joe. Do whatever you need to do."

My stomach lurches when I think about what I've already done. "Red, I left Colton in the past. I—"

Red holds up a hand. "Don't tell me anything I'd have a duty to report."

"Okay. I'll just be going then." But still, I hesitate.

"What are you waiting for?" Red pushes me toward the back stairs.

I race down the steps, grab a wad of cash, and shove it inside my bra. Then I ditch the duffel bag on the floor. I don't need it anymore. I'm going to 1985, then 1962, and then I'm done with missions.

Maybe forever.

I set my watch, and I'm gone. When I land, it's October 13, 1985.

CHAPTER 28

The Harvard Club is a four-story building, almost exactly one block south of where Tyler stole Abe. The club is sandwiched between a hotel and a brownstone that's been converted to apartments.

A car rolls down the street with its windows open and Madonna's "Like a Virgin" blaring. It reminds me of my mom. A redhead with a ponytail on the side of her head sits in the passenger seat, her head rocking from side to side as she sings along. Another group of girls brushes past me on the street. Two of them have on neon shirts and leggings, and the other—a girl with black, lace fingerless gloves—gives me the once-over. Because I'm in 1985 wearing a dress I purchased in 1962, and we're way too early for the vintage resurgence.

There's a lock on the heavy wooden door where people who belong here can use their fancy membership keys, and a telephone call box for the rest of us common folk. I pick up the receiver and press the call button.

"Harvard Club," a friendly female voice crackles through the box. "Are you a member?"

I lean in. "Yes, hi. I'm meeting my father for lunch. His name is"—I make a static sound.

"Sorry, I didn't catch that."

"I said"—more static.

"Why don't you just come in?" The door buzzes, and I open it. I step into a wood-paneled foyer. There's a group of men having brandy and cigars in a bar just to my left. Both of them have sweaters draped over their shoulders. I walk straight into a larger foyer with red carpeting—Harvard crimson, I suppose—and more wood walls. There's a fire going in a fireplace, and the whole feel is very old-school New England.

"Hello," a woman behind a desk says, standing to greet me. Her bronze name tag says Kimberly. "I'm sorry, there must be something wrong with our call box. Who did you say you're here to see?"

"My father." I look past her into a ballroom that's even more opulent than the one in Leighton's house. Its walls are two stories high, and there are marble floors and crystal chandeliers. Beautiful. Then I lock eyes with a man on the other side of the room, sitting in a chair by the staircase, looking up at me over a newspaper. I raise my hand and wave, a big, goofy, back-and-forth motion like I'm in a parade. He tilts his head, but then returns the wave. "There he is." I turn back to the woman. "I'm a little late. He doesn't like to be kept waiting."

Kimberly looks from the man to me. I smile at him and give another wave while the woman isn't looking. He has a confused expression on his face, which I see him try to cover up with a false look of recognition. Good. Let him think I'm the daughter of an old college buddy or something.

"I've got it from here," I tell her and walk away before she can question me.

"Hi," I say to the man. "I haven't seen you in a while. Not since my father's party, oh, when was that, two summers ago?" I peek over my shoulder. Kimberly is still staring.

"I'm sorry," the man says. "I'm having trouble—"

"I'm Laura. John's daughter." Then I give the man my warmest smile.

"Oh," he finally says. "Oh right. Laura. How is John these days?"

"You know my father," I say. "Always up to something. He's at his cabin in New Hampshire for a long weekend." I peek behind me. Kimberly is back at the desk, with a phone receiver pressed to her ear. I turn back to the man. "Well, good to see you! I'll tell Dad you said hi!" Then I hightail it up the stairs.

I step off the last stair into . . . another foyer? How many foyers can one place have? Honestly. There are a few employees milling about, wearing jackets, ties, and the same bronze name tags as Kimberly's, but I skip over all of them. I need someone young. Someone who won't ask too many questions. I find a kid who looks like he might be in college himself, rolling a cart of silverware into a room with a black-and-white checkered floor.

"Excuse me," I say, rushing over to him. And then I take a deep breath. I have only one shot at this. "I'm looking for Joe Caldwell."

The guy looks at my dress, so I decide to play the part. I channel Jackie Kennedy and toss my shoulders back and click my heels together. "He's expecting me," I say in my best Brahmin accent. I pray my voice sounds authoritative because the truth is, I'm not even sure that Harvard Club is the right HC. I mean, my gut is telling me it is, but I don't know for certain.

I get the confirmation I need. The guy nods at the staircase. "I know they have him set up in a meeting room on the third floor. The Saltonstall Room, maybe? It's the most private. Far back corner."

"Thank you," I say, giving him a small smile with my mouth, not my eyes. Very Boston proper. I wait until he's done wheeling the cart into the room before I sprint up the stairs once more.

I stop and get my bearings. There are four meeting rooms up here. As the guy downstairs promised me, the Saltonstall Room is tucked away in a back corner. The door is shut, but I can hear voices inside.

"Can I help you?"

I turn around. There's a uniformed man staring at me. No name tag. He's older, with silver-flecked hair and a face full of laugh lines. His smile is polite, not distrusting, and he's looking at my dress with a smile, like it brings back pleasant memories. I instantly read him as not being a threat.

But still, do I tell him I work for Joe? If it gets back to Joe that someone claiming to be an assistant is loitering around, I'm done for. No, I need something more subtle. "Yes, hi. I'm with"—it's 1985—"the phone company. I'm here about adding new lines for the Internet." Even though we're about ten years too early for that.

"What's the Internet?"

"It's the wave of the future. Management wants to run the phone line through that room." I point at the Saltonstall.

"Oh no, I'm sorry. There's a private meeting going on in there. It just started, and I'm not sure how long it will last. They've requested the utmost privacy"—he says the word British-style with a short *i*—"so I cannot allow you access."

I look at the room. The ladies room shares a wall, but I'm sure it's pretty well insulated.

"I could let you see the pantry. It's where we keep place settings and linens, but it's adjacent to the Saltonstall Room. Would that work?"

"Yes!" Damn, I sound too eager. "That would be acceptable."

"Only for a minute," the man says.

I'll take it.

He leads me around a corner and into the pantry. Shelves of plates, bowls, and glasses line the walls. There's a pocket door leading into the Saltonstall, and I can hear the murmuring of voices.

I walk over to the corner, underneath three windows, and drop to my knees, pretending to look for something. "I won't be long."

I don't hear the man's footsteps leaving, so I look up to smile at him. "I just need to take a few measurements and test the signal in here." I'm talking total nonsense, but I can tell the man doesn't know enough to call me out.

He nods once. "Very well. Please take care not to disturb anything."

"You got it." I smile at him again. "Thank you very much."

And then he's gone. I don't waste any time. I scoot over to the pocket door and slide it open an inch. Just enough to peer inside. Joe sits at the head of the table. He's so young, barely older than Colton is in the present. Their resemblance is scary.

To Joe's right is—my heart skips a beat. It's Joe's Secret Service agent. He's much younger, obviously, but I recognize the bulky frame, the lack of neck. And then it clicks. He's the man who took Bonner. *Of course.*

There are two other men. One of them is unfamiliar, but I assume he's a high-up government official, just based on his presence here. The other—I swallow the lump in my throat—is Zeta. Joe is speaking. "I've put together a list of potential targets." He slides a paper across the table at Zeta, and I crouch lower on the ground.

Zeta clears his throat. "You do realize this is a little premature. What you're talking about will take years to hurdle the red tape."

Joe jerks his head toward the paper. "As I was saying, that's a short list I've come up with."

Zeta looks down. "David Berkowitz. John Wayne Gacy. Ted Bundy." He looks up. "Gacy and Bundy are both sitting on death row. Surely you know this. They'll answer for their crimes."

"They will, but how many bodies did they leave in their wake? How many men, women, and children raped, tortured, and terrorized?" His voice is rushed, even pained. "There's one more name on that list."

"Albert DeSalvo." Zeta sets the paper down. "Mr. Caldwell, I'm aware of your personal history. However, and forgive me for being blunt, I'm not interested in leading Annum Guard on a course of vigilante justice because you harbor a vendetta."

"Well, forgive *me* for being blunt, Mr. Masters." I inhale sharply through my nose. Joe knows Zeta's real name. "But the last I knew, you weren't even in the running for the new leadership position. I reached out to you, but I can go above your head. You boys even organized yet?" He chuckles, and I realize that the second generation of Annum Guard hasn't started yet.

Something else clicks. My father quit the Naval Academy in 1985, and suddenly I realize why. Second generation is about to begin. I bet Joe goes to Alpha and Alpha goes to my dad, and *BOOM*, my dad starts a life of crime at twenty-one.

Zeta pushes his chair back. "Do as you like. We're done here." He looks around the room once. "Saltonstall. I haven't been in this room in years. Not since an *alumni* planning event." I bite my bottom lip at the obvious dig at Joe. Zeta turns to the man I don't recognize. "Jack, it was nice to see you again." Then he turns to the man who took Bonner. "Mr. Hansen, pleasure meeting you."

Hansen.

"I'll walk out with you," Jack says, standing.

Once Zeta and Jack are gone, Joe jumps out of his seat. It's only then that I notice his clothes. I lean back. He's wearing a wrinkled suit made of flimsy, cheap fabric. His watch has a plastic band.

"Smug son of a bitch," Joe mutters. "So I didn't go to an Ivy League school. I still went to college. I work at the Pentagon. My damn wife works at the White House. How does he think I even know about his organization? I have the connections, but I'll never be good enough for his type."

There is no Eagle Industries yet. This date. This place. This is where and when Joe decides to form Eagle.

"So we're on to Plan B," Hansen says.

Joe sits back down. "We always knew we were headed toward Plan B." He nods toward the American flag standing in the corner, to the eagle atop the pole. My chest tingles. "Tell me what isn't admirable about what I'm trying to do. Going back in time— erasing serial and mass murderers before they have a chance to claim victims. Just think of what we could do if we take this global. Hitler. Stalin. Pol Pot. Pinochet."

I lean in closer. Joe's voice is passionate, excited. My brain is trying to reconcile this Joe with the Joe I know in the present. The Joe standing before me in this room seems . . . genuine.

"I'm doing this, Adrian. *We're* doing this."

Adrian Hansen. Gotcha.

"We're gonna build ourselves a pantheon, and you and me'll be the gods. Just you watch. They're all gonna worship us. Our names will be part of history."

"And if we make a little side profit, like we discussed?" Adrian says with a sly smile.

"That's the payment we're owed." Joe shuffles all his papers into a neat pile. "Plan B is in effect. You can set up a meeting with Ellis?" *Alpha.*

"He was two years below me, but I know he's still in contact with our old headmaster. I am, too."

This guy went to Peel? Is he already Secret Service? Or something else? Maybe at the Pentagon.

"Why don't you set up a meeting for all four of us?" Joe says. Then he stands. "This is the start of something. Something big."

"Don't I know it," Adrian says. "What do we do about Masters?"

"Ignore him. You heard him. He thinks we're a joke." Joe pauses and strolls over to the window. "But he'll come to learn."

There are footsteps behind me. I slide the door shut and push up off the ground just in time to see the man who let me in here walk into the pantry.

"Did you get everything you need?" he asks.

I nod. "And then some. You have no idea how helpful you've been, sir." I extend my hand, and he shakes it. I give him a firm squeeze. He has no idea that he's just played a huge role in helping to take down a number of corrupt government officials.

Now there's one more thing I have to do. I have to go to Washington. To finally connect the last of the dots. To the Cuban Missile Crisis.

CHAPTER 29

I project inside the third-floor ladies room at the Harvard Club. I set my watch for a little after four in the morning on October 27, 1962. The Club is dark and deserted as I slip down the stairs. The front door is locked, but there doesn't look to be an alarm, so I unlock it and open it. I start walking, hunching my shoulders and hugging my arms across my chest.

There are delivery trucks rumbling down the street and a few people. Working-class men, off to jobs, I assume. I feel fairly safe, but I don't need to advertise the fact that I have a wad of cash on me.

Joe Caldwell. I wonder how long it took for the corruption to waft, how long before he realized the money he could be making. And then, all of a sudden, I feel sorry for Joe the same way I felt sorry for Alpha. Two men who aren't exactly the pure evil my mind wants them to be.

No. I can't think like that now. Joe is still the enemy.

It takes a few minutes to flag down a cab, and the driver seems surprised I'm asking to go to the airport this early, so I'm going to guess packed 6:00 a.m. flights are a modern thing.

Logan is all but abandoned when we pull into the departures area.

"No luggage?" the driver repeats, even though we just had this same conversation when he picked me up. Does he think luggage magically appeared somewhere in the Callahan Tunnel?

"No," I say as I bend over to fish a five out of my bra and hand it to him.

I've never seen the airport like this. All of the ticket windows are closed, and the only other person I see is a woman with a broom and dustpan. I park myself on a chair, lean my head back, and close my eyes.

They're coming, Abe. Green and Violet. I try not to think about how every hour that passes means there's a day and a half I won't be able to see Abe. Well, less than that, actually, because I'm in the past, too, so I'm going to have my own catching up to do. I start to do the math—roughly three minutes in the present for every one minute in 1962, so three hours for one hour—and I soon realize that, even if Red finds Abe today, I'm still looking at weeks without him.

Damn you, Colton. And Joe Caldwell, the one I really need to be focusing on. I need proof. Solid evidence that he's behind Eagle. *I* know he is, but that meeting I eavesdropped on isn't enough. Colton's confession isn't enough. I need more.

In many ways, I'm going into this mission blind, which gets my heart pounding. I read what I could about October 27,

1962, when I was back at the public library. And by read, I mean skimmed. I'm not feeling confident by any means.

All I really know is that the Soviet Union moved nuclear missiles into Cuba as a threat to the United States. We found out about it and issued a blockade—which was called a quarantine for political reasons—to prevent the Soviets from bringing in more weapons. And then President Kennedy and Soviet Premier Khrushchev played a game of cat and mouse for thirteen very tense days.

On October 27, 1962, an American pilot was flying a surveillance mission over Cuba and was shot down by a Soviet surface-to-air missile. I think of what Ariel told me, how the US responded by launching an airstrike, how the Soviets then launched their nuclear missiles, and how we did the same. How Washington, DC, and Moscow were leveled. How fifteen million people were dead. How overnight, the world was plunged into an economic depression worse than the crash of 1929.

But Ariel changed it. He prevented it. And dammit all, I don't know enough of the details. Something about the space program and a fake telegram, and that's all I've got.

The amount of information I don't know makes me queasy, although I'm not sure if I've ever been fully prepared for an Annum Guard mission. This organization is a little insane. We hold *so much* power—the power to affect millions of lives—hell, the power to screw up millions of lives with one tiny misstep— and so often we blindly jump into the missions with no more than a silent prayer we'll get it right.

The more time I spend as a Guardian, the more I can't help but think that maybe Annum Guard shouldn't be my future. Maybe it shouldn't be anyone's future.

The Pan Am counter opens at seven, and I'm the first one there. I ask for a one-way ticket to Washington, DC, on the next available flight.

"Are you traveling . . . alone?" the ticket agent asks in a chirpy voice. She's wearing a skirt that's so short, I'm not sure how she bends over more than a few inches.

"I'm on my way to a funeral," I say, and I remember Tyler's joke. Not to mention, if I somehow screw up this mission, there will be millions of funerals on my conscience.

The woman's hand flies to her mouth. "Oh! Whose?"

"Er, my grandmother." Both of my grandmothers are dead. I never even got a chance to meet my dad's mom. My *bunica*, my mom's mom, lived with us in Vermont until she died when I was six.

"You poor, poor thing. I'm so sorry. And traveling alone at such a horrible time."

"It's fine," I mumble as I start to slide my ticket off the counter.

But then her hand slaps down on top of my ticket. "Wait a minute, let me see what I can do." I let go, and she takes the ticket, tears it in half, and handwrites another one for me. I glance at it. She has me in first class.

"Thank you," I say.

"It's the least I can do. You take care, okay?"

I nod, feeling like crap for getting bumped to first class on a fake grandparent's death. But it will give me a better chance to focus on a way to infiltrate the White House. I have no idea how I'm going to do this.

I mean, I know security is a lot more lax in 1962 than in the present, but it's still the damn White House. I doubt I can just break a window and climb in.

I make my way to gate C14, park myself on a seat to wait, and then have to stand up because I'm a bundle of nerves. A bundle of completely exhausted nerves. Since last night, I've been to last February, then 1865, then 1928, then 1962, 1810, 1811—I'm lightheaded thinking about this—the present, 1985, and back to 1962. I hurt. There's not one part of my body that doesn't ache. I'm breaking my body, one projection at a time. My mind is flying in a million directions at once.

Several businessmen head to the gate and immediately open copies of the *Boston Globe*. I glance at the top headline:

REDS RUSH WORK ON CUBA MISSILES; US WARNS OF TOUGH NEW ACTION

I look closer. The crisis in Cuba fills the entire front page. I close my eyes and take a deep breath. *I can do this. I have to do this. Focus.*

I open my eyes and bounce from my toes to the balls of my feet and back again. A family walks up to the gate. The father is dressed in a suit and tie, the mother in a gray tweed dress with pantyhose, pumps, and kid gloves. There are two children—a boy and a girl—both wearing their Sunday best. They look like a family on a black-and-white TV show in which children never talk back, money is never an issue, and the mom has dinner on the table every night at five thirty sharp.

The mother ushers her two children into chairs and turns to her husband. "I still think this trip is a mistake."

"Jesus, Helen, I'm not having this conversation again," he says in a hostile whisper that shatters my illusion of their perfect family life.

"I just have this terrible feeling that we shouldn't be leaving home with—" She looks to her children. Her son is engrossed in a Hardy Boys book, and her daughter has pulled out a Yogi Bear coloring book and a yellow box of Crayola crayons. She drops her voice. "With *the situation* going on. We're traveling right to the center of the storm, Carl."

"Jesus, Helen, it's my brother's wedding. What would you have me do? We're going." And then he drops into a seat opposite his kids, yanks out a newspaper, and snaps it open so that his face is covered.

Helen sighs. I feel her turn in my direction, so I look up to meet her gaze. She stares at me with worried eyes but doesn't say anything.

"It's going to be fine," I tell her with a smile. After all, assuming I don't completely blow the mission, it *will* be fine.

Helen's expression changes from anxiety to anger. "Oh, you kids all think you're invincible, but you're not. And let me tell you, you won't be smiling when you're running from a nuke. You probably weren't even born for Hiroshima and Nagasaki. You want your skin to melt off, do you? Like a stick of butter dripping in a hot July sun?"

I blink. *Jesus, Helen, I'm sorry for trying to help.*

"I . . . okay." It's not worth a fight. I wander over to the ticket counter to wait for boarding. They start with first class and, for a moment, I forget that's me. I have to go outside, then climb a set of stairs to board the plane on the tarmac.

I settle into the window seat, lean my head against it, and close my eyes. I feel someone slide in next to me, and I crack my eyes open, then close them again. I need to focus. I need a game plan. I need a way to break into the White House in the middle of the greatest nuclear crisis the world has ever seen. I rack my brain, but I come up empty every time. My best bet seems to be slipping away during a tour, but, one, I have no idea if there even were tours in 1962; two, if there were, I'm going to guess they're suspended right now; and three, it's the *White House*. You can't just slip away from a tour undetected. I'm screwed.

I open my eyes. There's a businessman next to me with jet-black hair and a sour expression. He nods once in my direction but doesn't ask why I'm traveling alone. He doesn't make any small talk whatsoever, just that one curt nod. It's refreshing.

Although it doesn't change the fact I'm still completely screwed.

We land in DC, and the weather is mild as I step off the plane onto the tarmac. The kind of weather I love to jog in, or to sit under a tree and read a book in. I wish I could be doing either of those things right now. I really should stop in a store and buy a new dress. The one I'm wearing smells faintly of the Charles. But I don't. I hail a cab.

"The White House, please," I tell the driver.

He swivels around in his seat. "The White House? Are you out of your mind?"

"No," I say, dragging out the word. "I have business to attend to."

The driver raises an eyebrow. "What's a girl like you—"

"Stop right there." That's what really drives me crazy about the sixties. The sexism, the condescension, the way everyone's assumption is that I'm just a dumb little girl who needs help or guidance. "It's really not your place or your right to ask why I'm in Washington." I press my lips together and meet his stare. "Why aren't you driving yet?"

He tosses his hands in the air in mock surrender and shifts the car into drive. We pass a movie theater. There's a poster advertising the recent release of *Cleopatra*. Liz Taylor is looking at me with expertly painted cat eyes. The whole look is smoldering and intense, and now I miss Yellow.

A little while later, we're on Pennsylvania Avenue.

"Where would you like me to drop you, your highness? Are they expecting you at the gate?"

"This is fine," I tell him. We're about a block away.

The cab driver doesn't argue. He pulls over. I pay the fare and hop out. He's shaking his head as he drives away. I turn toward the White House.

The crisis is like a dark, heavy cloud that hangs in the air with no breeze to blow it away. Two men hustle by me, and I catch one of them whispering about retaliation. The next group that passes me murmurs something about an ExComm. I push past a woman saying something about the Kremlin. I try to block it out. Block it all out.

I slow down when I get to the demonstrators. There's a mob of them. Hundreds. On the periphery is a girl with ironed brown hair, wearing black capri pants and a summery white sweater, and holding a sign that reads "Don't Invade Cuba." She looks at me and nods. I bite my lower lip and look past her to a man holding his "Invade Red Cuba Now" sign in front of his head.

Well, glad to see there's some agreement.

I look again. The guy arguing for invasion is vastly outnumbered. There are mothers pushing babies in strollers, holding signs that say "Negotiation Over Annihilation" and "President Kennedy, Be Careful." I wade through the crowd toward a group of college-age guys. Their black signs with white type say "No War with Cuba" and "Hands Off Cuba" and "Stop Bases, Stop Blockade." Other groups are carrying the American flag.

And in the crowd, wearing a short-sleeved, white dress shirt and high-waisted, pleated pants, is Tyler.

I run in the opposite direction.

There's a line outside the east gate and a sign pointing toward the White House Visitor's Office. Wait, they *are* still giving tours? I glance at the guards eyeing the protestors, then the yards of tall black gate going all the way around the White House. The tour is my only chance to get inside, so I queue up at the back of the line.

I have no idea if the line is longer or shorter than usual. Frankly, I'm still shocked they haven't canceled the tours.

I'm in line behind an older couple. The husband is talking about Cuba and how they shouldn't be here, and the wife is whining that she hasn't waited seventy years to visit the White House to be thwarted now. *Block it out. All of it.* The protestors, the supporters, the frightened people on the street, the group of young men in army uniforms shouting for the president to finally strike.

The line moves inch by inch, foot by foot. I shuffle and wait, shuffle and wait, all the while looking over my shoulder. But I don't see Tyler again. Finally, when I'm about seven people from the ticket window, the man inside leans out.

"Sorry, folks, it's noon. We're closed for the rest of the day. You can come back again on Tuesday. We open at ten."

"What?" I shout. "No!"

It's Friday. This mission will be long over by Tuesday.

Everyone in front of me turns to stare, their own grumbling forgotten.

"Please, sir," I beg, pushing my way up to the window. "This is important. It's for a school assignment."

"Sorry, miss, but we're closed." He starts to slide the window shut, and I reach my hand in to grab it.

"You don't understand. I need to be on this tour. If I'm not, I'll fail." He has no idea how true this is.

The man shakes his head. I keep my right hand on the window and reach into my bra as inconspicuously as I can with my left. It's time to speak the universal language. I pull out a twenty and slide it through the window.

"I can't afford to fail, sir. Please. I'm begging you. Let me on the last tour."

The man looks from me to the money, then back to me again. There's more where that came from. I'll give him whatever it takes. But twenty does it. He slips it into his pocket, and jerks his head toward the group of people about to follow a guide inside. I ignore the protests of the seven people I cut in front of and tear off after the tour.

One step at a time, I tell myself. *First, you get inside. Second, you get to the West Wing. Third, you find Ariel. Fourth . . . you'll think of something.*

I join the group of twenty or so people inside. It's a mixed bunch. Older married couples, parents with young kids, groups of friends, a few stray loners. And me. I hang in the back, staying as invisible as possible.

Meanwhile, I keep my eyes peeled for anything I can use to get me from the East Wing to the West Wing and for any sign of Tyler. Nothing, so far.

"In here, please," our guide says. He's probably in his mid- to late-sixties, and short, with thin, white hair. There's a proud gleam in his eye that tells me he loves this job. It makes him feel important. That's going to make things harder. I know his type. He lives to micromanage and tell people no.

The guide gestures for us to follow him into a room with a peach-and-white tiled floor, past an enormous bust of President Lincoln. There are framed photographs and portraits on the walls.

"This is the East Garden Room," he says slowly. "I'm sure you noticed the bust of President Lincoln, the work of American sculptor Gutzon Borglum, who is most famous for creating the monumental images of four presidents at Mount Rushmore. You will also find a number of historic photographs on the walls. Please do take a minute to look around."

No, I don't have a minute to look around. I poke my head out of the room and into a long corridor that leads—I get my bearings—west. My heart picks up its pace. There's a group of three men and one woman walking down the corridor, heading toward us. I don't know who they are, but the men are talking fast, and the woman trails behind them, furiously scribbling in a notebook. And then I notice she has some sort of badge clipped to her blouse.

Bingo.

That badge might not get me to the West Wing, but it will get me closer.

I step back into the East Garden Room and pretend to stare at a cluster of pictures on the wall. I'm out of the way now, but that group is going to round the corner and run smack into me in five . . . four . . . three . . . two . . . one . . .

"Oh!" one of the men says as he collides with me. "Uh!" The man right behind him launches a shoulder into his. I stumble backward and think of falling to the floor but decide against it. Even now, half of the people on the tour are looking at me.

The woman rushes forward. "Are you all right?" she asks the men, ignoring me. I stare at her badge. "PRESS" is written on it in large letters. Perfect. So perfect! I pretend to stumble and bump into her. I put my hands out and knock the notebook to the floor. "Ah!" I cry, and she and I both dive for it. I lean into her, snatch the badge, and slip it into my pocket.

Then I step back. "Sorry," I mumble, keeping my head down. "I didn't see you."

The first man who collided with me stands up straight. He gives me one brief nod like he's accepting my completely fake apology. And then they're gone. Through the East Garden Room and away from me.

I shove a hand into my pocket and tighten my fist around the press badge. I can't believe I have it. The tour guide sidles up next to me. "Are you all right?" he asks in his dry monotone.

I keep my eyes on my feet and try to channel Yellow. Naive and innocent. "Is there a restroom nearby I could use? I just want to compose myself a bit."

He points behind me. "But the tour is continuing immediately down the east corridor toward the lower residence floor. We have schedules to keep."

"I'll catch up." I raise my eyes but don't meet his gaze. "Please, sir, I'll only be a minute."

"Very well." Then he looks past me and raises his hands. "This way, please. If you will all follow me, you will notice the windows that look out onto the east garden. The first lady worked with famed designer Rachel Lambert Mellon to landscape the lawn. Take special note of the topiary trees . . ." His voice fades as he leads the group away.

I dash toward the bathroom and pull the press badge out of my pocket. My name is Joanne Mulroney. I'm with *Life* magazine. Whoa. *Life* magazine. That was big-time in the 1960s. What if Joanne Mulroney is too high profile, too well known by everyone in the White House?

Then I shake my head. *Stop being so pessimistic. This is perfect.* I clip the badge to the front of my dress. Then I pinch my cheeks a few times to get some color into them, which makes me look older. I throw back my shoulders and practice a confident smile in the mirror. One that's friendly but assertive.

I walk down the east corridor into the residence area. My tour has wandered into a room on the left, a room with stark white walls, tons of decorative molding, and several portraits of the first ladies. I turn my face away from the door and speed past, down another long corridor. There are several people around, but after one quick glance at my badge, no one pays me a second look. This thing is magic.

And then suddenly I run into a swarm of reporters. They're all wearing press badges, and they're milling around, waiting for something. I cross my arms over my chest so that only the "PRESS" part of my badge is visible and push my way through. I get a bunch of weird looks, which I understand. I'm the youngest person in this room by at least ten years, and there's only one other woman.

And then we're all ushered into another room, and I instantly recognize it from television. It's the press briefing room. I've made it all the way to the press briefing room! I'm close, so freaking close.

I've only been in this room for about thirty seconds, but already it's clear that journalism in the sixties is a boys' club, which makes me feel really proud of Joanne Mulroney and whoever that woman is in the front, but also makes me way too obvious. I feel eyes on me. Dozens of them. Staring, questioning, trying to figure out who I am. I can feel their gazes penetrating my skin.

Then a tall, thin man with a handsome face struts in, and the room parts to meet him. He's also wearing a press badge. I don't know who he is, but he seems like the prom king of the group.

"Anyone know what this one's about?" he asks. "They finally decide to drop a nuke?" The way he says it—like it's a joke, like this whole situation is a joke—makes me recoil. There's some nervous polite laughter, but I gather most of the reporters feel the same way I do: there is nothing funny about this situation.

There's a shuffling of feet, and everyone scrambles to find a seat as a large man with a wide jaw and thick, black eyebrows enters the room and walks to the podium. The press secretary. I duck my head and slink to the back.

"Good afternoon," the press secretary says. "Earlier this morning, we were able to ascertain that three of the four MRBM sites at San Cristóbal and both sites at Sagua la Grande appear to be fully operational."

Every reporter in the room is furiously scribbling. I'm the only one who doesn't even have a notebook. But fortunately, everyone is too busy writing to notice me.

I need to get out of here. And then I look toward the door and see a very young Ariel dart past.

I quickly squeeze my way through two men and out into the hallway. Ariel disappears around a corner. I glance back in the room. All eyes are either on the press secretary or on a notebook. No one cares who I am or where I went.

I hurry after Ariel.

But then I hear a loud voice demand, "Are you from NASA?" I slide to a halt and press my back against the wall.

"I am!" I hear Ariel say. I peek around the corner. Ariel is surrounded by four men. Two are wearing military uniforms. The other two are in suits but are just as intimidating.

"Do you have the cable?" one of them asks. He's wearing an Army uniform with more insignia than I've ever seen—a general, no doubt.

"Right here." Ariel hands over a piece of paper, and the general reads it.

"This has been verified?" the man in the naval uniform asks.

"Yes," Ariel says.

The general nods once. "Follow me." Then the whole group heads toward a staircase leading downstairs.

I have to follow them. I have to know what's going on. But another flash of movement catches my eye. It's a walk I've come to know well. My father's walk. He's heading right toward me.

CHAPTER 30

There's nowhere to hide. I'm in a long corridor, completely exposed, and I clearly don't belong here. But at the last second, my dad ducks into a room. And then I breathe.

What do I do? Do I try to see what my father is up to, or do I follow Ariel? I can't be in both places at once. Hell, I don't even know if I can be in one of those places. This press badge has been a golden ticket so far, but for how much longer? Someone is going to catch me eventually, and it's going to take them all of about ten seconds to figure out I'm here with a swiped press badge. The tour guide might have reported me missing by now. Or Joanne might have figured out what happened to her badge. I'm going to wind up in a detention room with some serious explaining to do. What if Tyler makes his way in?

I don't know what to do!

My dad. It has to be my dad. He's the key to finding evidence against Joe Caldwell, and that's why I'm here. To bring down Joe and get everyone back.

And something is telling me that Tyler is trapped outside.

I take a slow breath, then turn my press badge around so it's just a blank white card. Maybe people will assume I'm the daughter of a congressman or an ambassador whose visitor's badge got turned around. *Yellow,* I think. *Become Yellow.* I plant a forced smile on my face that probably makes me look moderately insane, but it's as close to sweet and trusting as I'm going to get.

Another breath, then I round the corner. My smile fades as I run into a woman with deep-auburn hair and a bra that makes her boobs look like torpedoes. It's all I can do not to stare at them.

"Who are you?" she asks me, staring at my badge.

"Oh, um . . ." *Think!* "I'm here with . . ." And then it comes to me. I remember the training mission I went on with Zeta and Indigo, the one where I had to cause a senator to miss a cab. "Senator McCarthy!"

The woman scrunches up her face. "Are you his daughter?"

"His niece. I'm here on an assignment for my school paper. About . . ." I gesture in the air. "You know . . . what's going on."

She glances down at my turned-around badge, and I see her eyes twitch back and forth, like she's figuring out whether to push me further. I shift from side to side, trying to play up the naive thing.

Finally, she looks up. "How did you get over here? Shouldn't you be in the West Wing reception room?"

"Oh, um, probably." I'm deliberating raising my voice an octave. And I should start making everything sound like it's a question. That will make me sound young and naive, like I'm not a threat. "But I have to go to the bathroom? And I don't know where that is? It's kind of an emergency?"

"Are you here to see anyone in particular?"

"The, um, press secretary?"

Her eyebrow rises an inch. "Mr. Salinger is expecting you?" I can't read her tone. I'll be shocked if she is buying this whole story, but she's not giving anything away.

"I've already talked to him? But then he got called away to do a briefing? I watched some of it. Something about missile sites? But, like I said, I really need a bathroom."

The woman takes a second. Then another second. Then she points down the hallway. "Down there, on the right."

"Thank you!" The enthusiasm in my voice isn't fake at all.

I walk down the hallway, and it's not until I've gone ten feet that I hear the woman's footsteps start again. I pass by the room where my dad is. The door is open. He's there with three other men. They're just settling into chairs, like a meeting is about to start. I turn my head. The woman is gone, so I stop. Now what?

At Peel, they taught us confidence is everything. Act like you belong, and you have a better chance of not getting caught. It's human nature to trust that everything is as it should be. Our brains actually go out of their way to explain the abnormal, to try to make it fit within the parameters of our normal routine.

It's definitely time to drop the stupid schoolgirl act and get back to the "hell yes, I belong here" act.

There's a secretary pool several yards up. At least twenty secretaries are clustered at desks in the center of the room. Their heads are down and their fingers are rapidly firing against typewriter keys. *Clack clack clack clack clack.* I didn't think it was possible for anyone's fingers to move that fast. I rip the press badge from my dress and stash it in my pocket. Then I wander over.

One looks up at me, a girl in her early twenties. I give her a tight-lipped smile, and she returns it. So I test her. She has a stack of papers to the side of her typewriter. Probably a hundred sheets. I reach over and pick them up. She takes her hands off the keyboard. I flip through the first few. I don't bother reading them. I don't care what they say.

"Very well," I tell her. "Carry on." I turn and walk away. And wait for her to call out, to ask who I am and why I've just stolen a stack of papers from her desk. But she doesn't. Her *clack-clack-clacking* picks right back up.

Human nature. We're all way too trusting.

I pause outside the room where my dad is. Someone had shut the door. *Confidence.* I put my hand on the knob and swing the door open into a small conference room. There's a shiny wooden table with six chairs set around it. Two are unoccupied.

Four sets of eyes turn to look at me. The man sitting at the head of the table is wearing a naval uniform. Two men sit to his left. My dad sits to his right. There's a stack of papers next to my dad. Papers I need to get.

"Who are you?" the man in uniform demands.

"Sorry," I say. "I was asked to bring these." I hold up the pages I swiped from the secretaries and deliberately ignore his question.

"What are they?"

"I'm not sure. I didn't read them. I assumed they were classified."

"Leave them and go," the man says, waving his hand at the door. "And knock first next time."

"Yes, sir." I try to ignore how dizzy I am as I walk over to my dad. He's already turned his attention back to the man in charge. My hands are trembling. I'm stealing documents right from under my dad's nose in a White House conference room. There's no way I should succeed.

I eye the stack of papers near my dad. There aren't many. Five or so? I take five off the top of my stack and get ready.

The naval officer leans forward and presses the tip of his index finger into the table. "We plan to increase immediately the number of missiles aboard every submarine in our fleet."

"And Lockheed is ready and able to meet this increased demand," one of the other men says. I place the big stack of my papers next to my dad. "As you know, our Polaris missiles are the most advanced technology on the market."

"To date," my father says. He turns to face the military officer, who's now staring at the other two men. No eyes on me. I swipe my father's papers and replace them with the five I took from the top of the stack. "But I guarantee Pantheon can do better."

Pantheon. My head swims. That's what Joe said in 1995. He was building himself a pantheon.

Jackpot.

I bet Pantheon turns out to be a subsidiary of Eagle. Eagle wants a government contract to arm nuclear submarines. Of course they do. They profit off of wars and government contracts. That's their bread and butter.

As I turn to go, I glance down at the top page in my hand. Pantheon is there, and under it, there's a name. Joseph C. Caldwell Sr. *Senior.* As in Joe's dad? He somehow got his father in on this?

I need to forget Ariel and whatever he's up to, and let him do what history demands of him. *I* need to get the hell out of here. I open the door. I can't project in the middle of the White House, but it's good to be prepared.

I close the door behind me. I'm still dizzy. I have the evidence I need to launch the investigation into Joe and all of Eagle Industries.

I hurry down the hall, back toward the press briefing room. I pause at the staircase where Ariel followed those men and pray I haven't done anything here that would compromise his mission. Then I keep walking. I don't know any other exit than the way I came in. I'm close to freedom, so close to freedom.

But then I'm not.

A door bangs open behind me.

"There she is!"

It's my dad. He looks from me to the papers in my hand. "Stop her!" he shouts. "She must be KGB!"

My dad thinks I'm a Russian spy? Oh no. *Oh no!* You do not want to be captured as a suspected KGB agent in 1962!

Another man in a naval officer's uniform rounds the corner from the press briefing area.

"Stop her! KGB!" my dad shouts again.

No! I make a hard right and tear down the stairs. Footsteps thunder after me. Lots of them. I'm going to wind up with a bullet in my back. I just need to get out of sight so I can project. My dad can't see me project. He can't know I'm Annum Guard. It will blow everything. He has to keep thinking I'm KGB.

Because my dad has already seen me. Not for more than a glance and not while he was focusing, but he's seen me. That alone could alter the course of history—the course of *me*.

"Stop!" a man shouts.

I don't stop. I tear to the right, then to the left. There are more stairs and a maze of doors, and I'm completely lost somewhere in the West Wing. I make another right.

"KGB on the loose!" the same man shouts. I can't tell where he is. Somewhere behind me. "Young! Female! Dark hair! Capture immediately!"

Doors fly open. Guns are drawn. I freeze. *No!* I can't project right now. Not in front of these people. I'm screwed. Completely screwed. And then the door directly in front of me opens. One of the men I saw Ariel with steps out. I look past him. Ariel is staring at me, and I know I need help. I look at him and reach inside the top of my dress to grab my Annum Watch. It falls against my chest.

Ariel blinks.

I pray this decision didn't just mess up the future. The only reason I was able to take down Alpha in the first place was because Ariel helped me in 1963. Is that timeline screwed up? What if he won't help me then? What if he won't help me now?

Then I have my answer. Ariel pushes past the man standing in the doorway to get to me.

"What are you doing?" the man yells.

Lots of things happen at once. People rush at me from all angles. There are guns almost everywhere I look. Ariel dives into me.

"Go!" he whispers in my ear. Then he yells to everyone else, "I'll get her!"

His elbow thumps into my back, telling me to go, and I duck and somehow squeeze my way through a wall of men.

"She's getting away!" someone shouts.

And then there's a shot. And another shot. And a hailstorm of bullets rains down in the West Wing. I scream and round the corner, then whip open my watch face, spin the dial, and I'm gone.

CHAPTER 31

Going forward wasn't an option, so I went back. Two hundred years, three hundred years. I don't know. I didn't count.

I land in a heap on the ground. I'm panting and gasping. The papers! I still have the papers. The ones that link Eagle Industries to Joe Caldwell. Well, that *will* link him with a little more investigation.

I force myself to take a breath and look around. I have no idea when I am, but I'm in a very primitive version of DC. There are a few small buildings, houses, and churches, and I'm standing in an open field where the White House will be built . . . at some point in the future.

I run. I ignore the men in white powdered wigs, the women in long, sweeping dresses, the children playing with wooden toys in the streets. The cries, the protests. I ignore all of it. I don't stop running until I'm alone and gasping for breath again.

Good enough. Then I pull out my watch and project to 1975. I pick the date at random. I need a time before there were airport screenings because I don't have any ID on me. I need to hop a plane and get back to Annum Hall. Get back to Abe. I feel like my entire life is riding on this.

I'm now standing in front of the Washington Monument. It's five in the morning. There are cars on the street and joggers on the sidewalks, but it doesn't look like anyone saw me project.

I book it to a sidewalk and raise my arm for a cab. Any cab. I just need to get to the airport. *Annum Hall. Annum Hall. I have to get to Annum Hall.* I have to trust that Red reached my teammates first. But what if Colton escaped? I still have his watch safe in my pocket, but what if Tyler found him somehow? What if . . . *no.* I didn't even think about the possibility that Colton might have a tracker! If they've moved Abe and the others, I might never see them again. Not after what I did.

Colton now has a vendetta against me. What if he took my teammates back hundreds of years—the seventeenth century, the sixteenth century, the *fifteenth* century? I could be seventy by the time Abe makes his way back to me. He might never catch up. There's a lump in the back of my throat and I retch.

No. *Positive thoughts.* They're fine. They're all fine.

I wave my hand in the air, and a cab stops. I press my evidence tight against my chest and hop in.

"Where to?" the driver asks.

"The airport. *An* airport. I don't care which one. Dulles or Reagan. I just need to get to Boston as soon as possible."

The driver's brow furrows. "Reagan? What's that? Do you mean National?"

"I . . . um . . . yes." Stupid me. Of course the airport isn't named Reagan yet. He wasn't the president until the eighties. "I'm a little flustered. I just need to get on a flight."

The driver looks at me for another second. His expression is mostly one of distrust, but there's a hint of compassion peeking through. I prey on it. Time to pull out the big gun, the one that hasn't failed me yet.

"I have to get to a funeral. Immediately."

That does it. The driver turns and shifts the car into gear. The old-fashioned gearshift is up by the steering wheel. "National's gonna be your best bet. They have more flights."

I murmur a thank you, then watch the trees blur as we head down the highway. Again, I have to wait for the ticket counter to open. I pace around. My training is failing me. I'm all in my head and I can't shut off the voices. The voices telling me I've lost, that Colton won, that Abe is gone, that I'll never see him again.

By the time the counter opens, I'm frantic.

"I need to get to Boston," I pant to the ticket agent. Uniforms have changed since the sixties. Her skirt falls to her knees. She doesn't budge, so I throw out a "funeral."

"Oh," she says in a soft whisper, then issues me a ticket on a seven a.m. flight. I run to the gate, even though I still have an hour to kill.

By the time we board, my hands are shaking.

The flight feels four times longer than it actually is. The second we reach the gate, I push my way through the other passengers so I'm the first one off the plane. I ignore the stares and the comments. I know I'm being rude, but I don't care. I'm on a mission.

Literally.

I lock myself in one of the bathroom stalls and pull out my watch. I click the knob on top that will send me to the present, and before I know it, I'm in my time. I have no idea what day it is, how much time I lost. Is it July? August?

It doesn't matter.

I cut to the front of the cab line. I push right past a businessman stepping off the curb and launch myself into the car.

"Funeral!" I bark, but I don't bother to apologize. "I need to get to 34 Beacon Street now! By the State House!"

"Beacon Street?" The driver turns to look at me. Why isn't he driving yet? "Ain't no funeral homes on that stretch of Beacon Street."

I give him a stern look. "It's a private memorial service."

We're off. I press my knees together and bounce my heels on the floor of the car. Up and down, up and down. Close. I'm so close. Indigo's still weeks behind, but maybe if Red got Abe right away, we're both caught up. He might be there waiting for me.

I manage to keep it together as the driver pulls up in front of Annum Hall.

I run up the steps. The door is unlocked. There's no one in the foyer. I run into the living room. Where is everyone? I spin in a circle. Yellow is sitting in the library, her nose in a book.

"Yellow!"

She looks up at me and wrinkles her nose. "What?" She sounds annoyed.

"Did you find them? Blue, Indigo, the others?"

"What are you blabbering about?" She goes back to her book and mutters, "Drama queen."

I blink. Once. Twice. It's like she has no idea what I'm talking about. And she's acting like the Yellow I first met, not the Yellow who's my friend.

The pop of gunfire erupts in my memories. *Wait. What if*—

"Hello," a voice says behind me. No. It can't be.

I turn.

It is.

Alpha smiles. "We weren't expecting you back so soon."

I choke. "What . . . what are . . . I don't understand."

His smile widens. "Rough trip back?"

"Where's Abe?" I sway slightly.

"Abe?" he asks.

"Stender," I say.

"Like Ariel Stender?"

"Yes! Like Ariel Stender!"

Alpha purses his lips and stares at me with intense eyes, and I'm reminded how intimidating he is. Or used to be. I don't understand what's going on.

Alpha squares his shoulders. "How did you find out about Ariel Stender? That's classified information."

I don't say anything—can't say anything.

His voice is firm. "I'm not sure why you're asking about Ariel Stender. If you know about his existence, you must know he's dead. He died on the very first Annum Guard mission."

I hear the sounds again. They're so loud, like they're not just in my mind anymore. The thunder, the popping, the gunfire. Ariel is dead?

But—no. That means he never met Mona—he never had children—he never—

Abe.

And then everything goes dark.

CHAPTER 32

I open my eyes. I'm still, but only for a second. Then everything comes rushing back. Ariel. Abe. A scream bursts from my lips before I can stop it.

The door flies open, and my mom is at my side. Her arms are around me, and she pulls my head into her chest.

"Amanda, shh, it's all right. Everything is all right. You're home."

I'm in my bed. In Vermont? They took me back to Vermont? How? When? I'm so confused. I want to yell at my mom for everything she's done, but I don't. She's warm and comfortable and everything I need in this moment. I sink into her arms. My hands slide around her waist. Her fuller, curvier waist. She's wearing a long skirt and a tank top. A little roll of flesh peeks out over the top of the skirt. Her wavy hair hangs down her back. It smells like shampoo. I feel how strong her arms are around me.

She's better. She got better. How is that possible? I don't know if I care.

I pull her closer. "Mom, I think I had the most awful dream."

She smooths my hair and leans down to whisper in my ear, "It wasn't a dream, Amanda. I don't know what happened on that mission of yours, but you're never going on one like that again. This was not part of the agreement. Your father's already heard an earful from me."

My . . . *what?*

I pull away from my mom and look around. I'm in a bedroom, but it's not mine in Vermont. It's not my room at Annum Hall either. There's a pale-aqua duvet on the bed and a folded pile of clean clothes in front of the closet. There's a giant butterfly mural on one of the walls, and a window that looks out over—

I gasp and rush to the window.

I'm staring at Commonwealth Avenue, at the park that runs the length of the street, splitting it north and south. I'm in a brownstone on Comm. Ave. The most expensive street in Boston.

Do I . . . *live* here? I look down at a small white desk under the window. There's a neon-pink picture frame set on top of it, and I snatch it up. It's a picture of me and a bichon frise sitting in front of a Christmas tree. I set the picture down next to a notepad that has "AMANDA OBERMANN" printed on top, right next to six yearbooks lined up on the desk, all with "Phillips Andover Academy" printed on the spine. A painting hangs over the bed. It's the scene of a sailboat gliding across a blue Mediterranean.

I do. I do live here.

Ariel is dead. Alpha is alive. My dad is . . .

"Did you say my dad?" I ask as I look back at my mom. She smiles at me with her big peridot eyes.

"He was at the Hall, but he'll be home soon."

"I . . ." *I what?* I don't how to end the sentence. I don't even know how to start it. How did I even get here?

She reaches out and squeezes my shoulder. My very healthy, very stable mother.

"Are you taking your meds, Mom?"

She lets out a throaty laugh. "Like you even need to ask? I take the same combo. Every day. Just like always, baby."

"I think I need to be alone for a little bit," I tell her. My head is spinning. Everything is spinning. I can't focus on anything except that boat above my bed.

"Of course." My mom drops her hand from my shoulder. She's almost out the door when she turns back to me. "But I'm serious. No more missions like that." And then she smiles again. "And the law requires that you listen to me for about three and a half more months. My baby girl—almost eighteen. Crazy."

She shuts the door. I stare at it.

What the hell did I do?

I have a mother. I have a father. I have—I look toward my closet full of clothes and shoes, then to the Mac laptop on my desk—things. *Nice* things. Do I have brothers and sisters?

A phone rings, and I look toward the desk. I spot it right away. It has a turquoise case, and the screen is lit up. I grab it. Incoming call from Jess. Who is Jess? Do I answer or ignore?

I have to answer.

"Hello?" I say.

"Dude, what happened to you today?" The voice is female, and it's familiar. "Did the Molasses Disaster take a wrong turn or something? I mean, I knew it was going to be intense, but—"

"Hang on. *Violet?*"

There's a quick laugh on the other end. "Well, I guess if you want to be all formal about it, *Iris.* Seriously, are you okay? You don't crack like that. Your dad's going to flip. I mean, he already has. He left here like twenty minutes ago, and I've been trying to find a sec to call and give you the heads up. You may have escaped today, but you're in for one hell of a debriefing tomorrow."

A debriefing. Of course. Because I arrived back in the present completely confused and asking about someone who's been dead for like fifty years. I sink down onto my bed. Alpha's smart. I have to imagine my dad is, too. They know something is up.

"Amanda."

"Yeah?"

"You haven't answered my question. Are you okay? I'm worried about you."

"I'm fine. It was just like you said. The Molasses Disaster was a little more intense than I was expecting. But I'm fine. Promise." I hear voices in the hall.

My father is home.

"I gotta go," I say. "Thanks for calling. I—" There are footsteps heading toward my door. "I'll see you tomorrow."

I hang up as my door opens. My father stands in the doorway, and my heart is beating so loudly in my chest I don't know how he doesn't hear it. He's staring at me, really looking at me, and I have no idea what he's thinking. This man is a stranger to me.

"Hey, Princess," he says. "Rough day, huh?"

"That's an understatement."

He smiles. It's warm and relaxed. "We'll talk about it in a bit. I picked up dinner. Spicy miso soup and a mango, salmon avocado roll, just for you."

What do I say to that? I've never eaten sushi before in my life, and I can't even think about food right now.

"Okay, great," I say.

My father is still smiling. He raps the door with his knuckles—once, twice. "Your mom's going to meet with Leslie" —who?—"so it's just you and me tonight. Come on. We don't have to talk about the Molasses Disaster if you don't want. It can wait until tomorrow."

I can't get a read on this man at all. What did Violet say? That he flipped? The man in front of me is calm and collected. Is this a test? I'm so confused. Should I follow him? I think I should follow him.

I push up off the bed and follow my dad down a hall lined with paintings and into a kitchen that opens into a living room. The kitchen is sleek and modern, with white cabinets, a six-burner gas stove, and a stone backsplash. The living room has floor-to-ceiling windows that look out over Comm. Ave. There's also a gallery wall. I recognize my mother's signature on a few of the paintings. I stare down the hall, toward another open door that must lead to my parents' bedroom. I hear mom softly singing a Madonna song that was popular before I was born.

I drop onto a red leather bar stool and lean my elbows on the counter, next to a plastic takeout bag. Fragments of thoughts begin, but then they're ripped from my mind before I can blink.

My mother is well—*thought gone*. My father is alive—*thought gone*. I have a home—*thought gone*.

My dad takes the Styrofoam containers from the bag and slides a bowl of soup and a sushi roll in front of me.

I stare at the soup, a cloudy mess of broth and seaweed, and I think I might be sick. I push it away and stare at the sushi while my dad stares at me, almost as if he's waiting to see what I'm going to do. Or maybe I'm being paranoid.

"You know what? I'm really not hungry." I stand and tuck the stool under the counter. "I still feel a little out of it, so I'm just going to . . . go."

My dad nods slowly. "Of course, Princess. You do what you need to do." He kisses the top of my head.

I walk to my room as fast as I can without looking too obvious, then shut the door behind me and lean my back against it. I take a breath that comes out like a gasp.

What is happening here? This life—what is this? Two parents. Two seemingly healthy, functioning parents. They're the silent prayer I offered up to the universe more nights than I can count. Those nights Mom locked herself in her room and wailed so loudly I couldn't sleep, those nights I could have used a dad to comfort me, those nights I wished I had someone who loved me unconditionally.

No.

I do have someone who loves me unconditionally. *Abe.*

I've lost the one guy who's ever mattered to me. This life, this home, these parents—they're all an illusion. I can't stay here. This is not a dream. This is a nightmare.

And I need to wake up.

I will find a way to wake up.

Acknowledgments

Writing a book can feel like a solitary endeavor at times, but it is undoubtedly a team effort. And I am so grateful to have the following people on my team.

Thank you to everyone (really, *everyone!*) at Skyscape. Marilyn Brigham, for loving the series in the first place; Miriam Juskowicz, for taking the reins and making me feel like I was in great hands; and Robin Benjamin, for wielding a (figurative) red pen and transforming this book from a hunk of dialogue into a cohesive story. Thank you to Phoebe Hwang, this book's copy editor, and to Angelle Pilkington, this book's proofreader, for making these pages as perfect as possible. Many thanks to everyone who worked tirelessly to market this series, especially Erick Pullen, Timoney Korbar, and Andrew Keyser. And thank you to Cliff Nielsen, Katrina Damkoehler, and the entire art department, for designing such beautiful covers.

Thank you to my agent, Rubin Pfeffer, for your patience, wisdom, and ability to keep everything running smoothly behind the scenes.

Thank you to Kerry Cerra, Michelle Delisle, Jill Mackenzie, Kristina Miranda, and Nicole Cabrera. I am forever grateful I sent a random e-mail to a group of strangers a few years ago, asking them to take me under their wing. It was one of the best decisions of my life. And mountains of gratitude to Susan Dennard, Corinne Duyvis, Katy Upperman, and Jenni Valentino, for loving these characters but also for not being afraid to tell me when their plotlines were seriously lacking.

A special thanks to Christina Farley, Jessie Humphries, and Lori Lee. I couldn't have survived this crazy year without the support and encouragement of my Skyscape ninjas. Our chat sessions keep me going! And to the authors who make up the wonderfully supportive OneFour KidLit community, thank you for keeping me sane (and usually in a hilariously entertaining way).

Finally, I am forever grateful for my family. To my parents, thank you for your unwavering support. To Hilary and Patrick, thank you for the *years* of enthusiasm. To John and Jill, thank you for being the best in-laws I could ask for. To my husband, Scott, thank you for believing in me, even when I didn't necessarily believe in myself, and for giving me a good reality check when I needed one. And to my girls, Vivian and Audrey, thank you for inspiring me every day and pushing me to be better. I love you.

MEREDITH McCARDLE attended

the University of Florida and received bachelor's degrees in both magazine journalism and theater. She is also a graduate of the Boston University School of Law. She spent seven years working as a commercial litigator by day and writing at night before committing to writing full-time. She lives with her family in South Florida.

Learn more: **www.meredithmccardle.com**.